# Queen of Demons

## *A Novel*

## Haley Tyler

*"I wasn't lonely. I experienced no self-pity. I was just caught up in a life in which I could find no meaning."*

— Charles Bukowski

# Newsletter

*Join my Newsletter!*

**Stay up to date on title releases, cover reveals, preorder announcements, bonus/deleted scenes and chapters, giveaways, BETA and ARC sign-ups, content updates, sneak peeks, new project info, and more!!**

# Author's Note

THIS BOOK CONTAINS MATERIAL SOME READERS MIGHT FIND
UPSETTING.

*Depression, brief talk of weight/body, alluding to domestic violence,
sexual assault, swearing, explicit sexual content, violence, gore.*

# Julia

It had been like every other afternoon I'd had in the last five years. I walked the same route with the same women, talked about the same things, passed the same houses, and waved at the same people...

It was suburbia. Nothing ever happened.

"I can't believe he let her move in," Alison scoffed, pumping her arms exaggeratedly and not trying to keep her voice down as she glared at Mr. Miller's house.

"Disgusting," Margret agreed, then shrugged. "It should be illegal if you ask me." They smiled sarcastically and waved at Mr. Miller's young, pretty, new girlfriend as she climbed out of her car. She enthusiastically waved back, her smile bright and genuine.

Poor girl.

She had no idea she was just a sheep and they were wolves plotting their next kill.

As usual, I stayed quiet. I wasn't going to gossip with the two women who'd treated me the same way when my husband, Matthew, and I first moved into the neighborhood. The only reason I was even out with them now was for Sophie's sake.

I gave the girl a tight-lipped smile and turned my attention ahead again, anxiously counting down the steps until our afternoon walk was over and I could get away. Sophie craned her neck forward, straining to hear them as they whispered and snickered together, periodically looking over at the girl. Sophie so badly wanted to be a part of their crowd, and I understood why.

They were the popular wives on the street—they were the popular girls in high school who bullied us, but we still wanted to emulate them, if for no other reason than to just fit in. And that's all it really came down to, right? Fitting in. Fitting in with women who hated women, who tore them down to build themselves up. Fitting in with women who thought their opinions were more important, women who strived to out-Karen the next.

But these women, Alison and Margret, were sad, pathetic shells of the people they used to be. They sold their souls to suburban America while their husbands climbed the corporate ladder. And at night, when they finally got a moment together, they couldn't share two words because their lives were so disconnected.

Who would willingly choose that life?

"I think she's nice," Sophie chimed in, raising her soft, sweet voice to be heard. Both women abruptly stopped and slowly turned their seething gazes on her. I took a deep breath, readying myself to intervene.

"Nice?" Alison hissed, her eyebrows barely raising on her Botox-filled forehead. "You think that homewrecker is nice?"

"She ruined Lillian's marriage!" Margret screeched, her eyes bulging. She openly glared at the new girlfriend, not pretending to look friendly or pleasant anymore.

I let out a long, tired sigh. *Here we go.*

"I thought they started seeing each other after his divorce?" I said, folding my arms over my chest.

"Suspiciously soon after, if you ask me," Alison scoffed, narrowing her eyes at me. "He's old enough to be her father. It's disgusting. Don't pretend you don't think so, too, Julia." She spat my name like it was dirty—she said it like a slur.

I shrugged, feigning nonchalance as I glanced toward the house. "Who Bobby wants to be with is none of my business. If he wants to be with her," I shrugged again, "then good for him. I have better things to worry about than who Bobby's fucking." The women sputtered, and I couldn't help but grin.

I hadn't realized they could glare harder, but here they were, glaring harder.

With an irritated huff, Alison speed-walked away with Margaret tight on her heels. She sent a death glare my way over her shoulder, her eyes traveling over my body in a way that told me she thought I was worth less than the dog shit on her shoes.

Sophie gave me a watery smile as she sidled up beside me, her fiery hair swaying with her movements.

"She's been having a hard time at home," she said quietly, as if that excused Alison's shitty behavior. I looked at her from the corner of my eye, one brow raised skeptically. She stared after the women, a sad, longing look on her freckled face.

She was innocent and naïve but pretty. Her long, red hair flowed around her shoulders like she always had a fan pointed at her, making her look ethereal. Her skin was pale and creamy, with freckles sprinkled everywhere. She was curvy, and had a body I could only dream of having. And she was so sweet she made my teeth ache.

Her husband, Giovanni, could get fucked, though. I hated him. She tried to hide the bruises he'd leave on her, but I saw.

"She's just worried Vinny will do the same thing when he finally leaves her," I said, not trying to lower my voice. The whole neighborhood knew about her failing marriage and cheating husband; it was only a matter of time before he moved out.

The only reason I put up with these she-demons was for Sophie's sake, and I liked her enough to not let her face off with them alone. She'd only moved in about six months ago and desperately wanted to fit in. And I understood and sympathized with her.

I was like that in the beginning, too. But I quickly learned those two women had a weird power complex. The only control they had over their lives was bullying the neighborhood wives into submission. I felt sorry for them. It had to be hard to wake up one day and wonder what had happened to your life.

It *was* hard.

I'd been thinking that exact thing every day since I said, "I do." When I looked at them, I saw my future, and fuck if it didn't make me feel helpless. I felt like a trapped animal on the verge of attack. They spent their day's wine drunk just to numb some of what they felt, and I knew I was headed in that same direction.

The walk continued until we reached my house. I was quick to make it up the driveway, all but sprinting from them and their mind-numbing gossip.

"See you tomorrow, Julia!" Sophie chirped, and I gave her a thumbs-up over my shoulder, carefully avoiding Alison and Margret's glares, and slipped into my house.

Leaning my head against the door, I closed my eyes and let out a long exhale. I had a hard time believing this was my life—that this is what had become of me.

How had it all gone so, so wrong?

# Julia

After prepping dinner, I made my way to the shower. I stayed under the hot water as long as I could stand it, wanting it to ease my tense muscles.

I was so fucking tired.

Drained.

But also restless. I felt like I needed to run for miles and miles, not stopping until I felt free. I also felt like I needed to sleep for a month. The water did nothing but turn my skin red and make me dizzy. I couldn't force myself to get out, though. Something about hiding in the steam-filled shower made me feel like this was all a dream, one I'd wake up from at any moment.

I had only a few hours left before Matthew got home from work, and I wanted to enjoy them. It wasn't that I didn't love my husband or that I wasn't happy to see him at the end of the day...it was just that we'd become so distant. We lived together, but it felt like we led separate lives. I felt like I was sleeping beside a stranger every night.

And maybe that's why I was so quick to judge Alison's marriage and life because I didn't want to examine mine too closely. I was sure

Alison knew Matty and I had our problems. Not that I talked to her, or anyone else, about it. But it was apparent.

At some point, what he wanted outshone what I did, and the fighting just wasn't worth it anymore. So, I gave up and began silently following the path he laid out for us—for me. It made our marriage sail smoother, but I was miserable.

So fucking miserable.

I stood in the middle of my bedroom, leaning to the side to scrunch the water from my hair. My eyes roamed over my body in the full-length mirror hanging on the back of the door, and my stomach sank. I didn't recognize myself.

I was average-looking. Like, the housewife-of-a-semi-successful-husband average. I wasn't tall, but not short either. I was somewhere in between. *Average.* And I was thin. Thin in the way that made people worry. But it wasn't like I'd lost weight on purpose; depression just did that to people.

My brown hair used to be bouncy and full of life, but now it felt dull. And now my eyes—my mother's blue eyes—weren't as bright anymore. I didn't know how to bring the color back to my cheeks, or make my smile genuine.

Overall, I was content enough with my looks and had no desire for fillers or surgeries. Yet. But it was only a matter of time before I was like every other housewife on the block and filled my body with plastic.

Maybe if I did, Matthew would actually pay attention to me.

Glancing at my phone, I let out a long sigh. It was three-thirty, which meant I had only three hours until Matthew was home. I made my way to the living room with the current book club book. Alison created a book club a few months ago, and, surprisingly, it was my favorite part of the week. Anything that got me out of the house and let me use my brain made me happy.

I hated that the club was mainly used as a way for people to gossip and drink, and Alison and Margret used it to gather more intel for future smear campaigns. While most of the others used it to escape their lives—like me.

Sophie, a few other women, and I were the only ones who seemed to actually read the books every month. While it would've been nice to have a broader discussion, I was still happy to talk with the few of them about it.

The front door banged open as I walked into the living room. A scream ripped from my throat, and I instinctively threw my hardback book at the intruder. I turned, ready to flee down the hall and lock myself in the bedroom when Matty's scowling face appeared.

"What the fuck, Jewels?" he growled as he stormed further inside, slamming the door shut behind him, making me jump.

"Sorry," I breathed, putting my hand to my heaving chest. "You scared me. I'm sorry." Guilt washed over me. Not because I had hit him in the face with the book, but because I wasn't thrilled to have him home early.

I felt like I could never fully relax when he was home. He put me on edge in the worst way.

Matthew's light brown eyes narrowed, and I took a step back, inhaling sharply. His nostrils flared, and his lips flattened into a tight line before he began pacing in front of the fireplace. His heaving chest and tense muscles told me everything I needed to know about the mood he was in. He shoved his fingers through his short, sandy blond hair as he stopped in front of me again, glaring.

"Pack a bag," he demanded, his tone leaving no room for argument. My head reared back, and I pinched my brows together, confused.

"What? Why?" I glanced at my watch, noting it was barely three-forty-five. He wasn't supposed to be home until after six. It was Wednesday, and we never did anything in the middle of the week.

Oh, fuck. Who am I kidding? We didn't do anything on the weekend, either.

"Not now, Julia," he sighed irritably. I opened my mouth again, but he put his hand up, silencing me. "Just pack a fucking bag!"

Beads of sweat clung to his forehead and dripped down his face. His suit jacket was gone, and the first few buttons of his white button-down were undone, the sleeves rolled up to his elbows. His usually pristine, shiny dress shoes were scuffed and dull, and the hem of his dark, navy-blue suit pants were torn and dirty.

"What's going on?" I asked quietly, taking in his appearance again. "Is that blood? Matty—" He stormed past me, hitting my shoulder as he made his way down the hall. I turned, my eyes tracking him as he disappeared into the bedroom. Light spilled into the hall, showing his shadow bouncing around the room.

My heart was in my throat as I stood stupidly in the doorway, watching as he ripped drawers open, snapped hangers, and let things crash to the floor, uncaring that he was breaking our things. Finally, he turned to me and glared as he put his hands on his hips. He violently gestured to a bag on the bed with his hand.

"Pack," he ground out through clenched teeth, then turned back to shoving things in his own bag. My eyes widened when he put in four guns, then tucked one into the back of his pants, hiding it under his untucked shirt.

"What's going on, Matty? Where are we going? I don't know what to take—"

"Just pack, Julia! Jesus fucking Christ, do I have to hold your hand through everything?" Tears pricked the backs of my eyes, but I bit my lip as hard as I could to keep them in.

My chin quivered violently as I silently moved to the already open dresser. I pulled clothes out with shaky hands and a tight throat, trying to ignore Matthew stomping around behind me. He didn't seem to care that he was ruining our bedroom, and he didn't seem to care that I was upset.

Finally, when he walked out, I turned and covered my mouth with my hand. Our room was destroyed. My sobs bubbled up. I was unable to keep them down anymore, and I silently broke. A few hot tears slid from my eyes to my jaw before dripping to the carpet.

My shoulders shook as I cried. I wanted nothing more than to crawl into bed and hide under the covers. To hide from the world and pretend that my husband didn't just do everything he'd done. Pretend that he loved me, that I was happy, that I wasn't so alone.

Matthew had gone into the living room, but I wished he'd leave me here and go wherever he was taking us by himself. I didn't want to be near him, let alone trapped in the car with him.

His hands were white-knuckled on the mantel when I entered the room, his head lowered. I stood a few feet away, carefully watching him. Tension rippled off him in waves I was sure the entire neighborhood could feel. I watched him as you would a dangerous animal who'd gotten out—wary but calm.

"I'm sorry I snapped at you," he said in a low, gruff voice. I didn't respond.

It was always "I'm sorry" after the fact and never "Let me think before I speak or act." How many times could someone apologize before they were just empty words? How many times could someone forgive before they were just a fucking fool?

"What's going on?" I asked in a voice like ice. He straightened before turning to me, his eyes no longer holding the violent, erratic emotion he'd had since getting home. Now, with his body no longer tense and his eyes tired, his clothes even more disheveled, he didn't seem so mighty anymore.

"We can't talk here," he finally said, his eyes shifting around the room. "We need to leave. Now." He walked toward the front door, stopping to pick up our bags. "I'm sorry, Julia. Really, I am." He kept his back to me as he spoke.

The words were as empty as I felt.

He flung the door open and walked out, leaving me alone in our small house. It was our first house, and we'd made so many memories in it—some good, some bad, all empty.

It was the house that saw the beginning of our marriage and maybe the end. Looking around, I took a deep breath, and something swirled deep inside me that told me I'd never see this place again.

Not like it is now.

Not like I was now.

"Going on vacation?" A high, mockingly sweet voice asked as I locked the navy-blue front door. My hand tightened painfully around the doorknob as I took a deep breath, trying to ground myself.

I turned toward Alison, a fake smile already on my face. She was standing in the middle of our yard, her hands on her hips with one popped out to the side. Her eyes raked lazily over Matthew, and a wolfish grin spread across her face.

"Yeah," Matthew grumbled as he slammed the car's trunk closed.

"Where to?" she asked, her eyes following his every step. She arched her back, pushing her ass out to catch his attention.

*Good luck with that.*

He ignored her, like always. I bit my lip to keep from laughing at her expression.

"Don't know," I finally said, answering for him. "He's surprising me." I mimicked her high-pitched, off-putting tone, making her snarl at me before slipping her mask back on.

"How nice," she cooed tightly, then turned to Matthew, dismissing me. He stood on the driver's side of our black Lexus with his hand on the roof, his fingers tapping impatiently. "What do I have to do to get you to surprise me with a vacation?" Alison laughed, her tone dripping with desperation.

She'd been trying and failing to seduce Matthew for months. She wanted to get back at her cheating husband by having an affair with a younger, more attractive, more successful man. She tried to one-up him at his own game, and the fact that she'd be hurting me in the process only made her work that much harder.

"We're going to be late. Please get off my lawn," I said sweetly. Slowly, almost sinisterly, Alison turned her head toward me, that mask she always wore gone, showing the real her beneath.

"No need to be a bitch," she hissed. I smiled brightly as I walked toward the car.

"Right," I said, sliding into the seat. "Get the fuck off my lawn."

Matthew wasted no time as he peeled from the driveway and down the quiet, suburban street, leaving Alison fuming on our front lawn.

# Julia

Matthew turned the car down a long dirt road, and it was completely hidden from street view, so the only way he would've seen it was if he knew it was there. Unease swirled deep in my stomach, telling me something was very, very fucking wrong as we drove down the long driveway.

We'd been in the car for over two hours, and I was exhausted—mentally and emotionally drained. Matthew hadn't said a word to me the entire drive, letting me sit and stew in my thoughts and worries.

As we drove, huge, white plumes of dust billowed up around the car, and rocks crunched under the tires as we approached a small cabin. A few trucks and cars were scattered around the front, and my unease grew further.

"Where are we?" I whispered as I leaned forward, the seatbelt straining against my chest. Matthew stayed silent, and I wondered if he would ignore me, then he sighed.

"A safe house," he said. "Dominico Costa's safe house." My head snapped to him.

"Why would your boss have a safe house? And why are we at it?"

The air in the car grew thick as we stared at each other. Matthew's jaw ticked in time with my racing heart.

"I'll explain everything—"

"Now," I interrupted. "You'll explain everything right now." His eyes narrowed.

"I'll explain everything later, Julia." He said my name firmly, like a reprimand, and I took a deep breath. I didn't want to argue with him, but it was hard to keep my mouth shut. I managed. Barely.

Where had my sweet, fun-loving husband gone? I remembered how he was in our college days when he'd dance with me in the parking lot and stay up all night eating pizza and watching terrible foreign films. This guy, the one glaring at me so hard he was going to break a tooth, wasn't my Matty.

I lowered, then closed my eyes, trying to keep my conflicting and swirling emotions inside. I told myself this was just a rough patch. All couples had them, right? Everyone went through a terrible time in their marriage and came out stronger than ever. Right?

This felt different, though. This felt like I was on the precipice of something terrible, like one strong wind would topple me off the edge, and down I'd go. Down into a place of no return, where my marriage would be truly over. Then what would I do?

Matthew flung his door open and got out, slamming it behind him. It was a vacuum, sucking all the air from my lungs as I stared blankly at the now-empty seat beside me.

I forced myself to look away, to focus on my surroundings. My eyes found the cabin again, and I took it in with guarded eyes. It was small with a rusted, green tin roof and a chipped red door. Small windows sat on either side of it, planter boxes hanging under them full of dead leaves and long-forgotten projects.

A small metal rowboat was leaning against the wall on one side, a pile of chopped wood under it, sheltered from the elements. Other outdoor equipment sat scattered haphazardly around it, everything rusted and covered in moss and mildew.

My door opened, and Matthew offered his hand as he stared

down at me impassively, like he could care less if I took it or not. Swallowing down my hurt and rising anger, I slid my hand into his and allowed him to help me stand.

The cool Maryland air surrounded us, and the tall fir and pine trees shrouded me, hiding me from the evening sky. I inhaled deeply as Matthew let go of my hand. His warm touch used to bring me comfort, I used to miss it, but now it was a welcomed absence.

A security light flickered on above the cabin door, a faint buzz filling the still air. No one came out as I'd expected. Instead, I stood dumbly, staring at the light, then around the clearing. Absent-mindedly, I began moving forward, my eyes searching the wooded area around us.

"Watch out!"

Matthew's voice boomed and echoed through the trees. I barely missed a giant, rusty bear trap as I brought my foot down. It clamped closed, its ominous snap reverberating down my bones. My heart thundered in my chest, then lurched into my throat as I stared down at it, wide-eyed.

"What the fuck is this place?!" I threw my head back and arms out, screaming at the sky.

"My cabin," a calm, sensual, accented voice said from the door.

I snapped my head down, locking eyes with the shark that was Dominico Costa.

He was well into his fifties but still fit and handsome. Gray was peppered heavily throughout his black, neatly styled hair. He kept his face clean-shaven and his eyebrows perfectly arched. His thin lips were tipped up at the corners, and a glint in his dark, cold eyes told me to run. To run and not look back.

A shiver snaked down my spine, and my skin prickled. Looking into Dominico's eyes, I felt the predator lock his sights on me, and I needed to get away.

"This is Julia, my wife," Matthew said as he stepped beside me.

"Yes," Dominico purred, his eyes traveling over my body. "I believe we've met before. Although, I don't remember you being quite so beautiful." His words were sweet, but venomous slime coated them, and I barely managed a smile.

"Thank you," I said, the words tasting like ash on my tongue. I dropped my eyes, unable to keep his gaze. It was too much. Too knowing. Too lethal. Matthew rested his hand on the small of my back, his touch possessive. I glanced up at him, finding his shoulders back and jaw tense.

"Please," Dominico said, drawing my attention. He stepped to the side and elegantly swept his arm toward the cabin, "Come in." I looked at Matthew again, but he was as stoic as ever. He cleared his throat before straightening to his full height. Putting light pressure on my back, he urged me forward.

I didn't want to go. And I really didn't want to walk past Dominico. He tracked me, his gaze a brand as I moved down the dead, grassy path toward him. Stepping inside, I blinked rapidly, letting my eyes adjust to the dimly lit cabin. It was dark outside, but inside it seemed even darker, like any light that had been here was swallowed.

It wasn't what I'd been expecting. I had anticipated deer heads mounted on the walls and moth-eaten furniture. Fortunately, though, I saw none of those things. Instead, what I found was a quaint cabin.

It was small, but that was expected. The living room and kitchen were one large room, only separated by a small table. A worn leather couch sat in front of a brick fireplace, a handmade-looking coffee table sitting in the middle of the room. Two matching armchairs were off to the side, both looking worn and well-used.

The fire was burning high, the flickering flames causing shadows to dance along the walls. A set of stairs was to the back of the room, and two doors sat on the back wall next to them.

"What do you think, amor?" Dominico asked, his hot breath skittering down the back of my neck. I shuddered and tried to step away.

"It's nice," I squeaked, shuffling forward more.

"Let me show you around," he said, following me forward. "I'm sure you're tired. I can take you to the bedroom." He rested his hand too low on my back, and I stiffened. Glancing over my shoulder, Matthew stood like a statue, his eyes glued to where his boss was touching me. I silently pleaded with him to save me, to rip Dominico's hand off me.

He didn't.

He let his boss usher me toward one of the doors at the back of the cabin.

"Ah, Mathew," Dominico called over his shoulder, "go downstairs and see how the men are dealing with everything." His voice was dismissive. Authoritative. Arrogant. Cold.

"Yes, sir," Matthew said automatically, with no hesitation. I gaped at him, then my mouth fell completely open as I watched my husband drop our bags and walk toward the stairs robotically. He was leaving me alone with this monster.

This was low, even for Matthew.

Dominico swung the door open, letting it hit the wall inside. I stared into the dark room, my mouth bone-dry and breathing too loud in the still cabin. My feet were lead bricks, and even if I wanted to, I couldn't move. I knew walking into that room meant something terrible would happen, and I wasn't going to willingly let it—willingly let him.

"Please," he said soothingly, his hand sliding lower. His voice grated down my nerves, splitting them further. "You seem tired, let me get you to bed, and I'll be out of your hair." He laughed, the sound making my hackles rise. He gently pushed on my back, but still, I didn't move.

"I need my bag." I turned my back to the room, sliding away from him. "Matthew—"

"I'll bring it to you once you're settled," he said, smiling tightly. A cold, calculating smile that didn't reach his coal-black eyes. My hands trembled as I fell victim to his gaze.

"I need it," I insisted. He took a deep breath but kept his fake smile plastered on.

"Of course." He bowed his head slightly, then headed across the cabin, stopping where Matty had dropped our bags.

I thought about running into the bedroom and locking the door. Maybe I could push a dresser in front of it and barricade myself in. Perhaps it would keep Dominico out.

My chin quivered as I watched the shadow grow closer and closer. I smoothed my sweaty hands down the front of my leggings. I needed to decide.

And I did.

I rushed into the room, slamming the door and resting my hands flat against it. The pitch-black darkness swallowed me whole, chewing me up. One of my hands fumbled with the doorknob, realizing too late that there wasn't a lock. It began to turn, and I pressed my shoulder into the wood, digging my heels into the floor.

"Amor," Dominico called mockingly, "what game are you playing with me?"

"Please, leave me alone!" I cried, my voice hoarse. He shoved the door harder, and I was forced back. Quickly, I pressed my body against it, putting all my weight into it as I pushed the door closed again.

"I like the fight," he growled, banging on the door. "Let me in. Now." My stomach twisted as tears dripped from my eyes.

"I want my husband," I sobbed. "Matthew!" I screamed his name, hoping he'd hear me. Hoping he'd care enough to come for me. "Matty, please—" My voice broke as the door was shoved open. I fell to the floor, landing painfully on my side, twisting my wrist.

"That was very rude of you," Dominico snapped as he stepped into the room, ignoring my whimpers of pain. "Not the way a guest should act toward her host." He dropped my bag unceremoniously to the floor, the thud echoing around me.

His silhouette was imposing, swallowing all the air in the room. The firelight flickered behind him, making him look like a demon crawling up from Hell. I stared at him, my body trembling as tears raced down my face. He was a monster come to life. I opened my mouth to scream for Matthew again, but no sound came out.

"You should show more gratitude," he scolded, sounding smug. "I don't let just anyone into my safe house." I swallowed thickly. Had Matthew not heard me? Or did he just not care?

"I-I'm sorry," I stammered, my teeth clacking together. "I just wanted to be alone." I clutched my hurt wrist tighter in my hand, cradling it protectively against my chest. Another whimper left me, and Dominico's head tilted to the side animalistically. I hurried back, pressing my back firmly against the bed's footboard.

The hum of electricity hit me moments before the light flickered on, blinding me. I blinked a few times, squinting. As soon as my eyes adjusted, I wished they hadn't. Dominico's face was twisted in anger, but something else was heated in his eyes that made my throat dry.

"Your bag," he said as he kicked it forward. I didn't take my eyes from him, knowing if I did, he'd pounce.

"Thank you," I murmured, and he nodded once.

"Of course," he said, then extended his hand. "Please," he jerked it slightly, "let me help you." I quickly glanced at his hand, then back to his eyes.

"I'm fine," I said. Wrapping my hand around the footboard, I pushed myself up with a shaky arm, my hurt wrist still clutched to my chest.

Dominico's hands immediately went to my hips, his fingers digging into my flesh painfully. I stiffened, and my breath got lost in my lungs as I stared up at him.

"Please stop touching me," I said quietly. He squeezed me harder —so hard I knew I'd have bruises. "Thank you for your *hospitality*," I ground the word out, "but this is inappropriate." His lip curled slightly, then his throat bobbed as he swallowed and dropped his hands but didn't move away.

He pressed against me, and the wooden bedframe dug into the side of my knee. "Matthew doesn't know how lucky he is," he said, and I took a steadying breath. "You're very beautiful."

"Thank you." I tried to push him away, but he didn't budge. He grinned and pressed harder against me until I lost balance and slid onto the bed. I sat up abruptly and tried to get to my feet, but he crowded me, forcing me to stay seated.

His hand went under my chin, and he gently tipped my head back. "Even better from this angle." I jerked my face away from him, bile rising in my throat.

"Get away from me," I growled. Where was Matthew? His hand tightened on my jaw, his thumb pressing into my throat. "Stop fucking touching me!" I tried to pull my face away again, but he held me firm, forcing me to look up at him.

"You'll watch your tongue when you speak to me," he said, then roughly let go of me, throwing my head to the side. "And you'll remember your place while you're here."

He stalked from the bedroom, slamming the door behind him.

# Julia

I stared up at the ceiling, the hazy morning light shining brightly through the window. Matthew hadn't come to bed last night, and his absence was palpable. My safety, or lack of it, was even more palpable. The betrayal from him...I wiped roughly at my face as a tear slid from my eye into my hair.

What was even happening? My mind was still reeling over the fact Matthew brought me to a supposed safe house, then left me all alone. He let his slimy, terrifying boss touch me and let him be alone with me.

He left me alone.

He abandoned me.

I closed my eyes and tried to breathe through my emotions. I didn't sleep last night; I couldn't. Not when I was anticipating Dominico to come back at any moment. Every creaking floorboard, every slight rustling—any sound I prepared myself for him. Then I heard other men's voices, and my fear was heightened. I didn't know how many there were, and I hadn't heard any women, so I assumed I was alone in a remote cabin surrounded by men.

The room had no weapons, at least none that I could find. I

pushed the dresser in front of the door, but I knew that wouldn't keep anyone out. If Dominico, or anyone else, wanted in, they would get in.

A soft knock drew my attention to the door. I stared at it, terrified of what was on the other side.

"Julia?"

*Matthew.*

I let out a breath and slid off the bed, slowly shuffling my way to the door. Using my back, I shoved the dresser out of the way enough to open it. I found Matty looking more disheveled than I'd ever seen him.

"What's going on?" I said, not giving him a chance to ease into the conversation. My heart was shattering; my mind was spinning. I was drowning. I was out alone, cold and unsure of what was coming.

Matthew dropped his head and let out a long, tired sigh. "Can I come in?" His eyes lifted to mine, and for the first time since he'd come home yesterday, I realized how tired he looked. Bags were under his eyes, seeming to grow darker and heavier every second. The fine lines around them looked deeper. His lips were tipped in a tight frown.

I nodded and stepped back, letting him enter. He began unbuttoning his already half-unbuttoned shirt and shrugged it off his shoulders, leaving him in his white undershirt. He glanced around the room, not able to meet my eyes.

"Matthew," I croaked. Finally, he looked at me, his shoulders slumping. "Please." My voice broke, and he took a small step forward. He paused, and his jaw tensed when he saw my bruised and swollen wrist.

"What happened?" he asked. He grabbed my hand and brought my wrist to his face, inspecting it.

"I fell," I said as I pulled it away and held it protectively to my chest. "I fell when Dominico—" I cut myself off, my chin wobbling. "He shoved the door open, and I fell."

"He didn't—" he closed his eyes. "He didn't touch you, did he?"

"Beyond grabbing and hurting me? No," I said sharply. I was right, Dominico's fingerprints were imprinted on my hip, and a small bruise was on my neck from his thumb.

"I'm sorry—"

"I don't care," I said tiredly. "Just tell me what's going on." I was tired of his apologies, and I wanted answers, not more empty words. I wanted to know what the fuck was going on. I didn't care about his guilt—if he even had any.

He slumped onto the bed and rested his head in his hands, the heels of his palms digging into his eyes. His hair spilled forward, covering his forehead. Finally, he scrubbed both hands down his face as he sat up and looked at me.

"I fucked up," he said. "I got us in trouble."

I blinked at him, my throat tight. His expression was severe, if not a bit somber. He stared back at me expectantly.

"What does that mean?" I rasped. "Got us in trouble?" He sighed sharply.

"It means I fucked up, Jewels," he snapped, and I took a small step back.

"Matty," I said quietly, "just tell me." His brown eyes bored into mine, a swirl of emotion behind them.

"I was in debt," he began, his shoulders falling. "I was in so much fucking debt. I racked it up when we were still just dating. I thought I could pay it off by the time we were married, but...I couldn't."

Slowly, I moved to the bed and sank onto it beside him. I rested my hand on his forearm, squeezing it slightly. It was anchoring us together, whether we wanted it or not.

"I owed Dominico a lot of money. When I knew there was no way to keep you safe and pay him back, I came to him with an offer. I begged him to let me work to pay off my debt, and when it was all paid off, I'd be out."

"Out?" I croaked.

"Out of his Family," he said. "The Costa Family is powerful, Jewels. Really fucking powerful. And I didn't know then, but once you're in, you're in. There's no getting out. He didn't tell me that, of course, he just let me join them, work for him, and when the time came that my debts were cleared, he laughed in my face. Called me an idiot and told me I was never leaving the Family. I was a Costa now."

"Matty..."

"I know," he said, looking away. "Someone attacked us yesterday, a rival of ours called The Demons. They blew up some of our properties and killed a handful of our guys to send a message. They threatened our families. That's why I brought you here. To keep you safe."

My throat was nearly closed as I stared at him. How had I not known he was a part of this? How had I missed all the red flags?

All the times I asked him questions about his job, about where the money was coming from, why he took a gun to the office, came rushing back to me. He always told me to not ask questions; questions got people hurt.

I wish I would've pushed harder.

"I wanted to keep you out of this life," he said quietly. "But I couldn't, and I'm sorry for that."

"Why didn't you tell me sooner?" I cried, wiping at my face. "We could've figured something out. I could've helped you. We could've moved away—"

"There was no other way," he said. "It was either work for him or be killed. And I didn't want to leave you like that." I clenched my jaw to keep my teeth from chattering.

I never knew what he really did for work. He always said he worked in finance and left it at that. And I let him. I knew it was bullshit, that something was off, but I never pushed it.

Why hadn't I pushed him?

Maybe somewhere deep down, I knew I wouldn't like the truth. Maybe I always knew Matthew was tied up in something terrible with dangerous people. There was no way an accountant made the kind of money he brought home, no reason for one to carry a gun with him. There was no reason for one to be called out in the middle of the night because his boss needed help.

But he kept it from me to keep me safe.

That meant something, didn't it?

"So, you've been in his Family," I ground the word out, "our entire marriage?" He hesitated before he nodded.

I was a fool. A fucking fool. And he'd made me one.

"When can we leave?" I asked, steeling my spine.

"In a few days, maybe a week," he said, looking at me. "Jewels, I'm sor—"

"I can't do this right now," I said, shaking my head. "You've lied to me about this for five years, Matthew. Five fucking years. I can't—I need time." He stared at me for a long moment before pushing to his feet.

"Fine," he said coldly. "Take your time." He spat the words out, and tears pooled in my eyes. A coldness spread through my chest as I nodded. Something settled in my bones that told me this was it. That we were over. Truly over. This thing we'd tried to hold onto—that I'd tried to hold onto—was slipping away and crushed under the lies he'd just confessed.

His face shifted from sorrow to anger in an instant. I'd seen his swift mood change happen a million times before. But something about the anger behind his eyes this time had me shrinking away from him.

"You know what? This is bullshit," he snapped. "I'm the one who has had to endure this shit while you've sat at home." He began pacing in front of me. "I'm the one who has had to put my life on the line every day—"

"I never asked you to do that!" I shouted. He paused and snapped his head to me, his lips a thin line. "I never asked you to join his fucking Family! I—I never asked for any of this."

We stared at each other, both of our chests heaving. Matthew's hand tightened into a fist, then relaxed. I glared at him harder, all of the anger I'd felt over the years finally bubbling to the surface.

"And about me staying home?" I stood as I said, "Is because you wanted me to. I didn't!"

"What were you going to do instead?" he scoffed, shaking his head. "Paint?"

"Maybe," I said, nodding. "I could've—that doesn't matter. The point is I gave up what I wanted, what I could've done, because it's what you wanted, Matthew. You can't turn this around and say you joining his Family was my fault. I wasn't the one who gambled my way into debt. It was you."

His jaw tensed, then he nodded a few times. "This is exactly why I never told you sooner." My head reared back, and my brows scrunched in confusion. "You're a judgmental bitch at the best of times, but now—" he laughed humorlessly. "Now that you know what a loser I am, what kind of fuck up you're married to, you'll throw it in my face every chance you get."

My heart pounded in my chest, my palms sweaty. "You know what? You're right. You are a fucking loser. You are a fuck up. You fucked everything up."

He looked genuinely shocked for a moment. He'd tried to pull this shit before, calling himself a fuck up, but I'd never agreed. I'd always talked him down and stroked his ego until he purred like a cat. But now he knew the truth.

I thought he was a fuck up, and I thought he ruined everything. And I hated him for it.

"Whatever," he said, shaking his head. "Stay in this room, and don't get in my guy's way."

My mouth fell open, my eyes widening at the drastic change in him. His tone was authoritative, reprimanding almost, but cold and distant. Nothing in his tone would make anyone think the man speaking to me was my husband. I was just another person to him. Another woman he expected to obey.

He slammed the door on the way out, the hanging photo rattling against the wooden wall.

SOMETHING WAS BUZZING, AND IT WAS TOO LOUD. I CRACKED one eye open, groaning at the bright sunlight searing my retinas. My hand fell to the bedside table, and I clumsily patted around, trying to find my phone.

I knocked it off, and it vibrated against the wood floor. I groaned and slipped from the bed, crashing to my knees, the sheets still tangled around my waist. Ignoring the bite of pain in my knees, I grabbed my phone and answered, thankful the buzzing stopped.

"Hello?" I rasped as I rubbed my face.

"Julia? I'm so sorry. Did I wake you?" It was Sophie. A very chipper and very awake Sophie.

"You did, but it's fine," I said. "Is everything okay?"

"Oh, yeah. Just fine," she laughed breathily. "I wondered if you'd like to go shopping and have lunch. We could try that new vegetarian place that just opened!" I smiled as I pinched between my eyes.

Sophie was the only person who was considerate of my diet. She always made sure we went to a vegetarian restaurant, and if we didn't, she made sure we went somewhere with plenty of options for me.

She was too sweet and a great friend.

"I'd love to," I said, then looked around the unfamiliar room, and my heart dipped. "But Matthew surprised me with a last-second vacation. We'll be gone for a while."

"Really?" Sophie said. I could hear the smile in her voice. "That's great, Julia. Really. Alright, I'll let you go, then. Tell Matthew, Giovanni and I say hello. Have a great trip."

"You too, Soph," I said before hanging up. My heart felt lighter while I was on the phone, but now that I was alone with no distraction again...my conversation with Matthew came crashing back in full force.

Matthew lied to me for five years. Half a decade. I couldn't forgive that, could I? If he could keep something like this from me, what else was he hiding? Did he have another woman in his secret life? One that he cherished and loved more than me? One that knew what he was a part of? One he didn't lie to?

My heart sank painfully at the thought. Truthfully, I'd been so checked out of our marriage, of our lives, for so long that I think I wouldn't have noticed the red flags if he was cheating. I obviously didn't catch the giant, flashing signs that said he was lying to me about his fucking job.

I didn't understand how I could be so...stupid. So idiotic. So complacent. So okay with letting him take the driver's seat in my life. And I didn't understand how he could be so good at hiding things from me, at living a completely separate life.

I got to my feet and looked around the room, taking a deep breath. Earlier, I hadn't cared enough to pay attention to anything; I just wanted to sleep and forget the terrible conversation with Matty.

But now, with a detachment I'd never felt before, I looked around. It was basic with a plain bed and a patchwork quilt on it. The dresser, nightstands, and vanity all matched, all looking handmade. A small window beside the bed had curtains pulled back, letting sunlight in.

I walked to it and stared out at the evening sky, the forest, and the lake way in the distance. I didn't know where we were. Men I didn't recognize walked around, throwing things in the backs of the trucks and in the cars. I searched for Matthew, but he wasn't there.

They worked efficiently, robotically, like they'd been doing this their entire lives. And maybe they had. Had Matthew? Was he a part of this before his debt? Would this be the life he would've eventually chosen anyway? And if this threat had never come, when would he have told me?

There was so much I felt, so many conflicting emotions. So much anger and betrayal. I felt stupid. But a part of me thought maybe this was why our marriage was failing. The weight of keeping this secret pushed Matthew away, and now that I knew and everything was out in the open, maybe we could move on and grow together again.

But could I really live this life? One with safe houses and death threats? Of knowing my husband was in the Mafia? In a way, I'd already been living the life unknowingly. Now that the blindfold had been ripped away and I was fully aware of it, could I still be with him? Did I even want to be with him?

I turned away from the window, wrapping my arms around myself as I stared at the mostly empty room. I didn't feel as upset as I did earlier, but I was still hurting, and that would take a long time to rectify.

I just wanted our marriage to work, and I wanted it to last.

Even if Matthew hadn't taken them seriously, our vows meant something to me. Divorce wasn't something I wanted; it was 'til death do us part. But if I was miserable and in danger, I wouldn't have a choice, would I? I'd have to leave him. But I didn't want to. Did I? I loved him, and I didn't want to be without him.

It was a small mercy we'd never had a child or this would be a lot harder.

I got dressed slowly, trying to prolong leaving the room. But I could only take so long putting on jeans and a sweatshirt before going to the door. I knew I'd have to leave the bedroom eventually. Even if Matty had told me to stay here, there was no restroom and no food.

My hand hovered over the doorknob, and I breathed deeply, my eyes squeezing shut. I could do this. I could face whatever was on the other side.

I could fucking do this.

Without giving myself a chance to overthink, I pulled the door open and strolled out, trying to look more confident than I felt. A few men stood in a small circle in the kitchen, and when I approached, their conversation abruptly stopped, their smiles falling. I hovered awkwardly, flicking my eyes between them.

"I'm Julia. Matthew Blackwell's wife," I said, trying to sound friendly and not like I was terrified. "Do you know where he is?" The men looked at each other, each looking scarier than the other.

"Think he's downstairs," one man said, his voice heavily accented. "Boss is with him."

"Thanks," I said, nodding. A throat cleared when I turned to leave, heading for the stairs in the back.

"You're not allowed down there." He had a thick Jersey accent, and when I turned, he was the scariest of them all, with a long, wide scar on his face.

"Then can you please let him know I'm looking for him?" I asked, trying to stand stoically.

"No." He folded his arms over his chest and gave me a stern look, his eyes narrowing. "He'll find you when he wants to talk to you." I blinked at him. The other two exchanged a look, both trying to hide their smirks.

"Right," I said through gritted teeth. "I really need to—I'm not going to sit around and wait for him." My anger surged as he tilted his head to the side, shifting his arms as he glared at me.

"Don't know why he brought you here," he spat. "Should've taken you straight to the Westside. Bitches aren't welcome here."

"You're not married, are you?" I asked, choosing to ignore the bitches comment.

"I am," he said smugly. "But she knows her place."

"And where's that?"

"At home and out of my fuckin' business," he laughed, and the others grinned broadly.

"So, you're fine putting her in danger?" I said, lifting my brows. "My, what a big man you are." I scoffed and turned on my heel. His hand wrapped around my upper arm, squeezing tightly as he yanked me back.

"Watch your fuckin' mouth, bitch," he snarled. I struggled in his hold, trying to pull free, but he had an iron grip.

"Let me go, you bastard," I said, shoving his arm. "I'll scream."

"Scream all you want," he laughed, and the other two joined him. "No one here will give a shit. If you were my fuckin' wife, I would've beat you before I left—" I opened my mouth, ready to burst their eardrums with a scream, when Matthew and Dominico emerged from the stairs. Matthew's eyes widened when he saw me in this man's hold, then they narrowed.

"What's going on here?" Dominico asked as he strolled forward, sounding amused. The man's grip on my arm tightened.

"Your bitch is mouthy, Blackwell," he said as he shoved me forward. I stumbled and fell into Matthew's chest. He gave me a disgusted look as I righted myself, standing slightly behind him. "Check the cunt, or I will." My hands clenched into tight fists as I glared at him.

"I'll deal with it," Matthew said, his voice full of authority. I'd never heard him sound like that before. "Don't touch my wife again." My stomach twisted painfully as the man's face paled. "You understand me?" The man nodded, his eyes dropping to mine. He didn't try to hide his hatred for me, and I didn't try to hide mine from him.

Before I could say anything, Matthew grabbed my upper arm where the man had and pulled me back into the bedroom, slamming the door behind us. He shoved me forward, and I tripped over the rug on the floor. My hands shot out, and I caught myself on the bed, pain shooting up my injured wrist. He leaned against the door, his brows furrowed. I stood, then paced in front of him, my anger more palpable than his.

"Explain what that was about," he said. His voice was low, almost casual, but I knew better. He was about to explode.

"I came out to find you—"

"I told you to stay in this room," he snapped. I stopped pacing and slowly turned my head to look at him. "I told you to stay out of my guy's way."

"I wanted to talk to you!" I shouted, and he pushed off the door, storming toward me.

"You raise your voice to me again, and it'll be the last time you fucking speak." I blinked at him, my mouth going dry at the fiery rage in his eyes. "You're to respect me. Obey me."

"Fuck you," I spat. "I've obeyed you enough." He took another step forward, and I straightened to my full height to get in his face. "What? Are you going to hit me?" His hand clenched, then relaxed. "Do it." I taunted, following his face with mine. "Hit me, Matthew. See what happens."

"Like you could do anything," he said, laughing cruelly. I smiled at him, slow and cold, and his eyebrows rose. If I didn't know better, I'd say that was pride in his eyes.

"You lay a finger on me, Matthew, I'll fucking kill you."

He really did laugh at that.

"Sure, you will, sweetheart." He smirked down at me and it was anything but friendly. "Just keep your head down and mouth shut. Otherwise, you'll get hurt and have no one to blame but yourself."

I glared at him harder than before and swallowed thickly. I tried to keep my anger under wraps, and I needed to stay calm before this escalated any further. But it was so fucking hard to go along with what he said—to obey him.

And as much as I hated to admit he was right, he was. These men were clearly dangerous and apparently hated women. If I wanted to survive the next week, I'd have to play this game. But even if they weren't scary, sexist assholes, I still didn't want to be around them.

They weren't my friends. They were Matthew's friends. His colleagues; a part of his Family. I inwardly cringed, and all the rage I thought I'd gotten past came back.

"Fine," I ground out, and he gave me a condescending smile I wanted to slap off his face.

I'd heard people say they knew the moment they fell out of love, the moment they started to resent their partner, the moment that changed their lives. And for me, this was that moment. Staring into Matthew's eyes, seeing the lack of love in them, sliced me open. He didn't care one way or the other.

Why should I?

# Julia

That night, the bedroom door blasted open, startling me. I dropped my phone and nearly fell from the bed, my chest heaving. Matthew stood in the doorway, silhouetted by a bright light. I scanned him quickly, and my breath caught when I saw the holsters strapped to his chest, hips, and thighs.

"What—"

"Julia."

We spoke simultaneously, and the corner of his mouth tucked up. I stood from the bed and folded my arms over my chest, my brows furrowed as I stared at him, waiting for an answer.

"There was another attack. I need to leave. You're going to be here alone for a few hours." He tossed a gun on the bed. "Remember how to use it?" He jerked his chin at it, and I swallowed hard.

He'd taught me how to shoot when we first got married. At the time, he said it was because he thought everyone should know how to defend themselves, so I hadn't questioned him. Why hadn't I questioned him?

"Yes," I said, my heart pounding wildly. Sweat broke out across my forehead as I flicked my eyes to the gun, then back to Matthew. "I'm going to be here alone? None of the guys are staying?" I looked over his shoulder and watched as men scurried around the small cabin, hitting walls in random places to reveal little cubbies with guns and other weapons inside.

"We need them all," he said. "You'll be fine. No one knows about this place. You'll be safe." I glanced at the gun and gave him a questioning look. "Just in case." He shrugged as he took a step closer. "I'm sorry, Jewels. For everything." He dipped his head and kissed me. It was a hard, passionate kiss that left me breathless. It was a kiss I hadn't felt in years, and when he pulled away, my eyes stung. "I love you, Jewels."

As soon as the cabin was empty, I raided the fridge. The guys left quickly and efficiently, but I was shocked to see them all taking orders from Matthew. I guess he was more important than he'd let on, which I'd have to talk to him about.

I padded around mindlessly, pulling open cabinets and drawers to snoop, and found nothing interesting. Matthew and the others had been gone an hour, and I was starting to go stir-crazy.

Eyeing one of the walls, I shuffled closer. I looked around the empty cabin before using the side of my fist to hit random spots on the wall as the guys had. I felt like an idiot when nothing happened. I moved to another wall and tried again, and nothing. I tried a few more times on parts of the wall I was positive I'd seen men hit, but no hidden cubbies opened for me.

I gave up, noting it only killed about fifteen minutes. There was nothing in the cabin beside a small attic used as storage and a vantage point to see down the long driveway.

The sun was beginning to set, bathing the living room in pink and orange light and darkening the shadowed corners. It felt like eyes were watching me and the hairs on my arms stood on end. If I believed in ghosts, I knew this place would be haunted.

Maybe it was just the fact I was alone in a cabin in the middle of the woods, but I'd seen enough slasher films to know this was not good. The killer always came after the girl when nightfall hit. I wrapped my arms around myself, mentally scolding myself for thinking of a serial killer lurking in the woods.

Couldn't they have spared even one guy to stay with me? Not that I needed protection, I reminded myself. I was a badass bitch. Even if I had never been in a fight or used a knife for anything other than cutting produce and had only shot a gun once in my life...I was still a badass.

It was a pretty lie.

Once night fell, every corner of the cabin was dark. I lit a few candles but had underestimated the amount I'd need to fight off the darkness. I decided to exhaust myself by snooping.

Of course, Dominico Costa would have nothing of leisure in his safe house. Why would he? He's a fucking sociopath. I couldn't even find a damn book to read. With a violent eye roll, I ended up in the kitchen, snacking and reading the backs of pantry items. Riveting stuff, let me tell you.

Walking to the middle of the cabin, I stood with my hands on my hips and looked around the small space. My eyes caught and lingered on the stairs that led to the basement, and I nibbled my lip. The men said I wasn't allowed down there, but why? It's not like I'd tell anyone what I saw. Mostly because I had no one to tell.

Pacing in front of the stairs, I wrung my hands together, my eyes glued to them. No one would know that I went down there, and I could be in and out and back in my bedroom before they ever made it back.

I stopped and chewed on my thumbnail. I could see something I didn't want to see, learn something I wasn't ready to know. Against my better judgment, I took the first step down, silently hoping all the men were truly gone.

Was I really going to do this? I peeled the skin off my lip, wincing at the sting as I stared down the dark flight of stairs.

*Oh, fuck it.*

I fled down the steps on silent, bare feet and paused when I got to a massive metal door. It looked like the door to a bank vault, and it separated me from the basement, from the rest of the secrets, from diving deeper into this life Matthew had hidden from me.

My hands trembled with adrenaline as I pressed them flat against the door, the cold metal sinking into my skin as I pushed it. Slowly, it creaked open. I put all my weight into it as I shoved it the rest of the way, grunting with the effort. I was surprised it wasn't locked, but maybe they didn't think I'd be stupid enough to go inside. Or perhaps they had a trap in place for idiots like me who entered Dominico Costa's den uninvited. Either way, I wasn't going to risk letting it close in case it locked automatically.

The last thing I needed was to be caught locked down here.

The distinct smell of men hit my nose, and it took all I had not to gag. Trying to ignore it, I ran my hand along the smoothly painted cinder block wall, and when my fingers hit a little metal box with a small switch on it, I sucked in a breath, silently hoping it wasn't a fail-safe that would cause the whole place to go up in flames.

A faint buzzing sounded from overhead moments before fluorescent lights blinded me. I blinked a few times, then looked around the basement. Only, it wasn't an ordinary basement. It was a bunker. The walls had been painted a muted blue color, and rows of bunk beds lined both walls, forming a narrow aisle between them. At the end was a large door that pulled me to it like a magnet, my attention only on it.

With a deep, shuddering breath, I pushed it open.

The light turned on by itself, and my eyes widened. There were two rows of tables covered with monitors. In front of them, mounted to the wall, was a digital map of the state with flashing red dots. Next to it was a smaller map of Baltimore, again, with flashing dots. I didn't know what they meant, or where they were located, but it couldn't be good. I recognized most of the neighborhoods the dots were in and even some of the dots around the state.

Suspiciously, we'd been on weekend getaways in the area with the most concentrated of the dots. I had a sinking feeling I knew why. Had anything in our marriage been real? Had Matthew done anything for me, or for us, and not for this Family?

Three more monitors hung on another wall showing security feeds. The screens were split into four sections, and my breath caught as I looked at the first one.

It was the feed of the cabin.

One square showed outside. The others were in different rooms, including the one I'd been staying in. A shiver snaked down my spine at the thought of these strangers, these men, watching me without me knowing. It made my skin crawl. I felt violated.

The next one had a feed of a warehouse, but nothing was happening, so I looked to the next one.

I immediately wished I hadn't.

My eyes homed in on Matthew immediately. I'd know him anywhere. Something about the set of his shoulders and his tall, thin frame was imprinted on me, always letting me pick him out of a crowd.

He was using a baton to beat someone in the face. The man was kneeling in front of him, his face bloodied and unrecognizable, but Matthew kept coming down on him with his baton.

I couldn't tear my eyes away from the sight of my husband beating someone to death. Putting a shaky hand to my mouth, I watched in horror as the man finally fell, and Matthew repeatedly brought his heavy foot down on the man's head, leaving a heap of bones, blood, and brain in the place where his head should've been. Bile rose in my throat, and I tried to push it down.

I couldn't puke here. I couldn't let them know I'd been in here, that I'd seen this. Matthew couldn't know that I'd seen *this*.

Stumbling forward slightly, I braced my hands on the edge of the table, gripping it tightly. My eyes stayed glued to the screen. It was mocking me, showing me that I really had no clue who my husband really was or what he was capable of.

Silent tears rolled down my cheeks as two men walked toward him. He laughed at something one of them said. I recognized one as the brute from earlier, and my arms began to shake. They were laughing over a corpse—a dead man my husband had not only killed but obliterated.

Putting a shaky hand to my mouth, I forced myself to swallow back more sickness.

What was I doing?

I needed to get out of here.

I couldn't wait around until they got back. I'd be another one of their victims.

As I turned, Dominico caught my eye as he strolled casually toward Matthew, his usual unhurried arrogant walk in place. He clapped him on the shoulder and said something that made Matthew stiffen. Matthew nodded a few times, his eyes lifting to the camera. He stared into my soul, and I knew he knew I was watching.

He jerked his head at the men, and they quickly left them alone. Dominico and Matthew spoke quickly, their heads close together like they didn't want anyone else to see or hear what was being said. Periodically, Matthew's eye would find the camera again. And every time, my heart lurched.

Suddenly, Matthew turned on his heel and moved through the warehouse. I tracked him through the four quadrants until he was gone. I stood completely still, my eyes still glued to the screen.

What the fuck had I just witnessed?

Matthew killed someone.

If I thought I could live this life, I was so fucking wrong. I couldn't. I didn't want to. I didn't want anything to do with these people, with Matthew. I thought I could get past the lies, but this? Knowing he slaughters people? I couldn't stay married to a monster like that.

A muffled thud sounded above me, pulling me from my panic. I needed to get out of this basement before the men came back. I needed to get the fuck away from this cabin, from Matthew, and never look back.

I had to get away.

Now.

# Julia

I stormed up the steps after shutting the vault door. Heat immediately enveloped me when I got to the landing, and I froze. My eyes widened, and my chest filled with panic.

A fire roared in the cabin, and I looked frantically around at the tall flames. They flickered higher and higher, the heat searing my eyes. What the fuck had happened? Had one of the candles fallen, maybe?

I took a step forward, then paused, unsure. There was nowhere I could go; the fire was everywhere. I coughed as smoke invaded my lungs. Covering my mouth with the crook of my elbow, I squinted through the fire and smoke, trying to find an escape.

"Fuck!" I screamed at myself, my voice muffled. I coughed again and squeezed my eyes shut. "Think, Julia. Fucking think!"

Desperately, I moved forward again, and a sharp, searing pain shot through my foot. I jumped back, hopping on my good foot as I looked down at the burn. I couldn't tell how badly it had seared my flesh, but it was enough to really fucking hurt.

There was a semi-clear path to the kitchen, and I needed to get to it. Lifting my sweatshirt over my nose, I carefully moved toward the kitchen, paying better attention to where I was stepping. I made it unscathed and began yanking cabinets open with reckless abandon, trying to find a fire extinguisher. Surely there had to be one in a wooden fucking cabin.

Adrenaline and fear had my body vibrating. My thoughts were jumbled, and my heart was beating erratically. What the fuck was I supposed to do? There wasn't enough water to put this out, I didn't know where the fuck my phone was, and I couldn't find an extinguisher.

I turned toward the growing fire, freezing for only a moment before running back and grabbing a quilt draped across the back of the couch. If I could smother enough of the flames, I could get to the front door and out of the cabin. But when I threw it on the fire, it did nothing but swallow it and burn it to ash.

Smoke billowed around me in huge, sooty plumes, making me cough with each inhale. I pulled the neck of my sweatshirt over my nose and mouth to block some of it out, but it was too late. I needed to get outside. That was the most important thing.

The fire was growing dangerously close to the wooden furniture, and worse, it was about to trap me in a back corner of the room. I had to make a decision, and I had to make one quickly. I could go to the kitchen, the basement, or stand right where I was and watch the fire come for me.

I looked around again, my heart frantic, and my eyes caught on the window above the sink. It was high and small, but I could maybe fit through.

Moving to the kitchen, I leaned over the counter and banged my fists against the window. It looked too small for me to fit through, but if I could break the glass, I could scream for help. Or try to force my body through. Maybe there were neighbors close enough to hear me or see the smoke and call for help.

"God," I cried, tears dripping down my hot face. "Fucking help me!" I didn't want to die like this, in a fire. My arms swept across the counter, and everything crashed to the floor, the plates and bowls shattering, the food scattering, then getting swallowed by the fire. It was too close to me.

I climbed clumsily onto the counter, whimpering as the raw skin of my foot rubbed against the rough fabric of a towel. I searched for a latch on the window, my shaky fingers flitting quickly over it. But there wasn't one. I pressed my hands flat against the glass and tried to push it up, but it wouldn't budge.

The flames were growing closer and closer, trapping me in the kitchen. I needed something to break the glass with. As I looked around at the bare countertop, my heart was in my throat.

"Think," I told myself again and jumped off the counter, ignoring the sting of pain. I threw cabinets open, grabbing cans and anything else that looked like it could help. Climbing back up, I grabbed the towel and wrapped it around my hand, then grabbed a can, holding it in both hands.

Bringing it up, I reared my hands back and banged it against the glass as hard as possible. It didn't break. I hit it again. And again. And again. Pain seared through my wrist with each hit, but I couldn't stop trying. I had to get out of here. But no matter how hard I hit the window, the glass wouldn't even chip.

I balanced on my injured foot as I brought my good one up and slammed my heel into the window. I screeched in pain as my foot connected with the unbreakable glass.

More smoke was forced into my lungs, and I coughed, feeling lightheaded. I banged the can against the window again, feeling weaker. Using my fists, I hit the window repeatedly, begging someone to save me. Anyone.

There was a loud crash somewhere behind me. Everything was in slow motion as I turned, the room spinning around me. An unfamiliar man rounded the corner, his eyes wild and searching, then his gaze met mine, and it was hotter than the fire roaring around us. The smoke swirled around me as I fell from the countertop to the wood floor, and everything went black.

# Julia

My chest ached with each ragged breath. It felt like my lungs were shredded into ribbons, and my throat had been scorched. Every muscle in my body was sore, and my head was pounding. The pungent smell of smoke swirled around me, invading my nose, and my eyes snapped open.

*The fire.*

I shot up, ignoring the shooting pain that ripped through my head. I looked frantically around, trying to find Matthew or anyone familiar, but I was alone.

I didn't recognize where I was. I certainly wasn't in a hospital or any sort of clinic. I was lying on a small, uncomfortable cot in one corner of a tiny room. Blankets were thrown on the floor beside me like I'd kicked them off. A few full bottles of water sat next to it. My mouth was achingly dry, and I wanted a drink so badly, but I wouldn't drink or eat anything until I knew I was safe.

The room was small and mostly dark, but it was cool and smelled clean. There were no windows, décor, or anything remotely homey or comforting. A little light was plugged into an outlet on one wall, and that was the only light I had, other than the single lightbulb I could barely see hanging from the ceiling in the center of the room.

I could've taken a few large steps and been on the other side of the room—of the cell.

It was a cell, and it looked and felt like a cell.

Where the fuck am I?

The door slowly creaked open. As they walked in, I stared at the three shadows, my heart thumping wildly in my chest. One of them flicked the light on, and the dull yellow glow blinded me. I blinked a few times as my eyes adjusted. When they did, my breath caught.

A man stood in front of two others. He was tall, much taller, and bigger than Matthew. His shoulders were broad and square, his chest full and hard. And tattoos covered all of his visible skin.

He had on a long-sleeved black shirt with dark jeans and boots, but every inch of skin I could see was covered in black ink. He had a few on his face, all over his neck, the backs of his hands, everywhere. His dark hair was wavy and pushed lazily away from his face like he couldn't be bothered to do anything with it. It laid messily on his head but looked damp like he'd just gotten out of the shower. His jaw was square under a short, thick black beard.

He was...attractive, to put it mildly.

He studied me with his thick arms folded over his chest, his feet shoulder-width apart. My face burned when I realized what I'd been doing. I was checking him out. What the fuck was wrong with me? I was married, and this guy was clearly holding me prisoner in a cell.

"How are you feeling?" His voice was raspy and deep, and my toes curled involuntarily. I narrowed my eyes on him, then looked behind him at the other two men.

"Where am I?" I croaked, then winced at the pain that sliced through my throat. One of the men behind the big guy made a sympathetic face and flicked his eyes to the water bottles on the floor.

The other two men were complete opposites of each other. All three were ridiculously tall, but one had dark brown hair shaved close to his head, deeply tanned skin, and dark eyes. He didn't look mean, but he didn't look friendly. Tattoos covered his arms, and his muscles flexed as he folded them over his chest.

The other one looked sweet, innocent even. He had soft blond hair that was combed neatly to the side and a bit of stubble along his square jaw and dimple chin. He had a white t-shirt on with blue jeans and boots. He looked like a cowboy Disney prince.

"We ain't gonna hurt you," he said with a thick Southern drawl. I scooted back on the cot, pressing my back firmly against the concrete wall. It wasn't lost on me that they hadn't told me where I was.

The man in front hadn't changed his passive expression or stance. Apart from asking how I was feeling, he didn't care. Disney Prince took a step forward, his face soft. But just because he was looking at me softly didn't mean he wasn't dangerous.

"Pl-please," I croaked, "don't touch me." I held up shaky hands in a pathetic attempt to protect myself.

"Was just gonna grab you a water," he said as he crouched slightly and held his hands up, mimicking me. He jerked his chin at the bottles, and I shook my head, wincing at the throbbing.

"No, I don't want any."

"You need water," the big, tattooed man said. His voice was somehow rougher, more gravely, but his expression still hadn't changed.

"If she doesn't wanna drink, we shouldn't make her. Let her fuckin' die," the other scoffed, waving his hand dismissively.

"Cory," Tattoo Man reprimanded, and Cory clamped his mouth shut, but glared at me harder like I was the one who'd given the order.

"Ma'am, please drink somethin'," Disney Prince said, drawing my attention. "You've been out a long time, and you're dehydrated." I shook my head again and squeezed my eyes shut at the pain. It felt like my brain was rolling around, smashing against the walls of my skull.

"I don't want it," I whimpered.

"Why?" Tattoo Man asked, sounding genuinely curious. I pried my eyes open and stared up at him. "Why won't you drink the water? You clearly need it."

"You're strangers," I said quietly. "How do I know you haven't done something to it?" He narrowed his eyes at me, then, after a moment, he walked forward. I pressed harder against the wall, bringing my legs up to my chest, and held them tightly to my body. He crouched in front of me and grabbed a bottle. His eyes found mine as he roughly opened it and took a long drink. He held it out to me, but I shook my head, tears pooling in my eyes.

"Drink," he commanded, and I shook my head again. His head dropped as he let out a long sigh. "I'm not going to beg you to drink water." He pushed to his feet after putting the bottle on the floor again. "Drink it or don't. I don't give a shit."

Disney Prince glared at him as he strolled across the room. Flinging the door open, he walked out, our eyes meeting for a brief moment before he disappeared. Cory followed him, but Disney Prince lingered.

"Please, we're not gonna hurt you," he said again. "I'll need to recheck your bandage soon." He jerked his chin at my foot. "And the bruises—"

My heart raced as I stared down at my foot. I hadn't realized it was wrapped, but now that I was staring at it, I could feel the throbbing ache.

Then I realized I wasn't in my sweatshirt anymore. I was still in my jeans, but I was in a tank top that was too big for me. Had they changed my clothes and bandaged me? I didn't know how I felt about that.

"It's okay," I whispered, my hands shaking. He sighed before he left the room.

# Dean

"I'm not begging her to drink fucking water," I said as I stormed down the hallway. Micha was tight on my heels, his anger palpable.

"She's a scared, helpless woman," he snapped, his accent thicker. It always was when he was angry. It's how I knew he was actually pissed and not just annoyed. And right now, he was really fucking pissed. "She needs to know we're not gonna hurt her." I closed my eyes as I stopped in front of my office door.

"I'm not entirely sure we won't," I muttered. "She's one of Costa's women." I turned to face him, his jaw tense and eyes hard. "She can't be trusted, and we can't let our guard down."

He was a good kid. He was only twenty-five, but he'd been through so much shit in his short life that it had made him the best man I knew—the strongest and bravest. Which was why I trusted him to be my second in command and take over if I were killed, then Cory would be his second.

Even though we were only fifteen years apart, he was like a son to me. When Micha's parents were killed by Costa's Family, specifically

Dominico Costa's second at the time, I took him under my wing. He was just fifteen at the time.

I found him locked in a closet, dirty and terrified. He still hadn't told me the whole story; I don't know everything he saw or how long he'd been in that closet. All I knew was that when I'd seen him a week prior, he was a normal fifteen-year-old, and when he came out, he was a man haunted by demons.

His father, Drake, and I had grown up together and were best friends, closer than brothers at one time, but when he got his girl-friend pregnant in high school, they moved to Virginia to be closer to her family. When I took The Demons over from my father, I called him and offered him a job he couldn't refuse.

Drake was supposed to be my second, not his son. They were supposed to move back to Baltimore so he could help me clean things up; he was bringing them here for a better life. But he never got that chance. His son got a new life, though. One without his fucking parents.

"We have to help her, Dean," he said quietly.

He had a soft spot for women. Watching his mother be brutally raped and killed did that to him. He saw how terrified she'd been, how she'd fought for her life, and he was helpless to save her. He couldn't stand to see any woman with the same look in her eyes.

And the woman in the basement had the same look—the terrified, deer-caught-in-headlights look.

It could be an act. It wouldn't be the first time we'd tried to help one of Costa's women, only to have them turn on us.

"We can only do what she allows," I said gently. Micha glared at me, his blue eyes burning into me. We stared at each other until my phone rang in my pocket, breaking the tension. He flexed his jaw, then, with a huff, he turned on his heel and stormed away, his boots thudding on the floor. Pulling my phone out, I swallowed my annoyance.

*Matthew fucking Blackwell.*

"What do you want?" I said as I put the phone to my ear. I tried to sound bored, but this guy made it hard to keep my temper in check.

"Aw, what's wrong, Dean? Still cleaning up bodies?" he asked, his voice mocking. "How many was it again?" I clenched my jaw, the phone shaking from the rage I felt bubbling to the surface.

It was forty-five of my men. They were all fucking killed, *slaughtered*, by Costa's men for absolutely no fucking reason.

"How's the cabin?" I asked, my voice just as mocking. "A little warm?"

"Fuck you," he spat, and I smiled. "You have something that belongs to us."

"Do I?" I pushed the door to my office open, flicking the light on as I moved to my desk. "And what's that?"

"The woman," he ground out. "She's Costa's property."

"She's a woman, Blackwell, not fucking property."

"Same difference," he laughed. "Where is she?"

"Don't know," I said. "But what would I get in return if I did know?"

"Nothing, you fucking bastard," he snapped. "Where the fuck is she?" He sounded more angry than usual.

"Who is she to you?" I asked suspiciously.

"No one," he said. "Like I said, Costa's property. We want her back." I thought for a second. She could be Dominico's newest wife or a mistress. Or she could be his property, someone he was planning on selling... he'd surely want her back if that was the case. "What do you want?"

"What I've asked for," I said as I sat in the leather chair. "I want you to stop invading the Southside."

"Not happening."

"The Southside and peace. That's all. No more bloodshed."

"Fuck you. Not happening."

"Then you'll never know where the woman is," I said calmly. There was silence on the other end for a long time.

"Fine," he said. "Keep her."

The line went dead, but I kept the phone pressed firmly to my ear, shocked. Costa and his men were ruthless, but this was...I shouldn't be surprised. They'd been getting progressively worse since Matt took over for his father as Costa's second in command. Things had gotten a lot bloodier.

He was a true psychopath.

~

I LOOKED UP FROM MY PHONE AS MICHA STORMED IN, HIS DARK blond brows furrowed. I groaned as I watched him pace in front of the table.

"What is it now?"

"She still ain't eatin', and it's startin' to really piss me off," he said, punching his fist into his other hand.

"We can't force her," I said, shrugging and looking back at my phone. "If she's refusing food, let her starve for a bit. She'll eat when she gets hungry enough." The silence was palpable, but I chose to ignore him.

"I don't like this, Dean."

"You don't have to like it, Micha," I sighed, mocking his tone. I kept my eyes down as I leaned back in the dining chair. Just because she wasn't eating didn't mean I couldn't.

"We shouldn't be doin' this—"

"Micha," I snapped, finally looking at him. He inhaled sharply and stood a little straighter. "We have to question her. We need to know what she knows, why she was at that safe house—"

"She's terrified!" he shouted as he threw his arm toward the hallway, and I took a deep breath. "We can't treat her like one of them!"

"She *is* one of them," I said darkly. "She's a Costa." He stared back at me, his chest heaving with each breath. "We need to know what she knows."

"If we push her—"

"This isn't up for debate," I snapped. "Last I checked, I make the fucking rules, and you follow them, do you not?" His jaw tensed, and his lips pressed into a thin line. "And right now, I say we can't fucking trust her."

The door behind me opened, but we stayed glaring at each other. Chef came to the table, the smell of steak and buttery potatoes filling the room. He set a plate in front of me, one across me for Micha, and one beside him for Cory. Micha's eyes flicked down to the plate, then the corner of his mouth tucked up.

"Whatever you're thinking, don't do it," I warned. Micha looked at me, a wider grin spreading. "Don't do it." He ignored me as he grabbed his plate and left the dining room with a little bounce in his step. Cory eyed him as they passed each other and he grabbed the chair across from me.

"Was it the food?" Chef asked as we stared at the now-empty doorway.

"No," I sighed and grabbed my beer. "Probably taking it to the girl." Chef was silent for a moment before he looked down at me.

"You're keeping her locked in the basement," he quietly said, and I nodded. He hesitated before continuing. "Don't you think it's a bit..." he trailed off, then shrugged. "Don't you think it's something Costa would do?" I took a deep breath and squeezed the bottle in my hand tighter.

"Go back to the kitchen," I growled.

Keeping her locked in one of the basement cells was exactly what Costa would do, and I was well aware of my hypocrisy. But my guys didn't want her above the basement, and I didn't want her above the basement because she was still a Costa. We couldn't afford to have her snoop around. She'd give him all the information she could gather at the first chance.

It was dangerous to have her here.

"I meant no disrespect, sir," he said quickly, and I waved at him dismissively.

"I know," I said. "But I don't know what else to do." He stared at me a beat longer before hurrying back to his kitchen.

"You're doing the right thing, boss," Cory said and I nodded mindlessly at him, twirling my beer bottle in my hand. I knew I was doing the right thing, I didn't need Cory's approval.

Did I feel guilty that I was eating food prepared for me by my personal chef while she was down there starving? Sure. But was I going to starve with her?

Absolutely not.

# Julia

My eyes snapped open when I heard the hinges of the door squeak. I sat up abruptly, and the room immediately began to spin. Clutching my knees to my chest, I squinted as the light turned on.

"You're awake," Tattoo Man said quietly. My eyes flitted around the room, then behind him. He was alone. Why was he alone? "Still not eating or drinking, I see." He jerked his chin to the steak and the still-full bottles of water.

"Not hungry," I lied. He cocked his head to the side, his eyes narrowed. Then he shrugged.

"Shame to let that steak go to waste," he said casually. "It was an expensive cut of meat." Bile rose in my throat as I flicked my eyes to it, then back to him.

"I'd rather starve," I said, and I could've sworn I saw his lips twitch.

"Not a fan of steak, then?"

"Not a fan of killing other living beings," I said coldly. His dark eyebrows rose, the tattoo above his right one rising with them. He stepped further into the room and closed the door gently, his eyes never leaving mine.

"But you're okay turning a blind eye to it?" He folded his arms over his chest, his lips tightening into a flat line. My mind immediately replayed the images of Matthew stomping on that man's skull, and I squeezed my eyes shut.

"No," I said quietly. When I opened my eyes again, I kept them downcast. For whatever reason, I couldn't look at him. It wasn't like his judgment should affect me. His opinion didn't matter. But something in his searing gaze made my insides itch.

"What's your name?" He shuffled his feet wider apart, and I stared at his dull, scuffed Doc's.

"What's yours?" I lifted my eyes to him and found him smirking. It was barely there, but it was there.

"I asked you first."

"It's none of your business." His eyebrows rose again, and his head reared back, surprise flickering across his features. "When can I leave?"

"You can't."

"What?" My arms began trembling, only slightly at first. But when the weight of his words started to sink in, my entire body shook. "I *can't*?"

"Tell me what I want to know, then we'll figure something out," he said, shrugging. My chest felt like it was caving in as tears pooled in my eyes.

"What do you want?" I rasped. "Money? I don't have much—"

"I have plenty of fucking money," he snapped, and I squeezed my legs to my chest tighter. "I want you to stop invading The Southside. I want peace. I'm tired of the killings—"

"The—what?" He tilted his head to the side, his eyes narrowing.

"The killings," he said slowly. "This bullshit between us, between our people. I'm tired of it. I've told your—" he hesitated, his eyes narrowing further, "husband what I want, but he refuses to see things my way."

"You've spoken to my husband?" I felt a surge of relief flood me. He'd spoken to Matthew. He knew where I was, and he'd come for me. Surely, he would.

Then his words sunk in.

*He refuses to see things my way.*

"You want peace," I said, and his head barely moved in a nod. "And The Southside—"

"I want you to stop invading The Southside," he corrected, and I nodded mindlessly, my eyes roaming around the floor as I thought. Maybe if I could talk to Matthew, I could convince him to these terms and come home. Or, at the very least, they could come to some kind of compromise.

I had no skin in this game. I didn't care what was decided as long as I got to go home.

"The Southside and peace," he repeated. "The Southside is mine, and I need to know you will stop moving in on my territory. We can't afford to lose any more men—"

"Me?" I murmured. "I haven't—" I shook my head, mentally slapping myself. He thinks I'm a part of Costa's Family. "I'm not in The Family."

He took a small step back and dropped his hands to his sides. At that bit of information, he looked genuinely shocked. Then his face shifted.

"You expect me to believe that?" he spat. "If you're not in The Family, then who are you? One of Dominico's whores?" Ice coursed through my veins as I clenched my jaw. His eyes roamed lazily over me before he looked back at my face, a sarcastic smirk forming on his lips. "No," he said, shaking his head, "you're no whore. His whore's are —" he stopped himself, his eyes flicking between mine, that grin falling. "His whore's don't look like you."

"I'm not his whore," I said through clenched teeth. "I'm no one's whore." He glared back at me, his hands tightening into fists.

"Then who the fuck are you?"

"I thought you spoke to my husband?"

"Ah," he said, smiling coldly. "Mrs. Costa, is it, then?" I couldn't help the bark of laughter that ripped from my throat. His body seemed to vibrate.

"No," I said, shaking my head. Then all humor dropped.

Matthew didn't know where I was.

"Who's your husband?" He took a small step closer, and my eyes snapped to his. I pressed my back harder against the wall as I swallowed a whimper. He paused, looking conflicted.

When his eyes lowered to my arms, his jaw tensed. "Your wrist. It's swollen." Then he looked at my bicep, and I instinctively covered it, hiding the bruises that had formed from Matthew's manhandling of me. When his eyes lifted to mine, something flickered behind them. Something like fire. "Are you one of his girls?" he asked in a voice like death.

"I told you I'm not a whore," I said quietly, and he shook his head.

"His property..." he breathed, then closed his eyes. His hands tightened into fists again, his arms shaking. "Fuck." I wasn't sure what he was talking about or what he meant by property. "Where's your family? Where are you from?"

I pushed my eyebrows together, my mind reeling from his sudden change. "I—I don't have any. I never knew my dad, and my mother died a few years ago. I'm from here—" I glanced around the room, "if we're still in Baltimore." My unease grew as he dropped his chin to his chest.

"Do you have anywhere you could go?"

"I—" I inhaled sharply when his eyes met mine again. Gone was the anger I saw burning there, the distrust and curiosity. In its place was pity, and that was somehow worse.

"Can I just go back to my husband? Please?" His eyes flicked between mine.

"Who's your husband?" he asked again, then straightened, some of that same suspicion filling his face again. "Blackwell."

My stomach twisted, then dropped. Sweat broke out across my forehead as I tried to swallow past the cotton in my mouth.

"You almost got me," he laughed bitterly, shaking his finger at me. "Almost fucking got me." I wasn't sure what he meant, so I gave him a questioning look. "Oh, you can drop the innocent act now that I know who you are. Fucking Blackwell's your husband, yeah?"

"Yes," I breathed, and he rolled his eyes before nodding, looking more pissed than he had earlier.

"Of fucking course," he laughed. "Seems I did speak to your husband. He sends his coldest regards." He turned on his heel and left the room, slamming the door so hard behind him that the wood cracked.

*He sends his coldest regards.*

# Dean

Manipulative little bitch was fucking good at faking it; I'll give her that. She was good at faking being innocent and scared. And maybe she was afraid, but she should be. She was Blackwell's fucking wife, and she had the audacity to say that shit about killing living things? When her husband was a rightful fucking killer? That was the biggest load of bullshit I'd fucking heard.

When I got to the third floor, Micha was already at my office, pacing in front of the door. He shoved his hand through his hair as he turned to me, his blue eyes flaming. He had reason to hate the Blackwell's, but the fact that I was about to let my guard down for her made me irrationally pissed.

I'd thought she was one of the girls Costa and his men had taken and sold. She was pretty and young, and if she really didn't have family, she'd be the perfect target for them. I almost fucking believed her. The way she looked up at me, with those big, blue eyes, made me want to believe her. But she was just another lying Costa.

"She really his wife?" Micha asked, his voice low. I nodded. "Fuck!" He turned, banging his hand against the marble wall. It wasn't hard enough to break anything, but it looked hard enough to hurt. He was a grown man, though. I'd let him sort it out.

"Hate to tell you I told you so," I said as I unlocked the door. "But I fucking told you so, asshole. She can't be trusted."

He stayed silent behind me as we walked into the office. He shut the door firmly behind us as I rounded my desk and sat down. Pulling my phone from my pocket, I brought up the security feed to her room. She was curled on the cot. Her back was to the camera, and her body was shaking violently. I turned the sound on just loud enough to hear her sobbing. They were ugly, violent, barely-able-to-breathe sobs. Micha and I exchanged a quick look, then stared back at my phone.

Fuck.

Micha stared at my phone, then began pacing in front of the desk, his injured fist clutched in front of his mouth. He had every reason to be furious. It was Matt's father who made him an orphan overnight, and it was Matt who laughed in his fucking face about it only a few days ago.

I slammed my phone screen down, unable to watch her anymore. I couldn't be distracted when I called Matt. And I couldn't let her crying—her obviously *fake* crying—distract me. She was his wife, and she had to be as evil as he was. How else could someone put up with a monster like him?

Taking a deep breath, I called Matt and put it on speaker. I tried to calm myself as it rang. He'd know he won if he answered, and I was already furious. I shot Micha a look that told him as much, and he nodded, waving his good hand dismissively. He was vibrating as the phone rang, and I wasn't much better.

"Why, hello, Dean," Blackwell's cold and mocking voice tainted the air around us. "What do I owe the pleasure this time?"

"Cut the shit," I growled, and Micha shot me the exact look I'd just sent him. I took a deep breath before continuing. "We know she's your wife."

"Ah, she finally cracked. What did it take?" He laughed. He laughed like this was a game, like we weren't holding his wife. We could be doing anything to her, and he didn't seem to give two fucks about it.

If she was mine, I'd be tearing the world apart to get her back. I'd be slaughtering anyone in my path, burning everything to the ground to save her.

"Blackwell," Micha growled.

"The orphan's there, too?" he laughed again. "Let me guess," he mused, "you two double-teamed her, and she spilled everything? Not surprising. You should've known her in college. Real slut. It's why I married her. Although, she seemed to have lost that quality—"

"Shut up," I barked. Micha and I stared at each other, his jaw tense. I gripped the edge of my desk until the wood groaned and my knuckles were white. With another deep breath, I asked, "Do you want her back?"

"Depends," he answered. "Did you and your men stretch her out?" Micha growled, the sound deep from his chest.

"No one's touched her," I said calmly.

"Like I'm supposed to believe that," he scoffed.

"You have my word. No one's touched your fucking wife." He was quiet for a moment, and I took my chance. "Just agree to peace and The Southside, and you can have her back completely unharmed."

I flipped the phone back over and stared at the screen. Her body was still, and her chest rose and fell steadily. She was asleep.

"No," Blackwell finally said. I shot my eyes from one phone to the other.

"No?" I repeated slowly.

"No," he said. "We don't want peace. We want The Demons wiped off the fucking map, and we're not going to stop until you're all fucking dead."

I blinked at the phone after the line died, then slowly lifted my eyes to Micha. He was staring at me intently, his brows furrowed. We stared at each other, silently wondering what the fuck had just happened. His body was tense, his hand still clutched in front of his mouth, his other arm wrapped around his middle.

"We're sure she's his wife?" he asked slowly, and I nodded.

"She said she is." I looked back at my phone, finding her still asleep in a tight little ball.

"We should talk to her," he said, nodding to himself. "Maybe she can—"

"We're not talking to her," I said through clenched teeth. I stayed staring at the phone, at *her*. My mind was whirling. This could be a trap. If we lower our guard around her, she'll be able to gather information for them, and we'd be in trouble. We've only just started to recover from the last betrayal. Barely.

But something was poking at the back of my mind telling me there was more to her than this. There had to be more to her than just being Costa's property, more than just being Blackwell's wife. There had to be something more to her than this shell of a woman.

I could be looking at her too closely, trying to find something that wasn't there. But why? Why would I want to save this girl? She's on their side, not mine. No loyalty to me. There was no reason she wouldn't up and leave and betray me at the first chance.

No.

I couldn't let my guard down around her.

"She said she's not a part of his family," Micha said, and I sighed as I slumped into my chair. "She could help us—"

"No, Micha," I said firmly. "She's not to be trusted."

"We don't have to trust her," he said, and I slid my eyes to him. "But something isn't right." He jerked his head toward the phone. "A husband doesn't just give his wife up like that, no matter how monstrous he is. Even if he hated her, no husband would do that to his wife."

"Blackwell would," I said. "He's done a lot fucking worse."

"But this is his *wife*," he said, emphasizing the word.

"Doesn't matter." I picked my phone up, holding it sideways, and stared at her. At this mysterious woman. At this potential shark in my waters. At this wife who had been abandoned by her husband. At this scared girl. "We can't trust her."

# Julia

A new, mean-looking guard had brought me a meal earlier. I stared down at the tray. I wasn't going to eat anything because it was meat and because I didn't know if it was laced with anything. I drank from the water Tattoo Man had drunk from, but only that one. I rationed it, and when it was finally gone, I cried. Well, I wanted to cry, but no tears came out. Since being here, I hadn't even used the restroom, so I was way more dehydrated than I wanted to believe.

The days blurred together, so I wasn't sure how long I'd been here, locked in this cell. I hadn't eaten or drank anything, and no matter how long I'd be here, I wouldn't. I couldn't let myself become impaired and be left defenseless.

I sat up as the door opened. My head spun painfully, and I felt like I was going to be sick, but I clenched my jaw and tried to focus on Disney Prince's blond hair as he slowly approached. He stood a few feet away from me and took a deep breath as he stared down at the uneaten food.

"Why aren't you eatin'?" he asked, his voice low but not unkind.

"Not hungry," I croaked. My throat felt like sandpaper.

"You haven't eaten since you got here," he said. "Barely drank anything. This is the fourth meal you've been brought that you haven't touched."

"I'm not hungry," I said again.

"And still no water?"

"Not thirsty."

"Please," he said, looking into my eyes, "drink and eat somethin'." I tried to swallow, but I'd long since stopped producing saliva. I shook my head, wincing again. "If you eat somethin', I can give you medicine for the pain."

"I'm fine," I said, holding up a shaky hand.

"You're not," he said firmly. When he took a step forward, I clutched my knees to my chest, a small whimper leaving me. I hadn't meant to make the sound. It just came out. And then my body started trembling, even though I didn't want it to. He took a step back and quietly said, "I promise I'm not gonna hurt you, ma'am."

Any other time I would've laughed at being called ma'am. I'd never been called ma'am in my life, and now one of my captors was calling me it like it was supposed to lessen what was happening. As if he showed me the slightest bit of respect, I wouldn't be his prisoner.

"Is it the food?" he asked. "You don't like it? Told Justin to bring you more than that." I nibbled the dry skin off my bottom lip, ignoring the sting as the skin ripped open. On the tray was a chicken breast, and that was it. "What do you like?" I stayed silent, and he let out a long sigh. "What's your name?" I stared at him but didn't say anything.

He sighed again, dropping his head, looking defeated. After a few moments, he nodded solemnly and stooped to grab the tray. Without a word, he turned and walked for the door. Panic settled in my chest as I watched him leave, the lock clicking and echoing in the room.

I stared at the closed door for a long time and continued chewing my lips, enjoying the blood that pooled in my mouth. It was dampening my rough tongue enough to swallow something.

When I started to think he wasn't coming back, the door opened, and Disney Prince emerged with another tray and a folding chair in his hands. He set the tray on the floor a foot away from me and gently pushed it forward with the square toe of his boot. There were two bananas, two oranges, and two apples.

I looked from the fruit to him, confused.

"I thought you'd be able to tell if the fruit had been tampered with," he said as he opened the chair. "I can take a bite of each to prove that no one's touched it." I licked my dry lips, and my stomach growled. I was so hungry.

"Okay," I said quietly. "You eat it first." He let out a long, relieved breath and smiled at me as he dropped to the floor, crossing his long legs under him. I wanted to laugh. Why he was choosing to sit on the floor and not the chair, I didn't understand.

He looked so young, like a little boy, not like the man I'd been interacting with—not like the man keeping me captive. He pulled a small pocketknife from his back pocket and cut the orange into wedges. He ate one, making a whole production to show me it was fine. Then he handed it to me and moved on to slicing the apple.

As soon as the orange touched my lips, I cried. Sobbed. The juice was sweet and tangy, a little cold like it'd been in the fridge. I took a hesitant bite, ripping some of it off. I chewed slowly, savoring the taste. Then, I couldn't hold back anymore. I demolished the slice and quickly moved on to the rest of it.

I ate one of each fruit, not slowing down enough to taste anything. My stomach wasn't aching as much, and my mouth wasn't as dry. But I was still ravenous.

"Want the others?" he asked as he watched me finish the banana. I looked down at the other three, then at him. "It's all yours."

"Yes, please," I said quietly. "Can you take a drink of the waters, too?" He smiled gently before reaching for the bottles. He took a long drink of each before handing them to me. I gulped it down as he cut the fruit into more wedges. I was halfway through the second bottle when he gave me the food. I ate quickly, like a starved animal.

"I'll get you some more," he said as he pushed to his feet, brushing his hands down the back of his thighs.

"I'm okay," I said.

"That wasn't nearly enough." He lifted his brow, giving me a firm look. "You need somethin' more." I shook my head, wincing again. "What do you like to eat?"

"I'm vegetarian," I said shyly. "I don't eat meat." He stared at me for a moment, then nodded.

"Dairy's fine?" he asked, and I nodded a few times. "I'll be right back with somethin' else for you and some medicine." He turned and hurried to the door, a little excited bounce in his step.

"Julia," I murmured, and he paused. "My name is Julia." Slowly, he turned around, a giant smile already on his face. Something about the way he looked at me seemed familiar. I felt like I'd met him before, like I'd known him from somewhere. It'd been nagging at the back of my mind since I first saw him, but seeing him smile like that made me wonder where I knew him from.

"Micha," he said, putting his hand to his chest, bowing his head slightly. I smiled warily at him before he slipped from the room.

# Julia

Micha and I shared five more meals together. I was still wary of him and didn't trust him, but it was nice to have someone to talk to. The door opened, and he came in with two trays and a bright smile on his face like he usually did. I let him approach me all the way, which was something new for both of us. He gave me a shocked look, but it quickly faded into a happy one.

I was learning he was generally a happy, smiley man, and it made me uneasy.

"Thought I'd have lunch with you today. That okay?" Micha asked as he pulled the chair closer and sat, resting the tray on his lap. I nodded as I crossed my legs under me. "Not sure if it's any good. Had Chef make black bean burgers and fries." I snapped my head to him.

"Chef?" I asked, and he gave me a cheeky grin.

"Yeah, Chef," he said as he picked the burger up and took a small bite. He chewed thoughtfully, his eyes on the ceiling, then nodded. "Yeah, it's real good. Try a bite." He jerked his chin at my food as he took another, larger bite.

I eyed it warily. I was still waiting for the food or water to be laced, so I wasn't letting my guard down completely. "Swear on my Mama's grave nothin' was done to it." I slid my eyes to him, finding him serious. I wanted to trust him. I liked him. I was starving, and black bean burgers were my favorite.

Slowly, I grabbed a potato wedge and took a small bite. He watched me eagerly, a smile lighting up his face. It was the best thing I'd ever eaten. Buttery and salty with garlic and rosemary. I quickly finished them before lifting the burger to my mouth.

I hesitated, twisting it around to look at it from all angles, then sniffed it. He hid his laugh with a cough, and I glared at him as I took a small bite.

"Wow." I couldn't hold in my groan. I took a bigger bite, then another. Before I knew it, it was gone. My stomach ached at the fullness, but I would happily welcome that discomfort. It beats starving.

"Water," he said as he reached for one of the new bottles the new guard, Justin, brought me.

"You first," I said, and he laughed but took a long sip from each one before handing one to me. I downed it and grabbed another. I was starting to feel a little better, not as weak. I still felt terrible, but not like I was dying.

"Gotta change your bandage, Jay," he said apologetically. "Make sure it's not gettin' infected." I swallowed hard, the food threatening to come back up. "That means I gotta touch your foot." I took a deep breath, my hands shaking as I nodded.

"Only my foot," I said, and he nodded. "Alright." I turned on the cot and carefully held my leg out. He grabbed my foot gently and rested it on his thigh before reaching for a small box on his tray.

He peeled the bindings off, his eyes flicking to me when I hissed. He worked quickly and efficiently, cleaning the worst of the burn on the bottom of my foot. It wasn't as bad as I thought it would be, which I was thankful for. It was tender and a little raw but looked like it was already healing.

"You hurt anywhere else?" he asked as he wrapped a new bandage around my foot. I rubbed my sore wrist absently, and he held his hand out. "Let me see." I extended my arm, and he gingerly prodded at my wrist, turning it this way and that before twisting his lips to the side. "It doesn't look broken, but I can wrap it—"

"It's okay." I jerked it back to my chest, holding it protectively. "I'm fine." He let out a hard breath, his eyes sliding to my wrist, then to my arm.

"The other bruises," he said quietly. "What happened?"

"Nothing," I said, lowering my eyes from him. "I—I ran into the wall. Clumsy." I don't know why I lied to protect Matthew or the other man. But I did. And Micha knew I did.

"Funny lookin' bruises for runnin' into a wall," he said, his eyes boring into mine. "They look like fingerprints to me. They look like someone grabbed you." I wrapped my hand around my arm, hiding them.

His jaw clenched, then he nodded and let out a hard breath. Rummaging around in the little box again, he pulled out a little medicine packet.

"Just some pain killers, nothin' too strong," he said. "Ibuprofen. That's all it is, Jay."

"It's fine," I said again. He dropped his head, his shoulders slumping forward. He tossed the medicine on the floor next to the water bottles.

"For when you're ready," he said. I expected him to pick up our trays and tell me goodnight like he usually did. But he didn't. He sat back in the chair, locking his fingers behind his head as he stared intently at me. "What are your real ties to The Costa Family? Other than your husband." His tone wasn't angry or accusatory, just curious. I swallowed thickly, my heart galloping.

"I don't have any," I said. It was mostly true. I had no ties to The Family. It was Matthew who did, not me. Micha tilted his head to the side thoughtfully.

"We found you at Dominico's personal safe house," he said slowly. "And you're tellin' me you have no ties to The Family?"

"I didn't know he had a Family before this week," I said, spitting the words out.

"Why are you lyin' to me, Julia?" he asked darkly, and my eyes widened.

"I-I'm—" I didn't know what to say. "I don't know anything. Really, I don't. I don't want anyone to get hurt—"

"A child?" he asked suddenly, urgently. He leaned forward, resting his corded forearms on his knees. "Do you have a child?"

"No," I said, shaking my head. Then I mentally slapped myself. I could've lied, and maybe he would've dropped it.

"Who would get hurt? Matt?" he asked, and I shrugged. "We wanna help you." I barked a humorless laugh.

"You want to help me?" I mocked. "Then can I go home? Can I leave this fucking cell?" I threw my arm out, and he took a deep breath.

"Well, no," he said, wincing when I glared at him. "But we can get you help, and we can get you away from him—" I sighed and laid back down on the cot, curling my legs up to my chest.

"Please, just leave me alone," I said, my eyes stinging. I didn't need help. I needed my husband.

Even though he was terrible to me and treated me poorly during our last few days together...he was my husband, and I was scared.

"Jay—"

"Please," I rasped, my voice breaking. "Get out."

He swallowed thickly, his pronounced Adam's apple bobbing, then nodded. He collected the trays and empty bottles and left. Then, I was alone again.

What happened to Matthew? What was he going through right now? Was he scared I was dead? Was he looking for me? He had to be going out of his mind with worry; I know I would've been if he'd been taken.

And just because Tattoo Man said he'd *"sent his coldest regards"* didn't mean anything. He could've just been saying that to be an asshole, to make me second guess myself.

Maybe Tattoo Man hadn't even talked to Matthew. Maybe Matthew had no idea where I was or that I was even taken. Maybe he got back to the cabin and found it burned to the ground and thought I'd died inside. Or perhaps he thought I was the one who'd started it and then ran away.

I groaned and squeezed my eyes shut.

This couldn't be my life. I didn't want it to be my life. Maybe I shouldn't have eaten anything, then I could've just died. I wouldn't have to worry about anything if I was dead.

# Dean

"Bad day?" Micha asked around a mouthful of food. He was shoveling his dinner in, which surprised me since he'd been spending his meals with *the woman*. Cory shot him a look he chose to ignore, and I ignored them both.

I shook my head as I took a long drink. Tonight, I needed something stronger than beer. Tonight was a whiskey-for-dinner kind of night.

"You could say that," I said, swirling the amber liquid in the glass.

I'd been on the phone with Blackwell all fucking day, trying to work with him. Why the fuck I was working harder at returning his wife to him than he was, I didn't know, but it irritated me to no fucking end.

I told myself I was tired of having her in my fucking house, on my property, around my men. Truthfully, it was because every single fucking time I tuned into the security feed of her room, she was crying. She didn't know there was a camera in there; she couldn't be putting a show on for it, and that's what pissed me off even more.

"I want to interview the girl," I said when I lowered my glass.

Micha wouldn't tell me her name, but he sure as shit liked to gloat that he knew it. Asshole.

Slowly, he swallowed his food and sat back in his chair, crossing his arms over his chest. Cory watched us carefully, his dark eyes narrowed and body poised and ready to intervene if needed. It wouldn't be the first time he'd jumped between us.

"Why?" Micha finally asked.

"Need to know what she knows," I said, shrugging. "I need to know what her involvement with The Family is. Something isn't right. I don't know why Blackwell is fine letting his wife rot away here. If she was important to their operations, they'd want her back. And if she was trying to gather more information about us, she'd have already asked you something that gave off a red flag. She's been here a week and hasn't shown any interest in me, or The Demons, or—"

"I don't think she knows anything," Micha said, cutting me off. "Think she was just caught in the crossfire."

"That's what I'm starting to think, too," I sighed as I leaned my forearms on the table. Rubbing my forehead, I took another sip of my drink. "This is a fucking mess."

"Let me talk to her," he said, and I slid my eyes up to him. "She doesn't know or trust you."

"And she knows and trusts you?" I asked sarcastically, and he shrugged with one shoulder.

"We've spent more time together than you two have," he said. I don't know why that bothered me, but it did.

"Don't tell her we're interrogating her. I want to catch her by surprise so she won't have time to conjure up a story," I said, and Micha nodded a few times.

"' Course," he said. He pushed away from the table, ready to stand, but I lifted my hand.

"Let me talk to her tonight," I said quietly. "Let me have dinner with her." He stared at me for a moment, then nodded again. I glanced at Cory, but he was silent as usual. "What's her name?"

"Ask her." Micha smirked at me with mirthful eyes, then scooted back to the table. "Go on, you're not gonna hurt my feelings any." He jerked his head toward the doorway. My stomach tightened as I stared at it, anxiety settling deep in my chest.

"I can head down there with you," Cory offered as he tossed his napkin on the table. "Keep an eye on her. Make sure she doesn't attack you." Micha snorted and rolled his eyes.

"She weighs, what? A buck-ten sopping wet? She ain't gonna attack Dean," he said around his food. He pointed at the door with his fork as he glanced at Cory. "And Justin's down there."

"Fuck Justin," Cory scoffed. "Fucking piece of shit."

"Yep," Micha agreed, then focused on his plate again. I flicked my eyes between them, sighing. They were worse than bickering brothers.

Downing the rest of my whiskey, I dropped it on the table as I stood. "Tell Chef to bring us something." Micha nodded mindlessly as he ate.

"Boss," Justin said as he scrambled to his feet. He pushed his thin shoulders back as he straightened. "Everything okay? Haven't heard the girl—"

"It's fine," I said, waving him off. "I'm having dinner with her." His lips parted, then his eyes narrowed.

"Mike's been having dinner with her all week, now you?" He eyed me up and down, then glanced at the door.

"What're you really asking?" I said, turning to fully face him.

"It's just—" He let out a hard breath. "Is she really worth all this trouble? We never keep prisoners—"

"She's not a fucking prisoner," I growled. "I don't know what she is, but she's not a prisoner."

"The bitch is annoying," he said and I clenched my jaw. "She's uppity. Acts like she's better than me. She never says a word, not even a thank you or a fuck you when I take her ungrateful ass food—"

"You'll leave her alone," I said, and his eyes narrowed.

"I haven't bothered—"

"You'll leave her alone," I said again, jabbing my finger in the center of his chest. "You understand me?"

"I haven't—"

"Do you understand me?" I said again, emphasizing each word as I took a step closer. He tipped his head back to meet my eye and swallowed before nodding. I stared at him a beat longer, then turned toward the door.

"I just don't know why the fuck she's still here!" he said to my back, and I stopped. "Unless her cunt is magic—" I turned and grabbed his shirt, dragging him toward me.

"You say that shit again, you're fucking dead, you got me?" I asked, lowering my face to his. "You don't bother her. Don't fucking touch her. Don't talk to her. Don't even look at her." He nodded frantically, his eyes so wide that all I could see were the whites. "Leave her alone."

I roughly shoved him away, and he stumbled back a step before slumping into the chair beside the door. I turned toward it again and took a deep breath, trying to calm myself before going in.

Slowly, I opened the door and peeked my head inside. She was lying on her side, facing the door with her knees clutched to her chest. I stepped inside, but she didn't stir. Panic rose in my chest as I closed the door and took a small step closer.

"Miss?"

Her eyes flew open with a small gasp. She looked frantically around the room, and I tried to make myself smaller, not wanting to frighten her further. I'm a big fucking guy. I scare people when they're not in a fucking dark room.

"You're okay," I murmured, crouching slightly, and her eyes finally settled on me. We stared at each other for a moment, then she collected herself and slowly sat up.

"What do you want?" she snapped, and I lowered my head to hide my smile. She was fine.

"Just wanted to check on you," I said as I grabbed the folding chair leaning against the wall. Opening it, I turned it around and sat, resting my forearms on the back.

"You mean, you actually care how your prisoner is doing?" she said sarcastically, and I sighed.

"Why does everyone keep calling you a prisoner?"

"Maybe because I am?" She glared at me, but something else was there, something more.

"You're not," I said, and she narrowed her eyes. Sitting up, she pressed her back to the wall and crossed her legs under her.

"So, can I leave?"

"That's up to you," I said, and her face scrunched further in confusion. "I need some answers, then we'll talk about your freedom." She took a deep breath.

"If I'm not a prisoner, then I already have freedom. I could walk out of this room right now," she said, and I grinned.

"Go ahead." I waved my hand at the door behind me, still staring at her. She faltered for a moment, her eyes flicking to the door, then to me. "Of course, you'd have to figure out how to get out, get off the property, and then how to get back into the city. But, please, go ahead. I hope you're not scared of dogs. Or guards that are trained to shoot first, ask questions later."

Her throat bobbed, then she primly sat straighter, squaring her shoulders and lifting her chin. My eyes dropped to the faint bruise at the base of her jaw, and not for the first time, I wondered what happened. It could be a hickey, but paired with the injured wrist and bruises on her arm, I didn't think it was.

"What do you want?" she asked again, without much conviction.

"To have dinner with you," I said, and she narrowed her eyes.

"You didn't bring any—"

"One of the guys will bring it in shortly."

She tilted her head to the side, her lips tightening. "So, are you in charge here?"

"I am," I said, nodding. I opened my mouth to tell her who I was and what I was in charge of, but the door opened, and Justin came in. He set up a little table and chairs, left the room, and returned with trays. He glared at her periodically, so I'd have to reprimand him later. I told him to leave her alone, which included sending her death glares.

"Please," I said as I stood, holding my hand out for her. "Dinner." She stared up at me, her ocean eyes a little brighter than they had been when she first got here.

I kept my hand outstretched, never looking away from her. Swallowing hard, she took my hand, and my heart lurched. I needed to remind myself I was here to get answers from her, not fall all over myself for touching her. She was beautiful, but there were other women equally as pretty. If I wanted to get laid, I'd find one of them.

But why did the thought of being buried inside anyone else make me want to take a bath in bleach?

I gently tugged on her arm, helping her stand. I wanted to let go of her, but I couldn't. I didn't know why, and I didn't think I cared. So, I kept my hand wrapped tightly around hers as I led us to the table. I pulled her chair out with my free hand and waited for her to sit.

She gave me a weird look as I rounded the table and sat across from her. I ignored her as I nudged her plate closer, then pulled mine to me. When I looked down, my brows furrowed.

"It's ratatouille," she said, lifting her fork and knife.

"I know," I said sheepishly. "I have it as a side, or not at all. You don't get to be as big as I am eating vegetables." I gave her a cocky grin, and she rolled her eyes, but her lips twitched.

"I thought Popeye's whole thing was to eat your spinach to get big and strong? He never mentioned meat," she said, cutting into the food. She took a bite, then paused, her eyes growing wide.

"What's wrong?" I asked, worried. "Shit, are you choking?" I jumped up and moved toward her, but she grabbed her napkin and spat the food in it.

"You take a bite first," she rasped, her voice trembling. My brows drew together. When I reached for my fork, she pointed at her plate. "Of mine." I took a breath but stabbed the other side of what she'd just cut in half and ate it. She studied me for a moment, then nodded and waved at my chair.

"Wanna tell me what the fuck that was about?" I asked as I slowly sat back down.

Her eyes searched mine, my face, then down my body, and she closed down. She scooted her plate away and leaned back in the chair, wrapping her arms around herself. She looked away from me, her eyes trained on the floor.

"What is it now?" I sighed.

"Nothing."

"It's obviously not nothing," I said. "What is it?" She wrapped her arms tighter around herself like she was giving herself a hug. Or like she was trying to protect herself from me.

"What's your name?" she asked, and I cleared my throat.

"Dean," I said. "Yours?"

"Julia."

"Beautiful," I murmured, then grinned when she snapped her eyes to me. Quickly, she looked around the room again.

"How long have I been here?"

"Eight days." She sat a little straighter and held my gaze again. Her throat bobbed as she swallowed heavily, then she cleared her throat. Her teal eyes began to sparkle, tears lining them.

"Are you the leader of The Demons?" she asked nervously. My eyebrows shot up, and I took a long drink of water.

"So, you know something," I said as I leaned back in the chair, folding my arms over my chest. "What do you know about The Demons?"

"Just that they're a rival of The Family," she said, then her face got hard. "And that they're monsters. They threatened Costa's men and their families. Sending death threats to women and children is low, even for scum."

"Wow," I laughed, but it was anything but friendly. "You certainly are a hypocrite if you think we're monsters." She stared at me for a moment, her lips tightening before she squeezed her eyes shut.

"You're all monsters," she whispered, her voice thick.

"And your hands are clean, Julia?" I asked in a low voice, and she looked up at me through her lashes, her head still bowed.

"I don't know," she admitted. "I don't know anything anymore."

"Tell me what you do know."

"That's it," she said, lifting her head. "I don't know anything else. Just that you and your people attacked Costa's men."

"You said your husband was the one to take you to the safe house," I said. "Do you know how unusual that is?"

"No," she said slowly, giving me a standoffish look. "Why is it unusual for a husband to protect his wife?" It took all I fucking had to not laugh in her face.

"Because The Family doesn't protect their women," I said, almost growling the words. "They don't care if they die."

"That's not true," she said. "I've been kept safe for years."

"Women are seen as a way for the men to have sons, nothing more," I said. "They're used, abused, then sold or killed when they become a burden." She was shaking her head as I spoke.

"That's not true," she croaked.

"Were there other women at the cabin?" I asked, leaning forward. It was clear she hadn't thought about it because her brows tightened. "I'll take that as a no. Do you want to know what really happened?" I asked conspiratorially. She leaned forward, nodding as if in a trance. "We threatened *them*, not their women, not their children. We asked them to stop coming on our territory, to stop killing the men who wouldn't leave and join them, and we asked for peace. They retaliated by killing a dozen of my men and their families. They blew their homes up after slaughtering everyone inside. After the attack, they went into hiding like the pussies they are, so we had no choice but to attack their warehouse, where they killed forty more of my men. So, no, Julia, we aren't the monsters."

# Julia

Dean and I stared at each other, my heart stuck in my throat. What he was saying couldn't be true. But...there hadn't been other women at the cabin. I was the only one there. Why hadn't I pushed Matthew for more answers? Why hadn't I thought it was weird to be the only woman?

I didn't want to believe Dean, but with the way he'd said it, with such fierce conviction, I felt myself believing him. The way the men looked at me, treated me, called me Matthew's bitch...I ground my teeth together.

"Why would Matthew tell me you were the ones to attack first?" I muttered, mostly to myself. But he leaned forward more, resting his arms on the table and giving me a firm look.

"What do you know about your husband?" he asked, and I furrowed my brows.

"What do you mean?"

"Cut the shit," he growled, and I scooted back, the chair scraping against the cement floor. "I can't tell if you're just a really good actress or if you really don't know anything."

"I don't know anything," I rasped, tears stinging my eyes. "Really—"

"What do you know about your husband?" he asked again, and I took a deep breath.

"I didn't know about this world before the cabin," I said, lowering my eyes. "I didn't know Matthew was a part of anything or that he was in The Family—"

"How?" Dean asked, his eyes narrowing. "How could you not know what your husband was doing?" Slowly, I lifted my eyes to him.

"I didn't ask."

"You didn't ask?" he scoffed. "You're full of shit and a terrible fucking liar—"

"I'm not lying!" I shouted, and his eyebrows shot up. "I've hated my fucking life for the last five years. I didn't care enough to ask what my husband was doing. I didn't care enough to want to know about his life outside of our home. I didn't fucking care!"

I shot to my feet, my arms wrapped around myself. I was shaking, and I felt cold. Then the dam broke, and the tears I'd been trying to keep in began to fall. I kept my back to him as I cried, not wanting to look more pathetic.

"How is it possible he hid this from you?" Dean asked. He sounded closer, but I couldn't make myself turn to see where he was.

"The more he was out of the house, the more comfortable I felt. When he was gone, I could breathe. And—" I finally turned toward him, finding him standing by the table, his hands balled into tight fists. "And I've felt guilty for that. I've felt like a fool for not knowing who he really was. I know it doesn't sound believable, and I know you must think I'm an idiot, but you couldn't possibly begin to even understand how I felt—how I *feel*."

He stared at me for a few tense moments, his hands still tightly clenched. Neither of us spoke, but the room was tense with unsaid words and unasked questions.

"I felt trapped," I finally murmured, and he dropped his head, resting his chin on his chest.

"If you leave here, are you going back to him?" he asked, and I tilted my head to the side. I hadn't thought that far ahead. I wanted to get out of that cell, but I hadn't thought past it. Of course, my knee-jerk response wanted to be yes, that I was going back to him. But the more I sat with that thought, the more my chest tightened, and the more panicked I began to feel.

No, I couldn't go back to him.

I had a cousin. We'd been close when I was a kid, but he left after his girlfriend got pregnant when they were in high school. Maybe I'd find him. Maybe I'd try to rekindle our relationship. He was the only family I knew I had left.

"I don't know," I said, and his eyes lifted to me. "I don't know where I would go." His eye twitched, then he squeezed them tightly shut before nodding.

"Right," he sighed. "Can you tell me anything helpful, Julia?" My stomach twisted as I sank onto the cot.

"I watched him kill someone," I said. "Matthew."

"In front of you?" he asked, taking a small step forward.

"They had an underground bunker at the cabin," I said, lifting my eyes to him. "It was where all the men slept, I guess. But there was a control room with monitors and files and—I watched a security feed of Matthew beating a man, then stomping his head flat." Bile rose in my throat, and I covered my mouth with my hand. Dean stayed where he was, but he bounced on his toes a few times like he had too much energy.

"Who gave you the bruises?" he asked, and I shook my head. "Does he—did he do it?" I shook my head again, my chin trembling. "And your wrist—"

"Dean," I whispered, looking up at him. His mouth snapped shut, his eyes widening slightly. "It doesn't matter." He stared at me and opened his mouth but closed it again.

"You'll tell me if you think of anything else," he said, and I nodded. Without another word, he left me alone again.

# Julia

"Know how to play Hold'Em?" Micha asked as he walked into the room, kicking the door closed behind him. My eyes snapped open, and I groaned as I brought my hand to my head. It was pounding, and my lungs still ached. I coughed as I pushed myself up.

"Yes," I rasped.

"Great," he said, clapping his hands. I winced, then gave him an annoyed look. "Oh, shit. Sorry." He reached into his pocket and pulled out another packet of medicine. He tossed it onto my cot without a word, then sank to the floor in the middle of the room.

I still hadn't taken what he'd given me the other day, but he kept bringing me new medicine every time he visited. I'd been using mealtimes to track how long I'd been here, but everything was starting to blur together.

I inspected the packet closely, tilting it around to get a better view in the light. My head was killing me today, and I was willing to take a chance at being drugged if it meant getting rid of this killer headache.

When I was sure nothing had been done to it, I ripped it open. Micha laid the cards out but paused and flicked his eyes up to me, then down to the open medicine pack. He cleared his throat, a small smile on his face as he looked down at the cards again.

"Come on," he said, waving his hand. "Let's play. Gotta be boring as shit in here." I barely smiled and slowly pushed to my feet. Even though he'd been wrapping my foot and I'd been eating and drinking, I was still aching.

He showed me to the bathroom the other day, and I took the chance to explore my surroundings, but there wasn't much to see. There was a chair right outside my door, and I assumed it was because I was constantly being guarded. There were other doors, but they were all closed, so I wasn't sure what was inside.

*Maybe more captive women.*

The bathroom was nice—way nicer than I'd been expecting. It had polished floors and high ceilings. I didn't understand it. The ceiling in my room was maybe seven feet because Micha told me he was six-four, and his head wasn't close to the ceiling. Although, if he reached up, he could touch it. The bathroom ceiling was well over ten-feet high.

I'd been able to shower and change into new clothes, and they fit better and were more comfortable than what I'd had on. I was just thankful I could shower daily now. The soaps looked expensive and felt luxurious. It was at complete odds with my cell.

I didn't know the men other than Micha and Dean. Sometimes Cory would bring me meals, but mostly it was Justin who did that. Really, I only had Micha. He was nice to me and never treated me like a prisoner, even though we both knew I was. I wanted to ask him more questions, but that would mean answering his questions, and I didn't know if I was ready for that.

"Why are we playing cards?" I asked as I sat on the floor across from him. Looking down, I scrunched my brows. "Where are the chips?"

"Thought we could play for answers," he said, not looking at me.

"Micha," I groaned. "There's nothing I can tell you. I don't know anything."

"About The Family," he said. "But you never said *you* were off-limits."

"Dick," I laughed, then paused, my eyes growing wide. He grinned broadly, his eyes twinkling.

"If I win, you answer anything I want," he said.

"Within reason."

"What's off-limits?"

"Anything about Costa's Family," I said. "I think that's it." He laughed as he shook his head.

"Alright, nothin' about The Family, then," he said. "Nothin' is off-limits for me."

MICHA WON THE FIRST THREE ROUNDS AND LEARNED WHERE I went to college, that I had my first kiss at twelve, and that my favorite food is baklava.

This round, though, I was feeling confident. He grinned at me as he laid his cards out, and I pretended to pout, but I was doing a happy dance inside.

"Alright," he tapped his chin thoughtfully. "Hm. What do I wanna know?"

"You'll have time to think about it," I said as I laid my cards out between us. Royal Flush. His eyes widened comically, his mouth falling open.

"No way!" He shook his head, gawking at the cards. "You cheated."

"Did not," I huffed, crossing my arms. "Don't be a sore loser."

"But that's not—how did you—" He shook his head again, laughing under his breath.

"I think it's my turn to ask you a question," I sang, then laughed. Micha flicked his eyes to me, a crooked smile on his face. Being this close to him, I was able to see his eyes. They were a dark royal blue, similar to mine. I tapped my chin, mocking him. "Hmm," I grinned wolfishly, "how many girls have you slept with?" His face immediately flushed bright red.

"Why would you ask that?" he choked on a laugh.

"Not many?" I asked sympathetically.

"Not any," he said, laughing awkwardly. My mouth snapped shut, but my eyes went wide.

"You're not a virgin," I said, shaking my head. "No way."

"I am," he said seriously. "Waitin' for the right woman." I tilted my head to the side.

"So, your God says it's not okay to bed a woman before you marry her, but it's alright to kidnap them and hold them captive?" It was a low blow, and I hadn't meant to say it aloud. It just slipped out.

He cleared his throat, looking uncomfortable. "Not quite waitin' for marriage, just someone I love. You're not a believer, then?"

"I haven't had much reason to believe," I said quietly.

"I haven't either. But in my darkest times, my faith has been the only thing to help me through it."

"So, why work for someone who kills people? Who kidnaps them and holds them in a cell against their will?" I asked, my anger spiking.

"My boss is a good man, Jay. Even if you don't think so," he said. "He's been like a brother—well, no, more like a father to me, and he's the best man I've ever met. Sure, our line of work is...unsavory, but I'm right with God. I know where I'm goin' when I die."

"And your boss? Does he know where he's going?" I started to worry I'd been kidnapped by a cult of religious fanatics.

"He ain't a believer, either," he said, shrugging. "Don't bother me, though. Y'all have y'all's beliefs, and I have mine." As I opened my mouth, the door opened.

Dean walked in, then froze as he stared at us. Our eyes locked, and I swallowed thickly as I straightened my spine. Micha barely turned and glanced over his shoulder, then when he saw who it was, he sat up straighter. He must've thought better of it because he quickly pushed to his feet.

"Ah, Boss, hey," he said. "Was just checkin' on her." I quirked my brows at him, but Dean stayed staring at me. He looked impassive, but something in his eyes told me he was anything but.

"I see," he said. He scanned the cards laid out on the floor, and the corner of his lips twitched. "Hold'Em? Really, Micha?" Micha's shoulders slumped as he let out a long breath. "You know how to play?" I flicked my brows up at him, and he grinned.

"Yeah, I know how to play," I said. "I just beat him." Dean threw his head back and laughed, his tattooed throat bobbing.

"Deal me in, then," he said as he sank onto the floor beside me far too gracefully for a man his size.

Micha and I stared at him, then at each other. He wanted to play with us? He ignored us as we gaped at him and leaned back on his hands, stretching one of his long legs out to the side. Micha cleared his throat and slowly sat back down, his eyes shooting to mine.

The fun we'd just been having was gone with Dean's presence. I didn't know or trust him. Not like I did Micha, and I barely trusted him.

# Dean

I didn't know what the fuck I was doing or why I'd decided to play with them. Maybe because I wanted to learn more about Julia. Or maybe it was because I was bored and a little lonely. I don't even know why I'd come down here to begin with. I just found myself wandering, then in front of her door.

I'd been in contact with Matt again, but he wasn't interested in getting her back, and I didn't understand why. If I was being honest, it made me feel bad for her. What had her marriage been like if he wasn't trying to get her back? Had it been so bad that she was more okay with sitting here playing poker with us, the men holding her captive, than trying to convince us to get her back to Matt?

I stared at her and wondered, not for the first time, what a girl like her was doing with a man like Blackwell. Even when she glared at me, she looked sweet, and in other circumstances, I might've tried to win her over. She couldn't be older than Micha, though, and even if I was interested, she was too young for me.

*But she wasn't too young to fuck.*

Her dark hair was thick and full and hung in loose waves around her shoulders. Blueish-purple marks were under her eyes, and her full lips were chapped. But her skin, apart from the healing bruises and few scrapes, was fair and smooth; it looked soft, like a rose petal. And her ass was nice, as were her tits. But that ass could get a man addicted.

"Where are the chips?" I asked as I looked around.

"We're playing for secrets," Julia said. She sat on the floor but made it look like a throne. She was elegant, with a long neck and slender fingers, but more than that...there was something about her that made me feel like I needed to bow to her.

"Secrets?" I flicked my brows up, and she nodded, her eyes glued to the cards.

When I walked in, and our eyes met, I'd been held captive. Even if I wanted to look away, I couldn't. She was...alluring. Maybe it was the mystery surrounding her, or maybe it was because she was beautiful. Perhaps it was just that she was a sad, scared woman who'd been left behind by a shitty husband. Maybe that called to my baser instincts as a man, and I felt I needed to protect her. Whatever the reason, I wanted to learn her secrets. Her desires. Her wants and needs.

"Winner gets to ask the losers questions," Micha explained. "The only subject off-limits is The Family."

"That's bullshit," I scoffed, and she snapped her head to me so fast I was scared she'd broken her neck.

"Then don't play," she said through gritted teeth. I swallowed, my smile falling.

"Right," I said, lifting my hands placatingly. I'd need to play nice and by her rules if I wanted to learn anything. "Nothing about The Family."

She glared at me a moment longer, then turned her attention back to the cards. She roughly gathered them and shuffled them before passing them back out. Micha and I exchanged a quick look, but the way he barely shook his head told me not to push her.

She won the hand, and Micha groaned. I couldn't help but smile. She had a good poker face, which told me learning anything vital about her would be tough. I couldn't help but think she'd be helpful, too.

"I'll ask you the same thing I asked Micha," she said, and he hid his laugh with a cough, holding his fist in front of his mouth. His eyes twinkled as he flicked them between us, his white teeth gleaming in the low light. "How many women have you slept with?"

"What?" I laughed. "That can't seriously be your question."

"It is," she said primly, folding her arms over her chest. "How many?" Micha cleared his throat, his face bright red.

"What was his answer?" I asked, jerking my chin at Micha.

"None," she said.

*Fuck.*

He'd told her the truth and would know if I was lying and would no doubt call me out on it. I tried to look casual but couldn't help the grin that spread across my face.

"Why do you wanna know? Planning on fucking me, darling?" I asked smugly, and she sputtered, her cheeks flushing red.

"No," she squeaked. "Just a question."

"I don't know how many," I said as I leaned back, tilting my head to the side to watch her. My eyes traveled over her body, down to her bare legs, and then back to her flushed face. "I haven't kept track." She snorted and rolled her eyes, and I grinned broader. She was a brat, but I liked that. It made me want to take her across my knee and spank her until she was crying, then fuck her tears away.

"Sure," she said, her eyes roaming over me. She tried to look like she wasn't impressed, but the way her delicate throat bobbed told me all I needed to know. She was *very* impressed. "At least Micha wasn't ashamed to admit he's a virgin. Lying is just sad." Micha and I threw our heads back and howled with laughter. She had bite, and I liked it.

*Fuck, I liked it.*

"I'd say somewhere over a hundred. Or more," I said, and she laughed, the sound sweet and genuine. And at that moment, I realized that was the first time I'd seen her laugh or smile, and I wanted more of it. I thought it was her ass that would make a man addicted to her, but I was wrong. It was her laugh.

"That really is sad," she said, shaking her head. "If you're going to lie, make it believable."

"It's not a lie," I said seriously. "I had a lot of fun when I was young. European women are more...*open* than American women." Her eyes widened, her lips parting.

"Let's play again. I'm curious to know your answer," Micha said, grinning.

I clenched my hand into a fist. He was a nice guy and never fucking realized when he sounded like he was flirting. As much as he'd done and seen, he was still too naïve.

We played five more rounds before she lost. She learned I was from Baltimore, Micha from Richmond. We had no siblings or parents. I was forty, and Micha was twenty-five. My favorite color was red, and Micha's was blue. But now I won and it was my turn to ask her a question.

"Hm." I stroked my beard. As we played, she'd loosened up. She was sweet and fun, and I liked seeing her smile. "What's your maiden name?"

"Chamberlain," she said. Micha's body tensed, and I slid my eyes to him. The air in the room grew thick as he took a deep breath. "What?"

"Nothing," I said, still staring at him from the corner of my eye, waiting for his reaction.

His last name was Chamberlain. He knew his father had family here in Baltimore and had wanted to search for them but didn't want to get rejected, so he hadn't looked. But with Julia being a Chamberlain...

"Do you know a Drake Chamberlain? He'd be in his late thirties.

No, he would've just turned forty last month," Micha asked, his voice low and hurried. Julia's dark brows lifted, and she looked confused.

"Drake is my first cousin," she said slowly, flicking her eyes to me. "But I haven't seen him since I was a kid. He moved away—"

"Drake Chamberlain is your cousin?" he interrupted, and she nodded.

"How do you know him?" she asked, looking at me again. I subtly shifted my body toward her.

"He's—" Micha's voice cracked, and I clapped my hand on his shoulder. "He was my father."

I watched Julia carefully. This could be Drake, or it could be a random person. It could be a coincidence.

"He is?" she rasped, her eyes widening. She scanned his face, then down his body, and began to nod. "You look like him. But he wasn't blond. He has—"

"He had brown hair," Micha finished, nodding. "And blue eyes. I've been told I look like my mother."

"You're all Drake," she said, staring at him with a soft smile on her face. "Your mom is Natasha, right?"

Micha inhaled sharply, then cleared his throat. "Yeah," he said roughly. "Nat."

"Where is he? Is he here?" She looked toward the door like she expected him to walk in.

"He's—" Micha's voice broke, and he looked down before pinching between his eyes. "He's gone. Mama is, too." Her head snapped to him, her lips parting.

"Gone?"

"Dead," I said, and Micha cleared his throat again, then roughly wiped at his face.

"I'm sorry," he croaked as he pushed to his feet. "Just wasn't expectin' this. I can't—I gotta—" He turned toward the door, wiping at his face again as he pulled it open. Long after he'd shut the door, we stared at it.

"He's really dead?" Julia finally asked, and I slowly turned to look at her. "I wish I would've stayed in contact with him."

"Matthew's dad killed him," I said coldly, and her face paled. "Raped his mother, then let his men take turns." She shook her head as she put her fingers to her lips. "He watched the whole thing. He was a fucking kid. Only fifteen."

"Oh my God," she breathed, then looked to the door again. "Poor Micha." I dropped my head forward, letting my chin rest on my chest. Sliding my eyes to her again, I found tears in her eyes as she stared at the door like she could see through it, through the marble walls, and across the property to Micha's house.

"He'll be okay," I murmured and put my hand on her knee. Our skin contrasted too much. She was pale and smooth, unblemished, perfect. I was tanned and tattooed, scarred, imperfect. "He'll get through it."

"I shouldn't have asked," she said, shaking her head. Her voice was shaky, and a tear slipped from her eye, and she quickly wiped it away.

"You didn't know." I stroked my thumb back and forth, and she let out a shuddering breath. "He'll be okay." She finally looked at me, her throat bobbing.

"Will you tell him I'm sorry?" she asked quietly, and I smiled sadly.

"You can tell him yourself," I said, and she nodded, then dropped her eyes to my hand. Her hand shook as she put it over mine, and turned my hand, pressing my palm against hers, and rested my thumb across her fingers.

"It was Matthew's father?" she asked and looked at me again. I nodded a few times, then roughly cleared my throat.

"He wasn't a good man," I said, and she nodded.

"I know," she said. "I only met him twice. Once at our wedding, then again when he stayed with us for a few days. He was...I didn't like him."

"He was bad, but Matthew's worse. Things have been getting

bloodier since he took over a few years ago." I flicked my eyes between hers, needing to know how much she knew and how much was a lie. A small sob escaped her throat, and she squeezed her eyes shut.

"What does that mean?" she said, wiping her cheek as another tear fell. "Bloodier?"

"It means that ever since he took his father's place as Dominico's right-hand, more people have been killed, more women have been assaulted and sold, and more families have been ripped apart. He doesn't care who he hurts as long as it furthers The Family's agenda."

She stared at me, horrified. And I believed her. I didn't know why, maybe it was the expression on her face, but I believed she hadn't known that. She might know more about The Family than she's letting on, but she couldn't fake this reaction. It was pure, genuine horror.

I believed her, but I didn't trust her. I was starting to, though.

# Julia

The next night, my mind was still whirling from all I'd learned. Micha was my cousin's kid, which made him my cousin. The only family I had was the one who'd captured me and held me captive. And learning about what he'd gone through, all he'd seen and endured, made me respect him more and ache for him.

But the news about Matthew's father, about Matthew--it had shaken me to my core. I was still wrecked about it. I didn't want to believe that Matthew could be responsible for so much destruction, but I'd seen it. I saw him kill that man. And if he could do that, he could do so much more.

The way Dean had been gentle with me, touching me softly, looking at me with soft eyes...it confused me. I didn't want to examine whatever he stirred in my chest, and I couldn't let myself get attached to him. It was just a simple touch. But why did it feel right? Why did it make me feel grounded? Like I could finally breathe after years of suffocating?

It wasn't normal to feel like this towards a monster, towards a person holding you captive. It's not normal to have feelings for someone else when you're still married. And I didn't even know if what I was feeling for Dean could be considered anything more than infatuation. He confused and intrigued me, and I wanted to learn more about him.

That didn't mean I had feelings for him.

I hadn't seen Dean or Micha since last night, though, and I was starting to worry. I'd gotten used to seeing Micha at least once a day, and as much as Dean could annoy me, I'd been hoping to see him today. I wanted to talk to one, or both of them, about what we'd learned last night. But then they never came.

I spent most of the day trying to sleep or staring at the dark ceiling and walls. I couldn't quiet my mind. Too many thoughts were swirling around inside, and without having anyone to talk to, they stayed locked tightly in there.

I felt cold and abandoned and forgotten the entire time I'd been here, but today, being completely alone and disconnected from Micha and Dean...I felt even more that way.

The door quietly creaked open, and I sighed as I rolled over. I wasn't sure what time it was, but it was well past dinner. Justin, the mean guard, had brought me food, but I didn't touch it. I couldn't. The thought of food made my stomach roll with nausea.

"Why does the boss think you're so special?"

The door closed, and the click of the lock sent a bolt of panic through me. The only light in the room was from the faint nightlight in the corner. I swallowed thickly, my heart in my throat as I sat up.

"Why does he let Micha come in to talk to you? Play with you? Why doesn't he let me?" He growled the last few words, but the rest of them were slurred.

"I don't know," I said quietly.

Footsteps sounded, then the yellow glow from the lightbulb flickered on. I squinted, then blinked a few times as Justin emerged from the shadows. With the harsh shadows on his face and it twisted in anger, he was truly a sight. A fucking terrifying sight.

Slowly, he stalked forward, stumbling slightly. I wrapped my arms around my legs, forcing myself into a smaller ball. He barked an ugly laugh that made me jump. It was a laugh I'd heard Matthew make before—coincidently when I was hugging my legs to myself in the corner when he was angry and on a rampage one night.

"What's so fucking special about you? Is your cunt magic or something?"

I blinked at him, my chin trembling. I didn't know what to do.

"I think I'm gonna find out tonight." He laughed, sounding manic.

I screamed as his hand wrapped in my hair. He yanked me roughly forward, forcing my body to unfold and fall to the concrete floor. My hands and knees slammed into it, making me cry out and whimper in pain. He ignored me as he brought his hand down across my face, making my head jerk to the side.

"Shut the fuck up," he shouted. "You've given Micha and the boss some every fuckin' time they've come in here, haven't you? Probably even Cory. But not me. Why not? You got a problem with me? You think you're too fuckin' good for me?" He shoved me back, and my shoulder blades crashed into the metal railing of the cot.

"I hav-haven't touched them," I cried, tears streaming down my cheeks. "Please, leave me alone. I-I won't tell anyone you were in here. Just leave m-me alone." He laughed, grabbing my hair and yanking it harder.

"I'll leave when I'm done filling you with my cum," he said. "But you'd probably like that, wouldn't you? Sluts like you always do." I began thrashing on the floor, some of my hair ripping out of my scalp at the roots. I didn't care. He could rip it all out if it meant getting away.

"Stop!" I screamed as I scrambled to get my feet under me. He shoved me down, making me slide back on my ass.

"Open your whore mouth," he said, shaking my head by my hair. It forced my teeth to snap, and I bit my tongue hard enough for blood to pool in my mouth. Tears stung my eyes as I looked up at him, silently pleading with him to stop. His face was twisted in so much anger and hatred that I didn't know what to do. But I knew if I opened my mouth, he would hurt me. He might even kill me.

And I wasn't going to die. I wasn't going to be raped and killed by this fucking guy.

With a new sense of self-preservation and determination, I reared my fist back, then slammed it forward, hitting him straight in the dick as hard as possible. He howled as he dropped my hair to cup his crotch with both hands.

I tried to scramble away when he fell to his knees, but his hand wrapped around my ankle and yanked me back. I fell to my stomach and clawed at the cement floor. My nails broke, some peeling back and ripping the skin underneath. I kicked my other foot out, not caring what I hit. I kept kicking until I hit something hard, making it crunch satisfyingly.

I tried to crawl forward again, but his hold on my ankle tightened, then he grabbed the other one. He roughly pulled me back, my shirt rolling up, my body and bare breasts scraping along the floor. He landed on top of me, flattening me and knocking the breath from my lungs. He kicked my legs apart with his and pressed my face roughly into the concrete until it felt like my cheekbone would crack.

His fingers wrapped in my hair again, and he yanked my head back, my neck straining painfully. "You dumb fucking bitch." He spat on my face, and I squeezed my eyes shut. "You could've gotten off real fuckin' easy if you'd just opened your mouth. Not now. Now, I'm gonna fuck your ass until you fucking bleed."

I screamed until my throat was raw, until no more air would fill my lungs. He ground his hips against my ass, and bile rose in my throat. I bucked my hips back, trying to kick him off. He laughed and pulled my head back more.

"Look at that," he said smugly, "eager to have my cock in your ass?" He ground against me again, and I screamed as more tears streamed down my cheeks. Could no one hear me? Where was Micha? Or Dean? Cory? Surely one of them would be here to check on me soon.

But soon might be too late.

Justin's hand wrapped around the band of my shorts, and he roughly yanked them down. He squeezed my ass hard enough to bruise, then laughed when I screamed and sobbed again. He ran his finger between the cheeks and forced it into the hole.

"So tight," he murmured, his breath hot against my ear. "You ever been fucked here before?" He roughly shoved his finger in and out of the dry hole, making me cry harder.

"Stop," I cried. My voice was nearly gone from how much I'd been screaming. "Please, stop!" He ignored me as he pulled his finger out. I felt him fumble with his jeans, and I lowered my forehead to the floor, defeated.

This was happening.

There was no way for me to get out of this. It had only been a matter of time before one of them did this, and here it was.

The sound of his zipper was loud in the now silent room. He gripped my ass again, spreading me apart while his other finger dipped lower to my pussy. He shoved it inside, ignoring my quiet cries of pain.

"You're gonna love this," he panted. "You're gonna be begging me to fuck your ass every night—"

The door blasted open, shards of wood flying everywhere, and my head snapped up, hitting Justin's jaw. Tears and spit and blood were dripping down my face, and I'm sure I looked like a fucking wreck, but I didn't care. I didn't care who it was or what I looked like if they were here to save me.

Dean stormed in, his eyes furious. He lifted a gun, and I froze, my entire body tensing. I'd never had a gun pointed at me before, and I was even more terrified than I'd been.

"Get the fuck off her!" he roared. "Off. Now." He jerked the gun at Justin, and slowly, he pushed off me, but not before shoving my head down on the floor again. My jaw bounced off, my teeth biting through my bottom lip, and I whimpered. As Justin stood, Dean cocked the gun. "Julia, over here." He never took his eyes off Justin.

I half ran, half crawled to Dean as I pulled my shorts up. I slid onto my knees and wrapped my arms around his thick leg. My body was trembling as I rested my forehead against his thigh. His hand came down and rested gently on my head, his fingers gently stroking my hair.

"I told you to stay the fuck away from her," he said. "I told you not to fucking bother her."

"I—" I opened my eyes and slid my forehead against the rough fabric of Dean's jeans to look at Justin. His eyes were wide, and his face was pale. His eyes flicked to me, and I whimpered, pressing my face against Dean's leg again.

"Don't look at her," he shouted, "look at me!" Justin's eyes snapped back to him. Dean's body was vibrating with fury, but his hand on my head was a gentle caress. "Close your eyes, darling."

The shot echoed through the room.

# Julia

I didn't hear myself screaming. I didn't feel myself crawling toward Justin's bleeding, dying body. When I looked down, I was covered in his hot blood. I cupped it in my hands, scooping it onto his body.

"I can help him," I sobbed. "I can help him."

I was vaguely aware of Dean's gentle touch on me, his fingers stroking my hair. His voice was deep, but I didn't know what he was saying.

"It's okay," I said, watching hands that looked like mine but weren't mine scoop more blood in them and pour it over Justin's chest. "I can help him."

"Julia." Dean's voice was firm. He sank to his knees beside me. "Darling, look at me." But I couldn't.

Why was I trying to help Justin? He wanted to rape me, but I needed to help him. I had to. If I gave him his blood back, he'd live. I couldn't be responsible for someone's death.

"Look at me." A finger touched my chin, and gently, my head turned. "There you are, pretty girl. You need to breathe for me."

"He's dead!" I screamed, my aching throat raw. More tears leaked from my eyes. "He's dead."

"I know," he said softly. "Come here." He held his arm out and waited. My lips trembled as I looked from him to the blood on the floor, my body, and my hands.

I launched myself at him, and he took it, not budging even an inch. His arms were tight around me. Safe and sure. Unwavering.

"It's alright," he murmured over and over as he smoothed his hand down my back. "You're alright, darling. You're safe now. I've got you. I'm right here." I screamed into his neck, sobbing harder, and he held me through it all. When I finally calmed, he nuzzled his cheek against my head, then said, "I'm gonna pick you up now." I nodded, not taking my face away from his skin. He smelled good, like amber and musk, and that's all I could focus on.

I clung to him as he stood, then wrapped my legs around his waist. I didn't care that I probably looked insane, clinging to this giant man, covering him in blood--the blood of the man he'd just killed. For me.

He moved silently across the room and down the long hallway. One of his arms was under my ass to hold me up, while his other hand pushed a button on the wall next to an elevator. He pulled his phone from his pocket and sent a text. I watched his thumb flit quickly across the screen, but none of the words registered.

"Where are we going?" I rasped when we walked onto the elevator.

"My room," he said, still looking at his phone.

I didn't say anything else as I buried my face in his neck again, breathing in his scent. I slid my fingers under the neck of his shirt, and he caught my wrist, making me gasp.

"What are you doing?" he asked gently.

"I wanted to--" I paused. I didn't know what I had been doing. "Sorry." He paused for a moment, then put my hand on his chest over his shirt.

"Keep your hand here." I did. I closed my eyes and focused on his heartbeat, forcing mine to beat in time with his.

Finally, he put his phone back in his pocket and wrapped his other arm around me, shifting me from his side to his front. His hold on me tightened, and I whimpered.

"I'm sorry," he murmured against my hair. "I didn't want to scare you."

The elevator dinged, and the doors slid open. Dean swiftly walked down the hallway and opened a door at the end of it, shutting and locking it behind us. His steps were long and sure as he moved across the room. He lowered me onto a closed toilet and knelt in front of me.

Justin was dead. Dean shot him. He shot and killed him because of me. Because Justin had gone in to assault me. To rape me. To hurt me.

And Dean saved me.

My hands trembled as he stared at me. He pushed my hair behind my ear, his icy silver eyes flicking between mine.

"His body," I croaked and pushed to my feet. "We have to—his family. What do we do? I—I don't—I don't know how to hide a body! We have to bury him—"

"Relax," he cooed as he took my hands in his. "Micha's on it."

"Micha," I said, my voice barely a whisper. He nodded, his lips pressed tightly together as he scanned my face.

"Where are you hurt?" he asked darkly as he ran his thumb over my bottom lip. I winced when he brushed the hole my teeth had made.

"Nowhere," I said.

It was true. I wasn't hurting anywhere else. I felt nothing. I was numb. My chest was hollow, and my tears were dried up. But I couldn't stop shaking; my hands wouldn't stop trembling. And I was cold. So fucking cold. Why was I so cold? My teeth began chattering, and he swore under his breath.

"You're going into shock," he said, and I mindlessly nodded. "I need to get you a blanket or something—"

"No!" I reached for his hand as he stood, then slid from the seat onto my knees and wrapped my arms around his leg. "Don't leave me." His hand rested on the back of my head as he gently ran his fingers through my hair.

"Get up, darling," he said softly. I tipped my head back to look up at him. His face was soft as he stared down at me, his fingers never stopping their soothing touch. "Come on. Please get up." He tilted his chin toward the toilet, and slowly, I sat back down. He knelt in front of me again and pulled me against his chest, wrapping his arms tightly around me. I tucked my arms between us, nestling my head against his shoulder.

"I'm cold, Dean," I whispered.

"I know," he said softly. "Do you want a hot bath or shower? It might help." I nodded softly, my cheek brushing against the soft fabric of his shirt. "I'll have to take your clothes off. Are you sure you want me in here for that?" I nodded again, and his grip tightened. "Words, darling. I need to hear you say yes."

"Yes," I rasped against his skin. "Please don't go." I felt clingy and needy, raw and too vulnerable. And the only comfort I felt was from this giant, hulking, killing, tattooed man.

"I'm not going anywhere," he murmured and firmly pressed his lips to my temple. He held them there for a moment, and I further melted against him. "Bath or shower?"

"Bath," I said quietly. He stood with me in his arms, and my legs went around his waist again. Quickly, he moved across the large bathroom and twisted the handle on the giant bath, letting the water rush out of the two faucets.

"I need to put you down to take your clothes off," he said, and I nodded. "Words, darling."

"Okay."

He lowered me to the ground, but I kept my hand wrapped in his as he helped me get undressed. His eyes or hands didn't linger on any part of my body.

I stood awkwardly as he checked the temperature of the water and adjusted the handles a few times. Finally, he helped me into the tub, and I sank into the warm water, sighing. But when I closed my eyes, all I saw was Justin's body, and his blood pooled on the floor. The gunshot.

I bolted upright, the water sloshing over the side. My eyes frantically searched for Dean, but he was beside me, his face soft.

"It's okay."

He ran his fingertips lightly along my shoulder, back and forth, back and forth, until all I could do was focus on his touch.

"Tell me about your family," he said as he grabbed a bottle of shampoo. He poured some into his palm and lathered it in my hair. His thick, long fingers were gentle against my sore scalp, and I sighed. Every so often, I'd wince when he got to a tender spot. "Julia," he murmured, "tell me about your childhood. What did you like to do?"

"I liked to paint," I said.

"Paint what?"

"Anything," I breathed. "Everything. I went to school for fine art."

"Do you still paint?" he asked as he worked the soap into the ends of my hair.

"No," I sighed, closing my eyes as I leaned forward. "I haven't painted since college."

"Why?"

"Matthew didn't like the mess it made," I said mindlessly. His fingers faltered for a moment, then he cleared his throat. "My parents died in a car accident when I was fourteen, so I lived with my Nan until I went to college. She died two years ago. Started as kidney failure. She went downhill pretty quickly after that."

"I'm sorry," Dean said softly. "I—My mom died when she was giving birth to my little brother. He died with her." I turned my head to look up at him. "My dad was killed about ten years ago. That's when I took over."

"I'm sorry," I said, and he shrugged.

"I was never close with him. He wasn't a good man."

"You are," I whispered, and he smiled sadly at me.

"I'm not, but thanks for thinking so, darling." He wiped my cheek with his thumb, his eyes lifting to mine. Something passed between us, but I quickly lowered my eyes again and he cleared his throat.

We sat in silence as he rinsed my hair, then covered it in conditioner and twisted it in a bun at the top of my head. He worked efficiently, almost clinically. Maybe tomorrow I'd feel embarrassed about this, but right now, it feels right. I needed to be taken care of, and I thought he needed to take care of someone.

"I need to wash your body," he murmured, and I slowly opened my eyes. "Is that okay?" I nodded, and he let out a breathy laugh, dropping his head slightly.

"Yes, it's okay."

The soap he used smelled like him. I tried not to look at the bloody, murky water as he scrubbed the blood from my body. He didn't linger, his eyes didn't stay on any part of my body, and I thought I should've been ashamed that a man other than my husband was seeing me naked, but...

I didn't care.

He helped me from the tub and dried me off as I stood stupidly in the middle of the huge bathroom. He clearly had a lot of money. The walls and floors were dark marble, and a huge chandelier was hanging in the middle of the ceiling.

I felt out of place, and he should've looked out of place, being so scary and massive, but he didn't. Everything in the room complimented him like the room was an accessory.

He wrapped his hand around mine and led me to a massive closet, then waved his hand awkwardly at the clothes. I looked around, finding it full of t-shirts. All of them were black, and all of them long-sleeved. All smelled like him. I breathed deeply, letting *him* invade me.

"You can wear whatever you want." His hand tightened around mine slightly before letting go. I picked the closest shirt to me and slid it on over my head, and it swallowed me, falling past my knees. His lips twitched as he scanned me, but he didn't say anything as he grabbed my hand again.

We walked through his room again, and I finally looked around. There were floor-to-ceiling windows along one wall overlooking a small field of trees. It was dark, so I couldn't see much else, but it looked like there was a small village right outside his window.

A large bed with black bedding was in the middle of the room, the head pushed against a wall. Two nightstands sat on either side of it with lamps. The floors were dark, warm-colored wood, and the walls were a darker marble than the bathroom. Nothing was white. Everything was black or gray. The ceiling was vaulted, and the lighting was a soft glow that didn't hurt my eyes.

It should've looked small and felt cold, but it didn't. It felt warm and cozy. And safe.

*I felt safe.*

He led us to the double doors we'd walked through earlier, then gently tugged me into the hall after him.

"Where are we going?" I asked, my voice weak. I halted, pulling on his arm.

"To a guest room."

"I thought—" I stopped myself. I thought I was going to sleep with him? That he'd want me to sleep with him? He'd already done too much for me, and he didn't need me clinging to him all night.

*Stupid. I was fucking stupid.*

I kept my mouth shut, not wanting to embarrass myself more. But he stopped and turned to me, his eyes narrowed.

"Do you wanna sleep with me?" he asked, and I shook my head, lowering my eyes to the ground. "Julia." He growled it like a warning. "I don't want you to lie to me or hide what you're thinking and feeling. I want to know everything." I blinked a few times, my eyes stinging. "Darling, please look at me." Slowly, I lifted my eyes, and he cupped my face, gently stroking my cheek with his thumb. It slid lower to the faint bruise at the base of my jaw, and his jaw tensed. "Do you want to sleep with me?" I nibbled my bottom lip, wincing when I bit into the wound. He moved his thumb to it, gently tugging it from my teeth.

"Yes, please," I whispered. "If you don't mind."

"I don't. At all."

He led me to his bed and pulled the blankets back on the side closest to the windows. I laid down, and he helped me get comfortable, tucking the heavy, warm blanket around me. He smoothed my damp hair from my forehead as he straightened, then took a few steps back.

"You're not coming to bed?" I shot up, grabbing his arm.

I don't know why I felt like he couldn't leave me or like I needed to be by his side constantly. I didn't understand why I had to touch him, see him, or smell him. But I did.

All I knew was that I felt protected when he was with me. Maybe because he'd saved me, and now I was latching onto that. Even though he'd killed someone, he'd killed for me. And then he took care of me.

He cared for me in a way I'd never been taken care of before, and I felt...*something*. The closer I examined it, the more I understood that feeling was guilt.

I was with another man, lying in his bed after he just bathed me—after he just killed my would-be rapist. And Matthew was...where? Was he searching for me? Was he going out of his mind trying to find me? Did he think I was dead? Did he even care?

"Come with me," he said warily. "I'm just gonna take a shower. It'll be less than five minutes." I glanced at the bathroom door, then at him. "You can sit on the counter and tell me about your painting." I nodded, and slowly, he helped me up and led me back to the bathroom.

He picked me up like I was weightless and set me on the counter, then went to the shower. He stepped behind the dark fogged glass and threw his clothes on the floor. I could see his silhouette, but that was it.

It took me a few minutes to get into talking about art, but once I did, I found myself excited. Truthfully, I didn't think he was listening. But when he started asking questions, saying he wished he could see the pieces I'd painted, my chest warmed. He was actually listening, but more than that, he was *interacting*.

Matthew never liked to hear about art, mine or anyone else's, what book I'd been reading, or what Sophie and I saw on our outings. He'd barely listen or interrupt, not caring enough to even pretend to listen.

But Dean...

No. *No*, I couldn't do that. I couldn't compare them. There was nothing to compare, no reason to compare them. I needed to get back to my husband—I needed to get home.

Even if I was starting to feel attached to Dean, I couldn't let myself feel anything for him. He was nice and safe—that was it.

"Close your eyes," he said when the water turned off. I giggled quietly but put my hand over my eyes. "No peeking, Julia. I'm gonna get clothes."

"Alright," I said, smiling softly. "I'm not looking."

Clothes rustled as he pulled things on, then his feet slapping against the marble was all I heard. I jolted when he put his hands on my hips. I let my hand fall away from my eyes, and when I looked at him, my breath caught.

"Ready for bed, darling?" he murmured as he stroked my hair away from my face, tucking it behind my ear. I nodded, my head feeling heavy. We walked hand-in-hand back to the bed, and after he helped me in again, he laid next to me but not close enough to cuddle or touch me. Instead, he kept his hand wrapped around mine until I fell asleep.

# Dean

It wasn't the best idea to shoot and kill one of my own men, but when I saw what he was doing to her, red coated my vision until Julia was safely behind me. I should've left it at that, taken him to a kill room to kill him away from her. I shouldn't have shot him in front of her, but I was furious—no, I was more than furious. What I felt didn't have a fucking word.

It felt like my chest was being shredded every time she screamed. I hadn't even realized I'd had the sound on, but I'm fucking glad I did.

The first scream sent my heart racing. I didn't know where it had come from, but then I realized it was coming from the security feed on my phone.

When I looked and saw Justin in the room, what he was doing—what he was *trying* to do to her...I saw fucking red, and all I could think was that I needed to kill him.

And I wouldn't apologize for it.

I would've killed anyone if they were trying to do that to her.

At some point, she started to worm her way into my head and

now, apparently, my heart. There's a small piece of her in there, and I hadn't realized it until I felt her wrap herself around my leg, safe.

The fact that she worried about Justin's family afterward made my heart ache. He didn't have anyone—no wife, no kids, no parents, which is why he'd wanted to work for me. He'd been left as a baby at the hospital, no note, no sign of the mother, nothing. He'd just been dumped and forgotten. Then, forgotten again in the system.

He went down the wrong path, and it landed him in prison. When he got out, he found me and begged for a job. He wanted to go straight. He wanted to make something of himself and settle down. He was a hard worker, and I could've seen him working up the ranks.

That's if he hadn't started drinking again. As soon as he started drinking again, I fucking knew we'd have issues. And we did. Issues that ended with him dead.

Julia was sweet and was somehow tied up with us—with fucking criminals. Maybe Costa and his Family didn't care about who they brought into this life, about who they destroyed, but I did. I didn't want anyone to suffer or deal with this shit if they didn't have to.

*But...*

But I was feeling selfish. I wanted her. I really fucking wanted her. And I hadn't realized just how much I did until tonight. So, I was fine keeping her in this life. I was fine making her a Demon. I was fine with it, as long as she was by my side. I don't know what was drawing me to her, why I wanted her so badly, all I knew was that I did, and that was good enough for me.

Julia turned onto her side, facing me. Her lips were slightly parted, and her long, thick lashes were fanned across her high cheek-bones. Every so often, she'd scrunch her nose and eyebrows, making a cute little scowl.

I couldn't stop staring at her.

I should've made her sleep somewhere else, but the way she'd looked at me, like she trusted me, like she was safe, made me not want to break that. I wanted to protect her. And I'd be lying if I said I didn't want her in my bed. Of course, I wish she'd gotten in it for a different reason, but I'll take it. Now, I needed to figure out how to keep her in it.

Tomorrow, if she woke up and told me to fuck off, I don't know that I could. I don't know if I could give her back to Blackwell. I don't know if I'd be able to let her go, not after I'd had this revelation about liking her.

There was a soft knock at my door, and I sighed before running my hand softly over her dark hair, smoothing the strands away from her face. She nestled deeper into the pillow, sighing softly as her face and body relaxed. I kissed her forehead before slipping from bed, carefully tucking the covers back around her.

When I opened the door, I put my finger to my lips, telling Micha to be quiet, and shooed him back into the hall. He stepped away, a confused look on his face.

"Well?" he asked, folding his arms over his chest.

"Julia's in there," I said. "She didn't want to be alone." He nodded, his eyes darting to the closed door at my back.

"So..." he trailed off, looking at me again. "This means you're not givin' her back to Blackwell?"

"She's not some toy we can play tug-of-war with," I snapped, then scrubbed my hand roughly over my face. That's exactly how I'd just been thinking, wasn't it? Like she was something Blackwell, and I could yank between us. But if we did that, she'd break, and I couldn't let that happen. "Sorry, man, my head's just fucked right now."

"I get it," he said softly. I looked down at him, my eyes stinging from exhaustion.

"Did you get everything settled?"

"Yeah," he said, dropping his head back with a sigh. "The guys ain't happy about what happened."

"Knew they wouldn't be," I groaned. "I wasn't thinking, you know? I just saw what he was doing and reacted."

"They're not upset you killed him," he said, lifting his head to look at me, his thick, blond brows pushed tightly together. "They're upset the fucker was tryin' to rape her. We've killed our own for it before. You ain't the first to kill for it, probably ain't the last."

"You're right—"

A scream had us both stiffening. Micha's eyes went wide, and my heart pounded when we heard it again. It was a guttural, terrified, blood-chilling scream.

I slammed the door open and raced toward the bed, finding it empty. I frantically searched the room, spinning in a circle, not seeing her anywhere. *Where the fuck was she?*

A whimper came from the corner, and I whirled around, finding Micha crouched slightly as he walked toward her.

"Hey, Jay," he cooed, his voice soft. "It's me, Micha. You know me."

"Stop, don't touch me!" she screamed. Her knees were tucked under the shirt, and her trembling hands were out in front of her. The terrified look on her face was a sucker punch to the gut.

"Darling," I croaked, and her head snapped toward me. She let out a choked sobbing sound. "It's alright."

"Don't hurt me," she cried and scooted further into the corner.

"It's Dean," I said as I slowly approached. Micha tried to grab my arm, but I moved it out of his reach. She watched me warily as I crouched in front of her, trying to make myself as small as possible.

"Dean," she whimpered, her eyes barely losing some of the fear. "You—you weren't there when I woke up. You were gone." I hesitantly reached my hand toward her, and she let me rest it on her knee.

"I'm sorry," I murmured. "Micha and I needed to talk." She flicked her big blue eyes behind me.

"Micha," she said, and he let out a long, hard breath.

"Yeah, Jay. It's Micha," he said, shuffling forward and crouching beside me.

"I'm sorry," she whispered. "I don't know what's wrong with me."

"Don't apologize," I said. "You've done nothing wrong." She

stared up at me, her ruined bottom lip trembling. "You need some more sleep."

She glanced at Micha, her eyes still scared. She looked like a wounded animal, and I fucking hated it. There was something fragile about her, something that called me to protect her. But there was also something that told me she wasn't fragile at all. She just hadn't found her strength yet.

I'd help her find it.

"I can go back to my cell," she said as she lowered her eyes. "I don't want to bother you. I'm okay. I can go back—"

"No." Micha and I said together. I shot him a look, but he didn't notice. He was too busy staring at her. I roughly cleared my throat.

"No, darling, you'll stay with me," I said firmly. Then, hesitantly added, "Or one of the guest rooms." She nibbled her lip, and it took all I had not to reach out and stop her. "I should've never put you in that fucking room to begin with."

She looked between us again, her eyes guarded. Her throat bobbed as she swallowed, then she licked her lips. "Can I go home? Can I go back to my husband?"

Her words were a bucket of ice water over me.

"Is that what you want?" I asked, and Micha shot me a look I chose to ignore.

"Yes," she said. The look she gave me shattered me. "Please, Dean. Please, I just want to go home." Tears streamed down her face. She looked so fucking broken.

"Alright," I said, even though the word stabbed through my chest. Everything inside me was screaming at me to not let her go. "If you want to go back to him, we'll figure out a way to reunite you."

"Tomorrow?" she asked, hopeful. I hesitated for a moment, my breath caught in my lungs.

"Do you want to call him first?" I asked, my voice tight.

Maybe if I could get her to see what kind of monster he was, she wouldn't want to be with him anymore. Maybe I could convince her to stay here. With me.

# Julia

I paced in front of the large mahogany desk. Dean was reclined in the dark leather chair, his hands resting in loose fists on the desk's surface. He was tracking me as I paced. We were waiting on Micha.

Ever since Dean said I could call Matthew, Micha had been on edge. He hadn't looked me in the eye. He barely even said a word to me, and I understood. I was struggling with the fact that my father-in-law was responsible for the murder of my cousin and his wife. And the fact that Micha was my family still hadn't fully set in yet.

Finally, the door opened, and Micha strolled in. I let out a long sigh as I turned to him. He looked casual, but his tense shoulders and fiery blue eyes told me he was anything but calm. Dean watched us impassively, flicking his eyes from Micha to me.

"Can we call now?" I asked, turning to face Dean. I didn't know if I wanted to be with Matthew, but I wanted to be home. From there, I could decide what to do.

"On one condition," Micha said. "You listen. Don't make yourself known 'til one of us gives you the go-ahead. I want you to know what kind of person you're married to." I blinked at him, then nodded.

"I know he's done terrible things—"

"Then why do you want him back?" he snapped. His face flushed a deep red as he glared down at me, and I shrank away from him. The angry, crazed look on his face was one I'd never seen before.

"Micha," Dean said firmly, but he was ignored. Micha's body was vibrating, his hands opening and closing. I took a few steps away from him, and he squeezed his eyes shut.

"Why do you wanna go back to him when you know he's a shit person? When you know what he fuckin' did—" He gave me his back, his shoulders rising and falling with his rapid breaths.

"He's—" I paused and slid my eyes to Dean. He was watching me carefully, gauging my words and my reaction. I wanted to say he was my husband, that I had to go back. But I didn't, did I? "I don't want to go back to him."

They both froze, and, for a moment, I worried they weren't breathing. The air in the room was thick, but then Dean cleared his throat.

"Then why call him?"

"I want to go home, and I can't stay here forever," I said quietly and tried to ignore the way Dean flinched.

"Fuck," Micha muttered under his breath. "You think this is all— you think you can just go home after this? That your life will be normal?"

"Micha," Dean growled as he straightened in his seat, but Micha ignored him.

"You think Dominico won't come after you? You think he won't torture you for information about us?"

"But I don't know anything!" I said, stepping away. Tears burned my eyes, but I blinked rapidly. "I don't know anything about you," I turned toward Dean, "or you."

"He won't care," Micha scoffed. "He'll torture you until—"

"Micha!" Dean shouted, and I jumped. He pushed the chair roughly back, and it banged into the wall behind him. He stormed to us, stepping between Micha and me. "This isn't the time for that conversation. Let's just get this over with, then we'll deal with that shit later." Micha's eyes were flaming as he glared at Dean, then he dropped them to me.

"Do what I said." He walked to the wall and leaned against it, folding his arms over his chest. A moment later, Dean turned to me.

"You ready?" he murmured, and I nodded. "No talking until we tell you to." I nodded again, my throat dry and tight.

He didn't sit back down. Instead, he braced his fists on the desk and leaned heavily on it. He eyed both of us, then cleared his throat as he pushed on his phone screen a few times.

The ringing was loud in the quiet room. I stared at the phone, anxiously waiting to hear my husband's voice for the first time in over a week.

"What do you want?" Matthew barked as soon as he answered. It was his voice, but it didn't sound like him. Even when he was angry with me, he'd never sounded that cold. That...mean.

"Just wanted to ask if you've changed your mind," Dean said casually, his eyes locked with mine. "I just want peace, and you can have your wife back."

"And I told you to keep the whore," he sneered. My stomach dropped, and I pressed my fist into it. I was going to be sick. Tears blurred my vision, and my breathing was harsh.

"She's not a whore," Dean growled, and Matthew barked an ugly laugh.

"Whatever," he said. "I don't want the bitch back, used and stretched out. Keep her. Fuck her. Kill her. I don't give a shit. She was going to be your fucking problem anyway—"

"Matty?" I croaked, unable to stop myself. The room went completely silent. I felt Dean and Micha's eyes on me, but I couldn't make myself look at them.

"You fucking asshole! You bastard!" Matthew shouted. "She's there with you?" There was a crashing sound on his end. "Jewels, you know I don't think you're a whore, right?" I didn't say anything. I couldn't. My throat was too tight. "Julia!" Matthew barked, making me jump.

"Shout at her again, and the next time I see you, you're fucking dead," Dean said darkly. The threat hung in the tense air for a moment.

"Have you fucked my wife?" Matthew's words barely registered. Before Dean could answer, I moved closer to the phone, leaning heavily on the desk, my knees shaking.

"No!" I sobbed. "I haven't cheated on you, Matty!" My legs nearly gave out, but Micha wrapped his arms around me and held me against his chest. "Just do what he says so I can go home."

There was silence again.

"So, that's what this is about." Matthew laughed again, an ugly mocking sound. "You're working with them? You want me to agree to his bullshit conditions? You think I'm a fucking idiot, Julia?"

"What?" I croaked, looking up at Dean. He watched me carefully, his face neutral, but his hands were in tight, shaky fists. "I just wanted to go home."

"You want me to agree—"

"It's just peace!" I cried, and Micha's arms tightened. "Why wouldn't you want that, too? Why would you want to keep fighting if you didn't have to?"

"Because I want them all dead," he said without hesitation. My hands wrapped around Micha's forearms as they dug further into my stomach. "And if you're a Demon now, too, Julia, I want you dead." I opened my mouth, but no sound came out. What could I say? "You know what?" He laughed humorlessly and goosebumps rippled across my skin. "You're dead to me. You're nothing but a worthless Demon whore." He hung up, and the silence deafened the room. No one said anything for a long time. We just stared at the phone.

"Julia?" Dean finally asked hesitantly. "Are you alright?" I swallowed hard, my hands tightening around Micha's arms.

"Yes," I said, surprised that my voice came out smooth and not shaky. I was proud of myself for that, but I wasn't going to push it. If I said anything else, I'd break.

"Jay, we've got you," Micha said softly. I pushed at his arms, and he reluctantly let go.

They were silent, but I could feel their eyes on me as I slowly walked across the room. They called out to me when I carefully pulled the door open. I ignored them as I started down the hall.

I didn't know where I was going. I didn't know where I was. All I knew was that there was an elevator somewhere at the end of the hall, and I needed to get to it.

To that room.

To my cell.

Dean's rumbling voice echoed through the hall, but I couldn't make myself stop walking. I couldn't stop myself from wanting to get away from him. From Micha. From that room, that shattered whatever was left of me and my sanity. Of my marriage.

As I pushed the button for the elevator, a hollowness bloomed in my chest. It was a hollowness like I'd never felt before. It was like whatever was left of my soul was being emptied, and the only thing I could do was passively sit by and watch it happen.

Even after all the years of lies and manipulation, of the false and broken promises—even after learning his father was responsible for my cousin's death...I still loved Matthew, and I still wanted him. A part of me felt like I still needed him.

The doors slid open, and I walked into the cage. When I turned, I met Dean's storm-gray eyes. He was standing a few feet away, his face twisted in pain.

He watched as I pushed the button for the basement. He watched the doors slide shut, and when the metal was finally between us, when I couldn't feel his piercing, all-knowing gaze anymore...I broke.

# Dean

She went back to that fucking cell in the basement. I don't know why I ever put her in there in the first fucking place. It was a mistake. And why she felt more comfortable being back in there than with me didn't make any fucking sense.

It was where she was held as a fucking prisoner. It was where Justin—where he was fucking killed. But she was curled up on her cot, her knees clutched tightly to her chest. She was laying eerily still, and if it wasn't for the steady rise and fall of her chest, I'd think she was dead.

I should've gone after her. I should've coaxed her to leave the room. But I couldn't make myself move. A fiery rage was burning in my chest after that bullshit phone call with Blackwell. And the way she'd looked immediately broken, the way I saw the light flicker out of her eyes, fucking destroyed me.

Then it made me want to destroy him.

I wanted her to stay here, and I wanted her to know she was wanted here—that I fucking wanted her here. Forever. Fuck.

Her husband told her to fuck off in the worst way. And he'd

accused her of cheating when I know he's been cheating on her for fucking years. I'd never seen or heard of Julia but had seen other women on his fucking arm multiple times.

He'd said it to hurt her.

He was pissed at me, pissed that I had her, pissed that I had the upper hand for once, and he took it out on her. It made me wonder what else he took out on her and, more importantly, *how* he took it out on her. Was he abusive? Was that why she was so jumpy? Or was it just nasty words he'd spat at her?

Either way, I wanted to fucking kill him.

"She won't come out," Micha said as he stormed into the office, slamming the door behind him. He began pacing furiously in front of the desk. "Won't talk to me, won't even look at me. She just stares at the fuckin' wall."

"She needs time," I said, even though the words gutted me. He paused his pacing to glare at me, his face twisting in anger.

"She needs to know she's not alone. She needs to know we have her fuckin' back." I sighed and dropped my head into my hands, digging the heels of my palms into my eyes.

"Do I have her back?" I muttered. "I let her talk to Blackwell knowing he'd say some bullshit to her. I let Justin get close to her—"

"There's no way you coulda known he'd do that," Micha said as he slumped into the chair across from me. "She's scared."

"I know." Swirls of color and static were all I could see, but it felt good.

"Show her she doesn't have to be scared," he said. "Show her she can trust us. Show yourself that she can trust you." I finally looked up, blinking a few times to see him clearly.

"She's your family," I said quietly, and he dropped his eyes.

"She is." He nodded a few times as he picked at his nails.

"And you want her here."

"I—" He let out a hard breath. "I want whatever she wants."

"I want her here," I said, and he lifted his eyes, looking at me through his brows. "Does it make me an asshole that I don't give a shit that she wants to go home? I want to keep her here."

"You're always an asshole." He grinned when I rolled my eyes. "I see the way she looks at you, the way you look at her—whatever y'all have, it's real."

I smirked sadly at him, shaking my head. I didn't know what he saw. There was nothing between us. But I felt my chest loosen, like a worry I hadn't realized I'd even had was gone.

He tapped his fingers against the edge of the desk as he stood. Pausing, we stared at each other, then one side of his mouth tucked up. "Go get her."

I WALKED INTO THE ROOM, DETERMINED TO NOT LET HER STAY in there another fucking second. She kept her back to me, but I knew she was awake by the way her shoulders bunched.

"Darling, come with me," I said firmly. She didn't turn to look at me. She just stared at the wall, as Micha had said. "Julia, come on." She didn't move. She didn't speak. She didn't twitch. She looked like she was barely breathing.

Sighing, I crouched beside her and rested my hand on her head. She jolted and hugged her knees tighter to her chest, whimpering quietly. I softly stroked her tangled hair, smoothing it away from her face in a way I hoped soothed her.

"Julia, please come with me," I murmured. She finally looked at me over her shoulder, her eyes red and puffy, her lips swollen.

"I don't want to go anywhere," she said, her voice raspy. "I want to stay here."

"I don't like you in this room." She rolled back over, but I continued stroking her hair, hoping it would help her lower her guard. I needed her to lower her fucking guard and let me in.

"Please leave me alone," she whispered. "I'm not leaving this room." I paused but left my hand on her head. She let me, not trying to push it away. Her body shook with her silent cries, and I knew I had to do something.

I could either force her to come with me, kicking and screaming, or I could meet her halfway.

# Julia

The door slowly opened, and I wanted to scream. Why couldn't they just leave me alone? Could they not take a fucking hint?

Metal clanged behind me, something shuffled, then metal scraped against concrete. There was enough noise to pique my curiosity, so I slowly rolled over, pressing my back against the wall.

What I saw I hadn't been prepared for.

Dean was setting up a cot, one a little bigger than mine. He was tucking a blanket around the end of it. The head of his bed was only a few inches from mine, lined up against the other wall.

"What are you doing?"

"You won't come to me, so I decided to come to you." He sat on the cot carefully, and I waited for it to break. He looked like he'd been waiting for the same thing because he was wincing in anticipation. But when nothing happened, he relaxed and stretched his long legs out in front of him, crossing them at the ankles.

I pushed myself up and crossed my legs as I glared at him. "I told you to get out."

"And I told you to come with me," he retorted. "Seems neither of us is good at taking orders." I blinked at him.

"You can't be serious," I said. "Get out!" I threw my arm toward the door.

"I'll leave when you do." He shrugged and watched me impassively like this was a normal conversation. "When you decide to leave, tell me, and we'll go back to my room. Or you can have one of your own, although I must say I liked having you in my bed. But it's anything you want, darling."

"Stop calling me that," I snapped, and his eyebrows hitched high on his forehead.

"Darling?" He tilted his head to the side. "Why? It's never bothered you before."

"Just because I didn't say anything doesn't mean it wasn't bothering me." It was a lie. Honestly, it made me feel warm when he called me darling. I'd never had a name like that. Matthew called me Jewels, sometimes baby in the middle of sex, but otherwise...it was Jewels or my name.

Dean never called me Jewels, which I was thankful for. I hated the name. I absolutely fucking hated it. Despised it. Wanted to kill it.

But darling, I liked. I liked Micha's name for me, too. Jay. I'd never been called that, either.

"I brought something for you," he said as he reached for a bag. I hadn't noticed it on the floor, but it was large and overflowing with things. "I wasn't sure what to get since I don't know shit about art, but —" He pulled out a sketch pad and some pencils, then set them on the bed beside him. I watched wide-eyed as he pulled out some watercolor paints and brushes. "You said you paint, but I didn't know what you liked to use—" He held the paint out to me.

They hung between us, a lifeline that, if I only accepted, would change my life. Somewhere in my mind, I knew that. Somewhere I knew accepting these gifts from him, accepting his kindness, would mean something was changing, and I wasn't entirely sure I was ready for that.

So, I let them hang there, clutched in his huge, tattooed hand. His throat bobbed as he nodded a few times, his face falling in defeat. He shoved everything back in the bag.

"There's more upstairs," he said quietly, his voice rough. He sounded hurt. Not upset the way I'd anticipated, not yelling or blowing up. *Hurt.* Genuinely hurt that I hadn't accepted his gift. His truce. "I can get you anything else you want. Whatever you want—if you want an e-reader so you can read, I can do that. Or physical books. It doesn't matter. I bought you more paints and canvas—I bought everything I could find—"

"It's okay," I said, lowering my eyes to my lap. Guilt ate away at me. Why was I like this? Rude and cold to him when it wasn't his fault this was happening to me.

Well, not entirely his fault. He was a little to blame. He had kidnapped and held me captive, after all. The thought gave me pause, and I looked at him.

"How did you know about the cabin?" I asked. "There was a fire. How did you know I was in there?" He froze, then cleared his throat.

"We started the fire," he said, and I swallowed hard. "I didn't know anyone was still inside. If I would've known you were in there, we wouldn't have started it."

I said nothing as I watched him. He dropped the bag to the floor before sliding to the edge of the cot and bracing his elbows on his knees. His eyes bored into mine as he took a deep breath.

"I heard you scream," he murmured. "It was a scream I'd never heard before, like—like you were terrified, and hurt, and—and—and —" He dropped his head, his eyes squeezing shut. He took a moment to breathe deeply before he looked at me again. And this time, when his eyes met mine, I could see his pain. Feel it. "I asked Micha if he'd heard it, and when he'd said yes, I ran around the cabin, looking through the windows. I saw you hitting the window. I saw your face— you looked so small and scared. You looked like you were giving up. So, I ran inside. I got to you right after you fell off the counter and hit your head. You passed out. I felt guilty that we'd started it with you inside.

"I got you out of there and carried you to my car. All my guys were yelling at me, saying I was being too soft, that it was a trap, that I was an idiot to take you home. But, I don't know," he shook his head again, "I just felt like I had to take you. It doesn't make sense, but before you fell, our eyes met, and you looked sad. Broken. And I wanted to help you." He shrugged and locked his fingers together, twisting them awkwardly.

"After we got you here and set you up in this room, I realized that I was an idiot," he said, and I inhaled sharply. "I didn't trust you, and I didn't know you. You were my enemy. I thought we'd have you here for a day or two while we used you as leverage to get what I wanted."

"But that didn't happen," I said, and he nodded, turning his eyes up to me, but his head stayed bowed.

"That didn't happen," he repeated. "I'm sorry, Julia. Truly. I didn't know Matt was your husband, and I can't say I'm sorry for taking you away from him. He's an asshole. He's dangerous and not a good man. I'm sorry for everything you've gone through, for the pain you feel. But not for taking you away from him. I don't know how or why you ever got involved with him—"

"We were in college," I said defensively. Not defensive of Matthew, but of myself, of my choices. "We dated for about a year, then married six months later. That was five years ago."

"You married him knowing he was a part of The Family?"

"No," I said, shaking my head. "I didn't know he was a part of anything until we went to the cabin. He told me he had some debts he couldn't pay off, so he offered to work for Costa. But once he entered The Family, he couldn't leave. He said he wanted to—" Dean barked an ugly, harsh laugh.

"That's such bullshit," he said. "That's such bullshit, Julia. I'm sorry, but it is. He didn't have any fucking debts. He was taking over for his father." I blinked at him, nodding slightly.

"I know that now," I said quietly, and his sarcastic smile fell.

"Did he give you the bruises, Julia?" His voice was low, almost like he didn't want to know the answer. "Did he hurt you?"

I wrapped my hand around my arm mindlessly, feeling the faint pain of the almost-healed bruise. His eyes latched onto my hand, his jaw flexing under his beard.

"He grabbed me," I whispered, and his eyes shot to mine. "I fell and hurt my wrist—"

"Julia," he growled. "What happened?"

"Dominico was—" I sighed. "I tried to lock him out of the bedroom at the cabin, and when he shoved the door open, I fell and hurt my wrist."

"Why were you locking him from the room?" He scooted closer to me, his hands flexing. He looked like he wanted to touch me, but he didn't reach for me. "Was he trying to—"

"He was just being creepy, and I was scared. It was the first night there, before I knew what was going on. He was being forward with me, and I—I don't know. I overreacted and shut the door on him."

"Did he touch you?" he growled, and goosebumps rippled across my skin. "I'm going to fucking kill him." He gently grabbed my wrist and inspected it. It looked a lot better than it had. It wasn't swollen anymore, and it had just a faint bruise. The one on my arm was basically gone, and the one on my neck was gone. His eyes shot to my jaw, and I knew he was looking for it. "The one on your jaw."

"He didn't choke me," I said quickly, and his eyes widened. "But he had his hand wrapped around—"

"Motherfucker," he said under his breath. "I'm going to kill him. And Blackwell. Who else touched you?" He pushed to his feet like he was going to hear the name and leave the room to hunt them down right then. "You know what? Doesn't matter. They're all dead."

"Dean," I said and grabbed his hand. He stilled as he stared down at me.

"Did he ever hit you?" I shook my head, but he eyed me like he didn't believe me. It was true, though. Matthew never laid a finger on me, not until he'd grabbed me to take me away from his men. It was his words that hurt. "Don't lie to me."

"I'm not," I said. "Before that day, he'd never put his hands on me. And he only did that time because he was pulling me away from the other men."

"The other men?" Dean dropped to one knee in front of me, my hand still firmly wrapped in his. "What other men?"

"The men there," I said, shrugging. "They weren't happy I was there and that I was asking questions. One of them shoved me, and Matty caught me. He squeezed my arm too hard when he pulled me to the room. That's all. It wasn't anything bad. He didn't mean to do it."

"Why are you protecting him?" he murmured. "He's not a good man. He's not a good husband."

"He's—" I almost said he was amazing, but I stopped myself.

I was so used to praising Matthew to everyone to make my marriage sound better than it was. But right then, in that concrete room with no one around except for Dean, I didn't have to pretend anymore. "He's not. He wasn't nice."

"I'm sorry," he said, and I shrugged again. "He's not the only guy out there. Someone else will treat you well. Someone else will treat you better than he ever could. They will treat you like the queen you are." I stared at him, my chest heaving.

"Who?" I breathed, my eyes flicking between his. Slowly, he reached up and cupped the side of my face.

"I have to do this," he murmured as he pressed his forehead to mine. "If I don't, I'll never forgive myself."

Then, he kissed me.

# Julia

His lips were soft.

He didn't move them at first, just pressed them gently to mine, holding them there like he was waiting for me to push him away.

But I didn't.

Instead, I found myself pressing harder against him. I found my body unfolding as I shifted to my knees, resting my hands on his broad shoulders to steady myself. His hands dropped to my hips, and he gently tugged me forward until my knees pressed into his chest.

And when his tongue licked the seam of my lips, my mouth opened, and I eagerly let him in. He tasted fresh, like water and spearmint. His hands flexed before he dug his thick fingers into my hips. He groaned low in his throat when I sucked his bottom lip between my teeth, nipping at it.

He slid his hands under my shirt, his touch a feather-light caress that sent goosebumps rippling over my skin. I clutched his shoulders tighter when he slowly grazed his warm palms over my breasts.

"Can I?" he breathed, and I nodded, barely breaking our kiss to let him drag the shirt off over my head. He pulled away to look at my body, his eyes dark and hooded. "You're fucking perfect." He cupped my small breasts, then lowered his head to one, running his mouth around the hardened peak.

"Dean," I whimpered as he bit down on it, tugging it away from my body with his teeth. I ran my fingers through his thick, dark hair as I tilted my head back, pressing my breasts out for him. He moved to the other one, giving it the same treatment before finding my mouth again.

Sliding my hands down his hard chest, I dropped them to his belt. When I pressed my fingers against his lower stomach, he grabbed my wrists, stopping me.

"Wait," he said as he pulled away. "I—*shit*." He closed his eyes as he took a deep breath. "I have scars." I looked between his eyes as he opened them. "That's why I have the tattoos. To cover them. They're not bad on my arms, but—but they're really bad on my chest and stomach."

"It's okay," I said, sliding my hands back to his belt. "You can leave your shirt on." He let out a ragged breath as he kissed me again, harder. I pressed my hands to his stomach over his shirt, and his muscles flexed under my touch.

He wrapped his arms around me and pulled me off the cot as he sat on the floor. I straddled him, and his hands immediately found my ass, squeezing roughly. Circling my arms around his neck, I tugged on the ends of his hair, making him groan.

Somewhere in the back of my mind, I knew I shouldn't be doing this. If I did, I was nothing more than the whore Matthew accused me of being. But I was so caught up in Dean, so caught up in his scent, his taste, his touch, that I didn't care.

I'd be a whore for him.

I ground my hips against him, and he tightened his hold on me. "These need to come off right now." He tugged on the waistband of my leggings, letting the elastic pop against my skin. "Right fucking now."

I scrambled to my feet, and he tugged them off my hips, dragging them down my legs as I steadied myself on his shoulders. My face heated when his eyes dropped to my pussy. He was eye level with it, and I subtly tried to cross my legs, wanting to hide myself.

He didn't let that happen.

Instead, he gripped my hips and roughly pulled me forward. His mouth connected with my pussy, and I yelped as his tongue found my clit. He flicked it back and forth quickly, and I dug my fingers harder into his shoulders.

"Oh, fuck," I moaned as I dropped my head back. He let out a growling sound and threw my leg over his shoulder, pulling me closer. I would've fallen if he didn't have a tight hold on my hips.

"You taste fucking amazing," he said, the vibrations from his deep voice shooting through me. He dragged his tongue from my entrance to my clit, then roughly sucked it into his mouth before flicking his tongue over it again.

I ground my hips against his mouth as I ran my fingers through his hair, gripping it tightly in my fist as he hit a rhythm that had my eyes rolling back.

"Right there," I breathed as I pressed against his mouth harder. "Like that. Fuck, please don't stop. Please." He moved his tongue faster, driving my orgasm up. "Oh, god. Fuck, I'm—" I threw my head back, my cries echoing around the concrete room as I came. His tongue stayed on my clit through it, extending my pleasure until my knees buckled, and I fell to his lap.

Immediately, his mouth found mine, his hand cradling the back of my head. I'd never tasted myself before, but fuck if it didn't give me a headrush.

"I need to be inside you," he rasped before pressing his lips bruisingly against mine again. I whimpered as he gently pushed me back on his thighs so he could undo his belt and jeans.

"Wait," I said as I pulled more away from him. "A condom." He paused, then his shoulders slumped.

"Shit," he breathed. "I don't have one. You're not on the pill?"

"You've slept with a million women, apparently," I said dryly, and he laughed.

"I'm clean," he said, smiling at me. Gently, he brushed his fingers over my cheek, then tucked my hair behind my ear. "I got tested a few months ago and haven't been with anyone since." I flicked my eyes between his. I wanted to trust him—I really fucking wanted to trust him. "I can show you—" He reached for the bag, but I stopped him.

"It's okay," I said as I moved closer to him. "Just pull out."

"I'll show you," he said again and reached for the bag. "I have it on my phone—"

"It's okay, Dean." I cupped his face with my hands and pressed my lips gently against his. Reaching down, I slid my hand under the waistband of his boxer and tugged his cock out.

"Are you sure?" he breathed, stopping me. "Julia—"

"I'm sure," I whispered, then paused when I saw his dick. "Is that —your dick is pierced?" There was a silver curved barbell with beads on each end. It was right on the head of his dick. My eyes nearly fell from my head as I stared at it.

"Ah, yeah," he laughed. "Is that—are you—is it okay?"

"I've never seen one," I said. "It doesn't hurt?" I looked up at him, finding him smirking.

"Nah," he said. He reached down and gripped his cock, slowly stroking. "It won't hurt you, either, darling." I nodded a few times, my eyes dropping back to the piercing. "We don't have to—"

"I want this," I said, interrupting him. I lifted my hips and moved them forward until I felt his cock graze my clit.

"You're positive?"

"Dean," I groaned, "are you?" We stared at each other for a moment, then he nodded. He rested his forehead against mine, his arms wrapped around my waist as he held me. His head pressed against my entrance, and, even before noticing the piercing, I knew he was bigger than Matthew and would feel different from him. I whimpered as I pressed him inside me, our eyes locked.

"Fuck," he breathed, his hands moving to my hips. Slowly, I

pushed myself down, impaling myself on him. His hips lifted, shoving in more, and I cried out, digging my nails into the fabric of his shirt on his shoulders. "I'm trying really fucking hard to not turn you around and fuck you like a beast right now."

"Do it," I said, and he let out a raspy, harsh breath. I pressed the rest of the way down, and we both groaned, our hands on each other tightening. He filled me completely, almost too much, but I rolled my hips, getting used to him. "Fuck me how you want." He kissed me gently, forcing my hips in a circle again.

"Another time," he said against my lips. "This is perfect." He forced my hips up and down a few times, his piercing hitting a spot inside me that had me panting. "Your pussy is amazing. So fucking tight and wet, squeezing my cock—" I tightened around him, and he groaned, "Like that."

My hips rose and fell faster as I rode him. He had one arm wrapped around my waist while his other hand moved to my head, his fingers tangling in my hair. He roughly pulled my head back, forcing my body to arch. My chest pressed against his, the soft fabric of his shirt teasing my nipples.

"That's it," he murmured before gently biting my neck. "Ride my cock, baby. Show me how much you want it." I moved faster, rocking my hips back and forth, my clit rubbing against him. He kissed along my neck, down my throat to my breasts, making me moan. He jerked his hips up, hitting me deeper.

"You're so big," I breathed as he did it again.

"I know," he said. "But you're taking me so well, darling." I moved faster as he pulled my face to his, capturing my lips. "You feel so fucking good."

Suddenly, he flipped us, staying inside me. He pinned me on my back, the cold concrete floor biting into my skin. He sat on his knees and lifted my hips so they rested on his thighs, my back bent in a deep arch.

"Hands above your head," he said as he slid his hands over the curve of my waist. I did as he said, and he smirked down at me. "That's my good girl."

He gripped my waist tighter as he pulled almost all the way out, then slammed into me. I screamed and writhed under him as he fucked me harder, using his grip to hold me where he wanted. I wrapped my legs around him, holding on as he used my body how he wanted. His hand slid down my body, resting it on my lower stomach. He found my clit with his thumb and stroked it in fast circles.

"Love your tits," he said, moving his other hand to my breast. He roughly squeezed it, then pinched my nipple, making me cry out. "Love the sounds you make."

I wrapped my hands tightly around his wrist, silently begging him to stop rubbing my clit. He ignored me and slammed into me a few more times, then abruptly pulled out and began stroking himself.

"You want my cum, baby?" he grunted the words, and I nodded eagerly.

"All over me," I gasped as I cupped my breasts, rubbing my thumbs over my sensitive nipples. His eyes fixated on them, and he groaned, moving his hand faster. "Please, Dean. Please come all over my pussy."

"Shit," he breathed as he squeezed his cock, aiming it at my pussy. His cum spurted all over me in hot, thick ropes, and I spread my legs wider, letting him cover me. "Fuck, you're perfect."

# Julia

I sat in the middle of Dean's large bed and looked around his room. It was just as cozy tonight as it had been the other night. But today, I felt like I could enjoy it.

He brought me here, closed the curtains tightly over the large windows, and told me to take a nap. I hadn't done that, though.

I'd been too busy beating myself up over the fact that I fucked him.

I fucked Dean.

I shouldn't have. I know I shouldn't have. I should've told him to stop kissing me and laid back down on the cot. But I didn't. I gave in to him and to myself and let him fuck me.

Well, no. I didn't let him fuck me. I was an enthusiastic participant in the fucking.

Guilt ate away at me. I felt dirty, and like the whore Matthew had accused me of being. And maybe that's what Dean wanted. Maybe he wanted me to feel so bad, so guilty about betraying Matthew and our marriage, our vows, everything, so I wouldn't go back to him. So I'd stay here with Dean.

But I couldn't do that, could I? I couldn't let myself stay here, wrapped up in him. Because being with a guy like Dean, you'd forget who you were before. He took up all the space in your head and heart. He'd trap you with his big, warm, safe hands and soft lips, and sweet words.

I'd already allowed myself to die once, to forget who I was because of a man. I couldn't let it happen again. And even if the current man was...amazing. Gentle. Kind. Protective.

He was going to ruin me.

I knew he would. I'd be ruined, and then what? What would be left of me? As much as I wanted to ignore it, the blaring truth was that he was like Matthew—a killer. He was doing the same things Matthew did, even if his motivations were different. He was in the Mafia. He was the Don, for fucks sake.

But he hadn't lied to me as Matthew had. He hadn't made me feel worthless, or unheard, or like I wasn't good enough. Even when I first got here and was nothing more than his prisoner, he never made me feel worthless.

But Matthew? He made me feel like that every single day. And I think it wasn't until that moment that I realized just how far I'd fallen. Just how deep my wounds were and how far gone I'd been. Just how unhappy and miserable I was.

The door opened, and I numbly turned my head toward it. Dean froze in the doorway, his hand on the doorknob as he stared at me.

"Everything okay?" I asked quietly. His shoulders slumped forward slightly as he walked further into the room, closing the door behind him. He was careful as he approached the bed and sat on the edge, then turned to face me.

"Everything's fine," he murmured. "Just—" He stopped talking when I let out an irritated sigh. If this was going to work, whatever it was, I wouldn't let him lie to me. I wouldn't let him hide things. I wouldn't be made a fool of again.

I didn't know what this was—if it was just a quick fuck and he'd move on to another woman on his long list...*shit*. I hadn't even thought of that.

Was I just another notch on his belt? Had he always wanted to fuck a captive? Fuck a married woman? Fuck his enemy's wife?

I stared at him with new eyes and felt my gut twist.

Was that all it was? Revenge? Was I just a pawn in his game with Matthew?

"What?" he asked quickly, sounding panicked. "What's wrong?"

I didn't say anything. It's not like he'd tell me the truth anyway. With a deep breath, I forced myself to smile and fall into that complacent role I'd been in for the last five years.

"Nothing," I said, my voice cheerier than I felt.

His dark brows scrunched as he watched me. He dragged his bottom lip between his teeth before he nodded, coming to a conclusion.

"Come with me," he said as he stood.

"What?"

"Come with me," he said again and held his hand out. "I want to show you something." I hesitated as I lifted to my knees and grabbed his hand, shuffling across the bed.

"Where are we going?" I asked as he led me to the elevator, his hand wrapped tightly around mine. I still wasn't used to his house above the basement. The walls were dark marble, the floors a dark wood, and the décor—surprise—was dark with gold accents. Everything was totally Dean. There was no mistaking that this was his house—his *mansion*.

When the metal doors slid shut, he turned to face me. I tipped my head back to look at him, and he cupped my face, his thumb gently stroking my cheek. There was still a faint red mark there from Justin pushing my face into the concrete, and my lip still ached, but Dean's touch was gentle.

His touch was always gentle.

"Beautiful," he breathed, almost to himself, his eyes flitting over my face. My throat tightened to the point of pain, and my eyes stung. Tears welled in them as I stared up at this giant, tattooed, scarred, gentle giant of a man.

I shook myself.

See? This is what I meant. He'd make me lose sight of the important things. I thought he was using me to get back at Matthew, and all
it took was one word, one whispered compliment, and I forgot everything? I couldn't let myself get lost in him.

But it would be so fucking easy to do. With the way he looked at
me, like I was the only thing that mattered.

When the doors slid open, we stayed where we were, staring at
each other. Swallowing hard, I tore my eyes away first and looked
down the hall. It was the same one that led to his office. He cleared
his throat and put his hand out to stop the doors from sliding shut
again.

"This way, it's at the end of the hall."

With a deep breath, I walked with him. I wasn't behind or in
front of him. I was at his side. And something about that made me
feel...*something*. I felt like he saw me as his equal. He didn't want me
to lead him, but he didn't want me to follow him, either. He wanted
me to be with him, by his side.

Or maybe that was all total bullshit, and I was too in my head.

His hand landed on a doorknob, and he hesitated. "If you hate it,
I'll get rid of everything and get you exactly what you want."

I scrunched my brows as I looked up at him. His eyes were
guarded, like he was scared of my reaction. I nodded a few times and
then looked back to the white door.

Slowly, he turned the knob and pushed the door open.

I smelled the paper first.

Fresh, crisp paper. Paper that begged to be marked. I walked into
the dark room blindly, being led only by the scent of something
promising. When he flipped the lights on, my heart stopped.

"It's an art studio," he said quietly. "Well, the beginning of one."

I turned in a slow circle in the middle of the room, taking everything in. My mouth hung open, my eyes wide, but I didn't care how I
looked. All I could think about was the art supplies everywhere.

The ceiling was all glass, so the starry night sky shone overhead. Blank canvases hung on the walls; some were leaning against them, and others were sitting on easels. There were paints, brushes, acrylics, colored pencils, graphite pencils, watercolors, erasers, and oil paints... but the set of gouache paints on a little table drew my attention.

I mindlessly walked forward, my hands shaky as I reached for them. It had been five years since I'd held them in my hands, and I was trembling from excitement, from fear, from anticipation—every emotion I could feel, I was feeling.

"I have no idea what that is," Dean said from behind me, making me jump. "But online, it said it was a popular medium for artists, so I got a few sets."

"It's my favorite thing to use," I said quietly as I lifted each aluminum tube. "Gouache *was* my favorite—" I closed my eyes, tears stinging them. "I can't accept this. I can't accept any of this."

I dropped the tube on the table and took a few steps away, both from it and from Dean. His eyes tracked me as I walked back toward the door, his brows furrowed.

"What do you mean you can't accept this?" he asked as he turned to fully face me. "This is for you. It's all yours."

"No," I said, shaking my head slightly. "It's too much. It's—this was too much. It's expensive and—"

"I have the money," he said, taking a small step forward. "I have more money than I know what to do with. I want you to have everything you want." I wrapped my arms around myself as I dropped my eyes to the floor.

"I can't accept it," I said again.

His footfalls were muffled as he walked to me. I expected him to touch me, to reassure me, to stroke my hair, and say nice things...but he didn't.

Instead, he waited until I tipped my head back. He waited until I spoke first. He waited until I touched him.

"This isn't my home," I murmured, and he inhaled sharply as he straightened to his full height. "I can't accept this when I know I'm not staying here forever."

"You don't want to stay," he said quietly. "You don't want me." I flicked my eyes between his.

"It's not that—"

"Then what is it?" There was an edge to his voice. Anger. "You want fucking Blackwell?" he scoffed and shook his head, then shoved his fingers through his dark hair, making it stick up. "I—what we did," he threw his arm toward the door, "that meant nothing?" My chin quivered as I tried to hold in my tears. "That meant nothing to you? Because it sure as fuck meant something to me."

"Dean," I whispered, but he ignored me as he began to pace. He walked in front of me, up and down the large room. "I'm still married."

"You didn't seem to care that you were still married when you were riding my dick," he snapped, and my stomach twisted. "You didn't care you were still married when my mouth was on your cunt. You didn't—"

"I get it!" I shouted. "I get it! I'm a fucking whore, just like Matthew said. I don't need you reminding me of my mistakes—"

"Mistakes?" he rasped, blinking at me. "Mistakes? You think it was a mistake?"

"I don't know what the fuck I think!" I cried. "I've been apart from my husband for less than a month, and I've already fucked another man. I—I—" I ran my fingers through my hair, yanking roughly on it as I crouched down, burying my face in my knees.

"Julia," he said. His scuffed boots were in front of me, but he didn't crouch down with me. He didn't touch me. He stood above me and stared.

"I'm a whore," I muttered. "A cheating, lying, worthless, disgusting whore."

"Stop." His voice was hard. "Stop saying that."

"It's the truth." I tipped my head back to look up at him. His jaw was tight, his hands flexing at his sides. "He was right."

"No," he growled. "He wasn't fucking right."

Finally, he dropped to his knees in front of me and wrapped his arms around me. I fell into his chest, and he pulled me into his lap as he sat on the floor. I cried against him, my guilty tears soaking his shirt.

"He wasn't right," he said again, his lips moving against my hair. "Do you really think it was a mistake?" I pressed my face harder against him as I squeezed my eyes tightly shut.

*Did I think it was a mistake?*

I felt guilty, yes, but was I guilty because I'd slept with someone else, or did I feel guilty for sleeping with Dean? Did I regret *him?* Or would I regret it no matter who it was?

I tried to think about if I was single and slept with him, would I still feel guilty? Would I think it was a mistake?

And the answer was: no. No, I wouldn't feel bad about it. I felt something for him, even if it didn't make sense, and I probably shouldn't be falling for the man who'd kidnapped me; I still was.

He was dangerous and oversaw an empire. He was terrifying and could pull the trigger of a gun and take a life without thinking twice about it. He could be cold and mean...but warm, too. And funny, and sweet, and soft. He was hard and protective, serious. But he was everything I needed. Everything I wanted.

So, no. I didn't regret him, and I didn't regret what I felt for him. But I did regret proving my husband right.

# Dean

"No," she said quietly. "I don't think it was a mistake, but it still wasn't the right thing to do." I tightened my hold on her, squeezing her to my chest. "Even if I liked what we did, it was wrong. We should've waited. I'm still married—"

"Why are you still trying to be loyal to him when he said all he did to you? With everything he's done?" I suddenly asked, cutting her off.

Why was she so set on being faithful to a man like Blackwell? I understood some people respected the sanctity of marriage, but he ruined whatever they had when he'd refused to come for her—to save her.

If she was my wife, she wouldn't have ever been in the situation to get taken in the first fucking place. But, if she was my wife and somehow had been taken, I would've torn apart the fucking universe to get her back. I would've burned the world to the ground for her. I would've strung up every man and slaughtered them all if it meant getting her back.

And I still would.

If something happened to her now—I don't know what I'd fucking do.

"I can't just get into another relationship when I'm not even trying to get a divorce."

Her words were like a stab to the heart, and I pulled away to look at her. She didn't look at me.

"You're not trying to get divorced," I said slowly. "You want to stay married to him." She pursed her lips together, her brows scrunching.

"I haven't wanted to be married to him since the day after our wedding," she admitted quietly. "I've wanted out of it every day for five years. And now that it's finally here..." she shrugged, sounding sad. Broken. Lost. "I don't know what to do."

I put my knuckle under her chin and gently lifted her head. Her eyes were wide as she stared at me, and I couldn't help myself—I leaned forward and kissed her. It was a slow, languid kiss. A kiss I hoped she'd remember and feel forever. A kiss that told her I wanted her—I wanted her more than my next breath.

"Stay here," I rasped against her lips, my eyes still closed. I rested my forehead against her, breathing her in. "Stay with me, darling." Finally, I opened my eyes, finding her staring at me.

"You want me to stay?" she whispered, and I let out a breathy laugh as I pulled away.

I waved my arm around the room, "Isn't it obvious?"

Her eyes looked around, and the unmistakable glint of longing was in them. She wanted this—maybe not me, not yet, but she wanted everything in this room. She wanted to do something she loved, and I wanted to give it to her.

"If you don't want to be with me, if I'm too much too fast, I'll set up another room for you," I said quietly, even though it was the last thing I wanted. "If you want to be alone for a while—I'll leave you alone. Just tell me what you need, darling, and I'll make it happen."

"If I told you I needed a private jet so I could fly to Paris whenever I wanted?" she asked, grinning.

"Done."

"Whatever," she laughed as she shook her head. She looked around the room again, but I gripped her chin and forced her to look at me.

"Done," I said again, more firmly. "I'll have one ready for you by morning." She blinked at me, her lips parting.

"You're serious," she said, and I nodded.

"Anything you want, it's yours." Her throat bobbed before she lowered her eyes.

"You're a lot," she said, and my stomach dipped. "But I think I like you." She flicked her eyes up, looking at me through her thick lashes, a coy grin on her face.

"I think I like you, too, darling."

SHE WAS PACING IN FRONT OF THE BED. SHE HAD BEEN FOR THE last hour. It was nearly two in the morning, and I was fucking exhausted, but she was having a meltdown. Again. I barely held in my sigh as she chewed her thumbnail, her brows bunched in worry and guilt.

"I shouldn't have done it," she muttered. "We shouldn't—"

"Darling," I sighed, but she ignored me.

"I'm a cheater," she said around her thumb. "I can't believe I cheated on my husband."

"It's not like you two had the best marriage anyway. It was going to fall apart eventually." She paused, and slowly, she turned to face me. Her eyes were wide, her thumb secured between her teeth.

"You don't know that," she said. "We could've worked it out—" I scrubbed my hands over my face as I inhaled sharply.

"Then go work it out," I snapped. "If you want to be with a man who said he'd rather you be fucking dead than agree to my terms, then go back to him." She blinked at me.

I was done codling her. I was done trying to make her feel better about what we'd done. It made me feel like total shit that she felt guilty about us. Not because she was guilty, but because she regretted what we'd done. What we'd shared. And it wasn't fair. It wasn't fair that I was finally falling for someone after all these years, and she was pushing and pulling me around.

I was mad.

I was hurt.

I was sad.

"Is that what you want?" she asked, and I groaned.

"I want whatever you want," I said. "If you don't want me, then tell me that now because I'm not going to play this game with you. If you want to work shit out with Blackwell, then go. Leave. Stop dragging me around. It hasn't even been twenty-four hours and whatever the fuck this is," I waved my hand between us, "is already more stressful than it should be."

Her throat bobbed as she swallowed. "You're saying I'm more work than you want." I blinked at her, then laughed humorlessly.

"You're putting words in my mouth," I said. "I said whatever the fuck is going on with us is stressful. I never said you were too much work."

"But it's stressful because I'm trying to deal with everything. It's stressful because of me. And you don't want to—"

"Stop talking," I said as I pushed to my feet. "Stop fucking talking." She was silent behind me as I walked to the door. I leaned my hands on it, my head hanging.

I needed to get my head on straight.

She was my enemy's wife, yes. But also, whatever the fuck I felt for her was a lot more than I'd felt for anyone in my entire life. Not love, not yet. But could it be? Yeah, one day.

Could I see her walking these halls with paint splattered all over her clothes and smeared across her face? Her hair in a messy bun like it was now? Yes, absolutely. Could I see her dressed to the fucking nines and on my arm as we walked into some hoity-toity event? Yeah, and she'd fucking kill it. She'd be the best-looking one there.

Did I want her in my life, regardless of whatever drama she'd bring into it? Yes. And, most importantly, could I see her leading with me? Could she be a leader?

Slowly, I turned toward her and leaned against the door. Her face was flushed, and she looked pissed, but her lips were twisted tightly shut.

"I want you here. I want you with me, in my fucking bed, on my fucking arm. But if you want to go back, then go back." I stepped to the side and pulled the door open, letting it swing until it hit the wall.

She stared at me like she couldn't believe it. It was a gamble, and I knew it. If she walked out the door, I'd throw her over my shoulder and haul her ass back inside. I knew that, and she probably did, too. But it was a challenge, a test, to see where her head was. Where her heart was.

I wanted her to want me. I wanted her to choose me. I didn't want to live in Blackwell's shadow, and that's exactly where I'd be if she kept this bullshit up. I wanted her to choose to leave him, their life, their marriage, in the past.

"If I told you I wanted to go back to him, you'd let me?"

I took a deep breath and bit my lip hard enough to draw blood. "If that's what you want, then, yes." She stared at me, her eyes narrowing slightly.

"And if I said I didn't want to go back to him, but I didn't want to stay here either...what then?"

"I'd put you on a plane and take it wherever you wanted."

"And if I said I wanted to stay with you, see where this goes—"

"Then I'd bring you to bed and fuck you until we passed out," I said, and she laughed. It was a sweet, bright laugh. It was one I hadn't heard from her before, and it made my chest swell. "What do you want, Julia?"

She stared at me for a long time, her eyes flicking between mine. She was in deep thought, I could tell. I tried to keep my face neutral. I wanted her to make the decision on her own.

"What happens tomorrow?" she finally asked as she stepped forward. "We wake up, then what?"

"Well," I sighed as I rubbed my forehead, "I have to work some shit out with the families of the men we lost. Then, I need to start figuring out shit for our warehouses. How much we lost in damages and if we're able to rely on insurance at all for it. Boring shit."

"And me?"

"You can do whatever you want," I said. "I don't know what you're asking me, Julia. Are you asking if you can leave this room? Of course. I don't really want you to go back to the basement, but I won't stop you if you want to. But you will come out of that fucking room the first time I ask." I pointed my finger at her sternly as I stepped forward. She smirked at me, and I nearly lost it.

Yeah. I could totally fall in love with this girl.

"If you wanna spend all day painting, then do it. If you wanna lay in bed and binge Netflix, do it. If you want to explore, explore. You wanna go shopping? I'll give you all my fucking cards. Whatever you want."

"Can I go to work with you?" she asked, and somehow, I knew it was a challenge. I knew there was only one correct answer and that it was either going to save me or make me drown.

As much as I wanted her to lead by my side, this could backfire on me if she was still having doubts. And it wouldn't be only me who'd be getting burned—it'd be every Demon. Could I really have that on my conscience? Did I really trust her? Could I trust her?

With a deep breath, I said, "Yes."

Her shoulders slumped forward, and she let out a hard breath like she'd been holding it in. I took a few more steps toward her but stopped a few feet away. She'd have to come the rest of the way if she wanted me.

"If we're going to do this," she waved her hand between us, "then there will be no secrets. No hiding. No lying. No keeping things from me, and I won't keep anything from you. I want to know everything you do, and I want to be a part of it all. I want to learn everything. I want—"

"Julia," I said, cutting her off, and her mouth snapped shut. "Let's take it a day at a time, okay? Come with me tomorrow, meet the families, and then figure things out from there. One day at a time, darling." She nibbled her bottom lip, then nodded.

"Alright," she said. I sighed, feeling relieved. "What does this mean for us?" I lowered my head slightly, looking at her through my brows.

"If you wanna put a label on it, then label it. But you're mine now. That's all I know, and that's all I care about. You belong to me, Julia. And you might not be a Demon yet, but you will be." She inhaled sharply, her eyes fixed on mine.

"I'm yours?"

"Yeah, baby. You're mine. Every single person in this fucking world is gonna know—"

"Do you only want to be with me to get back at Matthew?" she blurted, her face reddening. My head reared back as I stared at her. My mouth opened, then closed.

*What the fuck?*

She couldn't possibly think I wanted her because of him. I fucking wanted her, regardless of who her asshole husband was—is. But did it cross my mind that it might make him mad that his wife was mine now? Obviously. Was it the only reason I wanted to be with her? Fuck no.

"No," I said firmly. "I want to be with you because I want you. Believe it or not, your asshole husband doesn't often cross my mind. My motives aren't all about him." Her lips barely twitched, then she grinned. "He's gonna know. He'll find out sooner than later, I'm sure, and you're gonna have to be okay with that, Julia. You have to be okay knowing he's gonna say terrible shit about you, about me, about us, about The Demons.

"We have a game to play, an image to uphold; so if you're mine, if this is what you want, then you have to play the game, too. You have to be mine. In public, it's a united front. We're hopelessly in love, even when Matt's around. There can't be a chink in our armor, or everything could collapse. This is bigger than just us, Julia. This is my entire empire. This is everything my family's worked for—it could topple if we let it. I need to know, are you ready? Are you choosing me?"

# Julia

*Are you choosing me?*

The words were heavy as I weighed them. Did I want to play this game? Did I want Dean? Did I want everything that came with being with him?

I took a small step forward, expecting him to close the distance. But he didn't. He stood stoically, carefully watching me. I took another step, a larger one this time.

It looked like he wasn't breathing.

Three steps were separating us. Could I take them?

Another small step, and I could reach out and brush my fingertips against him if I wanted.

"Julia," he murmured so softly it was barely audible.

*Two steps.*

I wanted him. I wanted this. I wanted to leave Julia Blackwell behind and become a Chamberlain again. I wanted to ignore the fear I felt swirling in my belly. I wanted to live a whole life again. I wanted to be where I was wanted, where I was loved. And I wanted to be somewhere where I loved...with someone I loved.

Not that I loved Dean. But I could. I felt it already brewing in my heart. I could love him. And it wasn't a learn-to-love kind of love like it had been with Matthew. This was an all-encompassing kind of love.

Another step forward. One left, and I was in his arms.

I slowly tipped my head back and stared into his silver eyes. They were unguarded and vulnerable. He was vulnerable. For me.

At that moment, something clicked. Something clicked, and the word *mine* screamed at me, a siren blaring in my head.

He was mine, and I was his.

I took the last step and hesitantly reached for his hand.

"I'm choosing you," I said quietly. "I'm choosing us."

He let out a hard breath like he'd been holding it and wrapped his hand tightly around mine. "Thank fuck."

I reached up on my tiptoes and shook his hand off so I could circle my arms around his neck. He let me tug him closer to me. He let me press my lips to his. He let me take control.

"I want you, Dean," I said against his lips. Pressing my forehead against his, I closed my eyes. This is what I wanted. It felt right. Perfect, even.

His arms wrapped around me, and I felt his muscles flex as he squeezed me. He held me like he never wanted to let go.

He stood straight with me in his arms, and I wrapped my legs around his waist, finding his mouth with mine again.

"The door," I breathed, and he nodded. He didn't break our kiss as he went to the door, closing and locking it before walking back to the bed.

I expected him to lay me down gently, to be soft with me. But he wasn't.

He threw me on the bed, letting me bounce a few times. I blinked at him, shocked. The look in his eyes was dark, and the set of his shoulders was tense as he stared down at me. He was shadowed in the dimly lit room, but I could see his intent clearly.

He wanted to own me.

"Take your clothes off," he growled, and my breath caught. It wasn't a voice I'd heard from him before, and it had my pussy dripping. *"Now."*

I scrambled to obey. I stood on the bed and quickly stripped my shirt and shorts off, then I was standing before him, completely naked. His eyes roamed over my body lazily, an arrogant smile spreading across his face. When his eyes found mine again, I lost my breath.

"On your knees." I dropped to my knees without hesitation as he took a step forward. "You're gonna suck my cock, then I'm gonna turn you around and fuck your tight little cunt until you can't remember any other man who has ever been inside you. It's just me, Julia. It's only me."

"Only you," I repeated as if in a daze. Dean's eyes held mine as he slowly unzipped, then lowered his jeans just enough to pull his cock out. He barely stroked it as his other hand reached for my head.

"Come here." His fingers wrapped in my hair, and he tugged me forward. I fell on my hands and arched my back, wiggling my ass for him invitingly. "Fuck." His hand left my hair, and he brought it down on my ass, smacking it hard enough to leave a mark.

I licked the tip of his cock, and he let out a startled gasp. Opening my mouth, I slowly slid his head inside and swirled my tongue around and around. He groaned as he gripped my ass. He was bent over me, his chest pressing into the back of my head. I moaned when his fingers dove inside me, stretching me.

"That's it," he said as he quickly pumped them in and out. I took him deeper, barely reaching halfway. Suddenly, his hips jerked forward, and the pierced head of his cock slid into my throat, gagging me. "Fuck, yeah. Choke on me." He held me where he wanted me, his fingers moving faster inside me. His thrusts were shallow but hard. Tears flowed from the corners of my eyes as he fucked my throat and pussy.

I couldn't do anything but take it. I tried to push back on his hand to get away from his cock, but he only pulled me forward again, forcing his cock further down my throat.

"Uh-uh," he chided, his voice thick. "No running away. Take it." His fingers slid from my pussy and immediately found my clit. My hips rolled, and my body shuddered as he worked his fingers quickly over it. I moaned as much as I could around his cock, and he groaned. His other hand came down on my ass again, making me scream.

"Are you ever gonna doubt me again? Ever doubt us again?" His hips moved faster, in time with his fingers. I tried to shake my head, but I couldn't. "Are you ever gonna think about leaving me to go back to Blackwell?" His fingers moved faster, then his hand came down on my ass again, harder. "You're my girl now, darling. You're fucking *mine*. And there's no way in hell I'll ever let you go now."

Tears and saliva dripped from my face and landed on the blanket below. My orgasm was so fucking close, but he pulled his fingers away. The cold air assaulted my soaked pussy, and I cried out around him. Suddenly, his hand came down on my pussy, and I screamed as much as I could. He did it again, slapping it harder.

"I'm going to pull my cock out of your throat, and you're going to tell me who you belong to," he growled as he slapped my pussy again. He thrust into my mouth a few more times, then abruptly pulled out.

"You," I said before taking a deep breath. "I belong to you."

"That's fucking right." He gripped my hair and yanked my head to the side. I stared up at him, into his hungry, demanding eyes. "I fucking own you. Turn around." His hand fell away from my hair, and I barely caught my breath before he wrapped his arm around my waist and turned me around, throwing me like a rag-doll. "When I give you an order," he slapped my ass again, "I expect it to be done immediately." Another slap.

Then, his cock filled me.

I screamed at the size, at the fullness. It was a delicious mix of pain and pleasure as he fucked me relentlessly. He rested one foot on the bed, his other on the floor, and fucked me harder.

"Dean," I screamed his name as my orgasm built again. "Please!"

"What?" he grunted. "What do you want?"

"I want—" My body shuddered again, so fucking close. He pulled out of me, his hand coming down on my ass again. "I want to come! Please. Fuck!" He shoved inside me again, fucking me harder. He was growling like an animal. The piercing on the head of his cock rubbed against a spot inside me that had my eyes rolling back.

"This is my pussy," he breathed, his hand tightening on my hip. "You're my fucking girl." He slapped my ass again, even harder than before. He gripped my hair and yanked my head back, making my back arch deeply. "Who the fuck do you belong to?"

"You!" I screamed. My hands came off the bed as he pulled me back by my hair. He kept slamming into me, his thick cock hitting me deeper with each punishing thrust.

"If you ever pull the shit you just did, telling me you regret us, that you want to go back to him, your ass will be so fucking red you won't sit for a week. You won't come for a fucking month." He pulled me back against his chest, his hand dropping from my hair to my throat as his other arm wrapped around my waist. "You're mine now, and I don't fucking share. Keep his name out of your mouth, out of your head. No games. No regrets. No fucking second thoughts. This is it. Only me."

He shoved me back down, letting me fall limply to the bed as he fucked me. He lifted my hips easily and pushed and pulled my body the way he wanted. Shoving my legs further apart, he hit deeper, and I cried out. I gripped the sheets in my fists above my head and held on as he rode me.

Another orgasm built, one I hoped I'd fucking have. I looked back at him, finding him already watching me. "Come for me, darling." I squeezed his cock, and his eyes rolled back. The sound that came out of him was my undoing.

I pressed my face into the bed as I screamed his name through my release. It was too much. It was the most intense orgasm of my life, and as I came down, my body turned to jelly.

He shoved all the way inside me, and with a grunt of his own, he filled me with his cum. I arched my back more, pressing him further inside me, letting him fill me. I'd never let Matthew come inside me.

I'd never let anyone do this. But with Dean, I wanted it. I needed it. And I think he did, too.

He stayed inside me until his cock softened completely. And even then, he stayed in a little longer. Then, slowly, he pulled out. I felt his hands part my ass, then his fingers as he brushed them over my clit.

"I want you to come again," he said as he slowly circled my clit. "Fuck, I love the way your pussy looks leaking my cum." He circled my clit faster, and I whimpered into the blankets.

When I glanced over my shoulder, I found him kneeling on the floor, so he was eye-level with my pussy. I felt exposed and raw. Vulnerable. He was seeing everything. I couldn't hide.

"Come for me again, baby." His fingers moved faster, and my stomach muscles tightened. That familiar warmth began to flow through me as he worked me up higher.

"Please don't stop," I cried, gripping the blanket tighter in my fists.

"I won't," he said. "Does that feel good?"

"Oh, fuck!" I screamed and dug my face harder into the bed. "It feels so fucking good."

"You like feeling my cum inside you?"

"Yes!" I screamed again, my throat raw. "Fuck, fuck, fuck—"

My screams were muffled by the bed as I came again. He was relentless, not stopping his assault on my clit. I couldn't catch my breath as I came down. I reached back blindly, and he grabbed my hand, pinning it to my hip.

"Again."

So, he flicked my clit until I came again. And when I was mush, he flipped me onto my back and filled me with his cock again. He fucked me into the bed, watching me writhe under him. Our eyes stayed locked. No matter where I turned, he was there. His silver gaze was there. All I could see, all I could feel. Him.

He fucked me until he came again, filling me even more. He didn't kiss me. He didn't say anything. He wasn't gentle, but not rough either. What he'd been doing before was punishing me, and what he'd just done was claim me.

"You're going to keep my cum inside you tonight," he said when he finally pulled out. I stared up at him, blinking a few times as he tucked himself away. "Let me see." Slowly, I let my legs fall open, and he groaned. "Fuck, what a pretty sight."

He lifted me and easily slid me under the covers. When he got in, he wrapped his huge body around mine. His hand slid between my legs, cupping my pussy possessively, and I stiffened.

"No more playing," he whispered against my neck. "I just want to hold you."

# Julia

I felt awkward and out of place. I stood beside Dean, Micha on my other side, as he tried to console a woman. We were in a neighborhood I didn't know, talking to people I didn't know. A small boy was clinging to the woman's leg, his eyes wide as he stared up at Dean. He didn't look scared—he looked mesmerized.

"He was a good man," Dean said softly, and the woman nodded her agreement. "I know this won't bring him back, but—" He held out an envelope, and the woman let out a broken sob. "Take it, Amelia. Take it and start a new life with your boys. Go somewhere safe, somewhere away from here." She nodded as she wiped roughly at her face.

"Thank you," she said, sniffing hard. She took the envelope from Dean; it trembled in her hand.

"What is it?" The little boy asked, and Dean tipped his head down to look at him. My heart ached for this woman and her family. Dean smiled and crouched down in front of the boy. He moved further behind his mother's leg but kept his curious eyes trained on Dean.

"A gift," Dean said. "Would you like one too?" The boy glanced up at his mother, and she nodded, still sniffing back tears.

"Yes, please," he said. He couldn't have been more than four. Dean pulled a lollipop from his pocket and held it out to the boy. He hesitated before reaching out and snatching it quickly from him. Dean laughed breathily, his eyes soft.

I'd never seen him look like that before. Soft and kind, of course, I'd seen, but the way he was looking at the kid, the way he was inter-acting with him, made me ache.

"What do you say?" Amelia said as she ran her fingers through the boy's hair.

"Thank you," the boy said quickly, and Dean smiled.

"No problem. I'll bring your real surprise over later," he whis-pered, but it was loud enough for everyone to hear. "What's your favorite color?" The boy hesitated again before he stuck his head out a little further from behind her leg.

"Blue."

"Do you know how to ride a bike?"

The boy's eyes turned into saucers. "My daddy was teaching me." Amelia let out another sob, turning her face away from her son. Our eyes caught, and I smiled gently at her before she looked away.

There was something in the way she looked at me, though—like I wasn't supposed to be here. Like I was intruding. And maybe I was. Just because I wanted to be here, and Dean wanted me here, didn't mean his people wanted me around.

Dean cleared his throat as he dropped his head before he nodded and looked back at the boy. "I'll teach you." The boy eyed him, then looked up at his mother. Her hand was over her mouth as she looked down at Dean with tears welled in her dark eyes.

"Okay," he said slowly, looking back at Dean. He scanned his large body, taking in all the visible tattoos on his hands and neck, scalp, and face. The boy stepped forward, his little fingers wiggling like he wanted to touch him. "Why did you color on yourself?" he asked, and Dean laughed.

"I didn't. Someone else did," he said, and the boy took another small step forward. Dean stuck his hand out, and the boy looked at the rose on the back of it. "You can touch it. It's okay." The boy stuck his little pointer finger out and lightly traced the rose, then dipped his head closer to get a better look. He rubbed roughly at it, then looked up at Dean curiously. "It doesn't come off, bud."

The boy looked thoughtful, then looked at the rose again before he shrugged and stepped back to his mother's side.

I didn't know what to do. I felt awkward and uncomfortable. I felt like I was spying on a private moment. I felt guilty, and I didn't know why. Maybe it was because I didn't believe that whatever was going on with Dean and I could last. Maybe somewhere in the back of my mind, I was counting the days until everything went to shit, and I had to leave.

Micha touched my arm, and I looked over at him, finding Dean, Cory, and him giving me strange looks. Amelia and her son had already walked away, leaving us alone, and I was too zoned out to notice. Which probably didn't win me any points with her. *Shit.*

"You okay?" Dean asked as he tucked some hair behind my ear. I smiled shyly at him before nodding. His eyes flicked between mine, his lips pursed. "You can rest when we get home. You don't have to be in the office with me. We're just going over insurance stuff."

I twisted my lips to the side as I looked up at him. Maybe I was looking too much into it, or maybe I was trying to find something wrong, or maybe I was trying to give myself an out—but why didn't he want me to be around for his *insurance stuff?*

Even last night, he seemed hesitant to bring me into that part of his life. And it's not like I wanted to know his finances or really help run his empire. I just wanted to know...*everything.* I didn't want there to be any surprises later.

"It's okay," I said. "I'm not tired."

He stared at me a moment longer, his thick fingers still in my hair, before he nodded. He and Micha shared a look I couldn't read, then he put his hand on my lower back, gently pushing me toward his car. He opened the door, and I slid in.

"What are you doing?" I squeaked as he grabbed my seatbelt. He didn't say anything as he buckled it, then tugged on the strap a few times. I sat, shocked, as he pressed a quick kiss to my temple.

Micha got into his truck in front of us, a few other men getting in with him. Cory gave me a quick glare over his shoulder before he got into the passenger seat of Micha's truck. Dean slid into the driver's seat, then slid his dark sunglasses on.

"What was that about?" I asked, and he barely turned his head toward me. His hand wrapped around my thigh as he turned the car on and leaned slightly toward me, resting his elbow on the center console.

"What?"

"You put my seatbelt on."

He looked at me again, then ahead and put the car in the drive when Micha's truck began to move. "I just wanted to make sure you had it on."

"I'm capable of doing it myself."

"Just because you're capable of it doesn't mean you have to do it," he countered, and I narrowed my eyes. "Why do something when I want to do it for you?" When he looked at me again, he laughed. "If you think any harder, you'll wear a hole through your damn skull. Relax, darling."

I stayed staring at him. When was the other shoe going to drop? Guys like him didn't exist, did they? They didn't fuck you senseless one second, then put your seatbelt on and treat you like a cherished, fragile prize the next.

Right?

But here he was, doing just that.

His hand tightened on my thigh as he came to a slow stop. "I'd appreciate it if you'd stop staring at me." My lips parted, then he smirked, and I rolled my eyes.

"Why did you do it?" I eyed him, anticipating his answer. I was waiting for a lie or some grand reason.

So when he sighed and said, "Because I wanted to." I hadn't been prepared.

"Because you wanted to?" I squinted at him, then shook my head. "That's not an answer."

"Well, it's my answer." He stayed looking ahead, his fingers tapping mindlessly on my inner thigh. "What's the real problem?" I took a deep breath.

What was the problem?

So what? He put my seatbelt on for me. I'm sure plenty of men did it for their girlfriends. But was I his girlfriend? After the claiming last night, I assumed I was.

"Did I take a freedom away from you? Or make you feel less than? What?" When he stopped at a traffic light, he turned his head to look at me, his dark brows raised expectantly.

"No one's ever done that for me before," I said with a slight shrug. "That's it."

"Are you going to bite my head off when I do it again?" he asked, his lips twitching. He looked ahead again and let the car slowly roll forward.

"I didn't bite your head off this time, did I?"

"No, but you were about to," he teased. "I just like taking care of you, Julia. I like knowing you're safe. And in our world, that's important to me."

I hadn't thought of that. Nodding, I looked ahead again as a car weaved between Dean's car and Micha's, and I waited for the road rage. But it never came.

Sneaking a glance at him, he looked calm. He was relaxed. Well, as relaxed as he could be when we were on the way to give money to another one of his men's wives.

"What?" he finally asked, glancing at me. He slid his hand up my thigh and grabbed my hand, stroking his thumb along my fingers.

"I thought you were going to yell at that car," I said, laughing slightly. His brows bunched, so I continued. "Matthew had pretty bad road rage."

"Oh," he said, then cleared his throat. "I try not to, but I'm only human." I nodded again. I was learning that. He wasn't at all like the person I thought he was when we first met.

That person had been uninviting and cold. But he was the total opposite. Even if he didn't think he was a good man, everyone else around him could see that he was. I think that was important to him, to be a good man. I hadn't known him long, and I didn't know him well, but I knew that.

"I want to talk to Micha when we get home," I said, and he nodded a few times.

"Alright," he said, shifting in his seat. "What about?" I laughed breathily.

"Oh, about the weather," I said sarcastically, and he snapped his head to me. "We just found out we're family. Don't you think we should talk about it?"

"He's not one to be open with his feelings," he said. "He might not want to talk about it."

"But we can't continue on like we were," I said, and he shrugged.

"You could let him come to you," he suggested, but I shook my head.

"No," I said. "I want to talk to him."

# Julia

Walking onto the deck, I took a deep breath. Dean's property was a lot bigger than I thought it was. His most essential guys lived here with him, but all had their own homes. And they weren't small homes, either. Micha's place was closest to the main house, so it didn't take long for me to walk here.

Cory escorted me, which surprised Dean and I. Dean had some business he needed to take care of, and I wanted to talk to Micha before I lost my nerve. Cory offered to walk me since his place was right past Micha's.

"Text me before you leave, and I'll walk you back," Cory called. He was gruff and abrupt, and I wasn't at all surprised he was single and had never been married. As much as he wanted to do the right thing, he was an asshole.

"Sure," I said, waving at him. He gave me a stiff nod and stalked toward his house. I watched him for a moment, trying to steady my breathing before knocking on the door.

With a deep breath, I turned and raised my hand. I hadn't given myself time to think about what I was going to say. I just wanted to be here. But now that I was, I was starting to doubt myself.

What if he hadn't come to talk to me about it because he didn't want to get to know me? What if he didn't want to be family? What if he blamed me for what Matthew's father had done?

A small part of me blamed myself for it. I wouldn't be upset if he did, too.

I knocked softly at first. All the lights were on, and country music was blaring, so he probably couldn't hear me. I knocked again, a little harder, and the music stopped.

There was a window on Micha's front door that was fogged. I could see his shadow walking toward the door, but I couldn't see his face. What if he was upset I was here? He probably wanted to unwind after a stressful day, and here I was, about to drop this on him?

It was too late to change my mind, though.

Micha opened the door, and surprise flashed over his face. He stuck his head out the door and looked around like he expected someone else to be with me.

"Just me," I said with a small laugh. "Sorry to disappoint." His head snapped to me and his dark blond brows bunched.

"Not a disappointment, just a surprise," he said as he stepped back, opening the door wider. "Come on in."

Smiling shyly, I stepped inside and looked around. It was totally Micha. A dark brown, very worn leather couch sat in front of a fire-place, a huge TV mounted above it. A football game was on, but I didn't know or really care who was playing. In front of the couch sat a coffee table littered with things, including the belt he'd had on today like he'd taken it off and thrown it on there as soon as he walked inside.

"I was just makin' something to eat," he said awkwardly, rubbing his hands together. I nodded and followed him toward the kitchen in the back. There wasn't much in his place. No photos or artwork hung on the walls, except for one picture of him with his parents.

I tripped but caught myself on his back. When I looked down, I noticed it was the boots he'd had on earlier. Did he just start stripping as soon as he walked inside?

"Shit, you okay, Jay?" he asked as he helped steady me. I laughed and waved him off.

"Fine," I said. "You need a maid." I kicked the boots out of my way and followed him the rest of the way into the kitchen.

"Probably," he said. "Beer?" He hesitated before opening the stainless steel fridge, his brows raised.

"Sure," I said. The countertops were a dark butcher block and were apparently very well-loved. Pots and pans hung from the ceiling above a small island in the middle of the room. He popped the top of the beer off and handed it to me before moving back to the gas stove and picking up his beer next to it.

"So," he said, his back to me. "What are you doin' here?" His voice was tight, and I knew he felt as nervous as I did. I cleared my throat as I slid onto a barstool and watched him stir whatever he was cooking.

"I just–with everything going on, we haven't had a chance to talk," I said, and his shoulders bunched.

"About?"

"Micha," I said, laughing breathily. He dropped his head forward as he let out a long breath. Alright, so he wasn't looking forward to this conversation. Great. "You know, we could do this another time." I stood and ignored the tightness in my throat. "Sorry to bother you."

"Jay, wait," he sighed. When he turned, the look on his face gutted me. The blue of his eyes stood out more from the red that rimmed them. His thick lashes were wet, but he quickly wiped his hand over his face. "There's been a lot of memories that have come up for me, and--it's been hard."

"I'm sorry," I said, taking a small step forward.

"It ain't your fault." He took another swig of his beer. It felt like my fault, though. I was the one who'd brought these memories up for him. I was the one to remind him about all that he'd lost. "Look, I don't wanna sound like an ass, but why are you here? What's there to talk about? So, what? We found out we're related. Happens to people every day."

My chin trembled as I lowered my eyes. He was right. I really didn't know what I wanted to talk to him about. Maybe I just wanted to feel close to him? Maybe I wanted to learn more about Drake. He'd left when I was only a kid, and the only things I knew of him were the stories our Nan told me. But he didn't owe me anything. He didn't have to tell me a damn thing about Drake or Nat. He had every right to kick me out of his house and never welcome me back.

But he sighed and finished his beer, then tossed it on the counter as he made his way to the fridge. He didn't say anything as he shut the stove off, moved the pan off the burner, and then moved toward the backdoor.

"You comin'?"

# Julia

The lights on the back deck automatically came on when the sun went down. Micha had gone inside to shut them off, and he grabbed us a few more beers and a blanket for me. He didn't have chairs or anything to sit on, so we sat on the wooden deck with our backs pressed against the side of the house.

"What was he like?" I finally asked. I was nearly done with my second beer, and since I never drank, I was starting to feel its effects. "Drake."

"I thought you knew him," Micha said flatly. His head rested against the wall, his eyes trained on the endless field of trees in front of us.

Cory's lights were on at his place, and I could hear heavy metal blasting through the speakers, but I didn't know where he was. I wondered if he ever got lonely, being in that house all by himself. From what Dean had told me, Cory mainly kept to himself. He'd have dinner with Micha and Dean a few nights a week, but otherwise, he was home when he wasn't needed.

"He left when I was five," I said, stretching my legs out in front of me. "Most of what I know is from what Nan told me. He called for a bit after he left, but..." I shrugged as I twirled the bottle in my hands. "I don't hold it against him. He had a family to take care of, and he couldn't keep calling."

"He said his dad didn't want us around," Micha said tightly.

"Yeah," I agreed. "He was an asshole." He turned his head and watched me, but I couldn't look at him. I didn't want to spill all the nasty things I'd heard my uncle say about the boy–*the man*–beside me.

"You knew him?"

"Unfortunately," I said, then risked a glance his way. "He was just a dick, that's all. Wasn't happy Drake got Nat pregnant."

"Dad never talked about you," he said. I twisted my lips to the side as I lowered my eyes again.

"Figured as much." I took a long pull of my beer, finishing it.

"He didn't talk about anyone," he added quickly. "I knew Mama's daddy, but that was it. I didn't have no one else."

"I'm sorry, Micha," I said, turning toward him. He shrugged and looked out toward the trees again. "Where is he now? Why didn't he take you in after they--after everything?"

"He died when I was young," he said. "Dean took me in when he didn't have to, and I can't ever repay him for that."

"He doesn't expect you to repay him." I rested my hand on his forearm, and he squeezed his eyes shut.

"It's what a man does, Jay," he said, sounding choked. "Repay his debts."

Micha wasn't indebted to Dean, but there wasn't anything I could say that would make him see that. I squeezed his arm slightly before taking it away, but his warmth stayed with me.

"So, my dad was your mom's nephew?" he asked after clearing his throat.

"Yep," I said, nodding. "She loved Drake. I know she would've loved you, if they would've stayed here."

"She didn't like Mama." His voice was hard, and his hands were trembling.

"She loved Natasha," I said quietly. "We all did. Everyone except Drake's dad. That's why they finally left, because he was protecting your mother from him. He didn't want either of you to be around him." Micha's brows pinched together, and he turned to look at me.

"You think that's why he left?" he asked, and I shrugged. I handed him an unopened beer, and he popped the top off for me. I took a long drink and thought about everything Nan had told me over the years.

"Your dad was a lot like you," I said. He made a choking sound, then turned his head away from me, hiding his face. "He was a good man and did the right thing. And when he found out he was going to be a father, Nan told me he bought a cheap ring from Walmart that night and asked your mom to marry him."

Micha's shoulders shook, but I didn't draw attention to it. I let him have his moment, but he needed to hear this. I didn't know if he ever knew it.

"He took that role seriously," I said, looking down at the shadowed beer bottle in my hand. "He took being her husband seriously. Nan said he'd fought with his father his entire life, but the way he'd protected Nat from him was something she'd never seen. And she said she had never been so proud of him before. She said she always knew Drake would be a great person one day, but the night he packed his truck up and took her away was when she realized he'd turned into a great man."

"Why did they leave? Why couldn't they have stayed here? If everyone liked Ma..." Micha asked, his voice thick. He wiped at his face before he turned toward me again. His cheeks were red, and his eyes were swollen. I scooted closer to him and wrapped my arm around his broad shoulders, and, surprisingly, he leaned into me and let me comfort him.

"Apparently, his father had accused your mother of cheating on Drake. He tried to tell your dad that you weren't really his baby, but Drake didn't listen to him. And when Nat told him that he'd gotten aggressive with her, your dad beat the shit out of his own father and took her away. Nan encouraged him to leave, not because she wanted him gone, but because she knew he could do so much more if he got out of the city. But when he stopped calling, it was right around the time you were born. Nan thought it was because she never asked to see you that he thought she was upset with him, but she wasn't. She just knew he had his own life and family, and she didn't want to guilt him into coming back here where his father was."

"I didn't know that," he said quietly. "I don't think he did, either." He looked out at the trees again, and I followed. There weren't a lot of lights on the property, so the stars shone brightly overhead. "Dad loved camping, but I never would go with him. Always begged me to, but I was an idiot teenager and wanted to spend more time with my friends than I did with my parents. Now, I want nothin' more than to hear him beg me to go with him again."

My throat got painfully tight. Dean told me what had happened, so I wouldn't ask Micha. If I had questions, I'd just ask Dean later or keep them to myself. There was no reason for Micha to have to relive that day. But when he sighed, I felt the air shift around us.

"When Dad told us we were moving back here, Mama was real happy," he started. "I didn't know Dean that well because he was too busy to visit us that often, but sometimes he'd stay for the weekend. Dad said he'd offered him a job and that we were moving back to Baltimore. I was pissed about it." He laughed bitterly and shook his head. I rested my head on his shoulder, tightening my arm around him. "I didn't wanna leave my friends, and you know what I told him the day he fuckin' died? That I wanted him to go by himself. Told him I never wanted to see him again." His voice broke on the last word.

Tears streamed freely down my face. His body was shaking, but he stared straight ahead. I rested my other hand on his forearm, wanting to wrap him tightly up and take away his pain.

"Costa's men broke into the house that night," he croaked. "Ma told me to hide, but I didn't want to. Then Dad grabbed me and shoved me in a closet and told me not to make a fuckin' sound. He said that no matter what happened, I needed to stay in there until Dean came. And I did."

I squeezed my eyes shut. I couldn't imagine the terror he must've been feeling. He was a kid. He shouldn't have had to go through that.

"They made Dad watch. Tied him up and beat him 'til he could barely move and made him watch his fuckin' wife be raped by a dozen fuckin' men." His voice was shaking, but it wasn't from crying anymore. It was from fury. He took a swig from his beer, then lowered his head as he took a deep breath to calm himself.

"I have nightmares," he said. "I hear her screaming. And sometimes, she looks at me and asks why I didn't help her. Why I just hid in the closet and didn't help her."

"Micha," I murmured. "You were a kid."

"I was a man," he said, shaking his head. "I was fifteen, plenty old enough to protect her."

"You were doing what your dad told you to do." He shook his head stubbornly.

"I should've done something, then maybe they'd be alive."

"Or maybe you'd be dead," I countered, and he shrugged.

"Wouldn't mind it," he said quietly. "At least I'd be with them. At least I wouldn't have to remember."

"I'm sorry," I finally said. His broad shoulders stiffened.

"Don't want your pity." I pulled away from him, my brows bunching. There was a knock from his front door, but we ignored it.

"It's not pity," I said. He nodded, then dropped his head again. The knocking grew louder and more frequent, but we still ignored it. I stared at him, waiting for him to say something. Somewhere behind us, his front door opened, then slammed shut.

"Micha!" It was Dean. "Julia!"

"Out here," Micha said, barely raising his voice. Dean stomped through the house, but his footsteps faltered when I glanced over my shoulder, looking through the open back door at him. His eyes flicked between us, confusion clear on his face.

"Everything okay?"

"Fine," Micha said, then gently pushed my arms away as he stood. He stooped and gathered the discarded beer bottles, and went inside. Slowly, I got to my feet and followed him, closing and locking the door.

Micha quickly cleaned the kitchen while we silently watched. I knew I should've said something, but I didn't know what. What could you say to someone that had gone through that? *Sorry for your loss* didn't seem to be enough.

Finally, he stopped and rested his hands on the island in the center of the room. His head was dipped low, and his eyes were closed. Dean and I shared a look, but we stayed quiet, waiting for Micha to speak first.

"Want a beer or something?" he finally asked Dean.

"Nah." Dean waved a dismissive hand. "Chef made a lentil shepherd's pie if you wanna come with us." Micha made a face, and Dean shrugged. "Per Julia's request."

"No offense, Jay, but that sounds fuckin' disgusting," he said, laughing.

"Offense taken," I laughed. "I'll save you leftovers."

"Please don't."

Micha smiled softly at me, then rounded the island and gathered me into a tight hug. It wasn't the ending to the conversation that I wanted, but it seemed that's all I was getting tonight. And I'd take it if it meant he was smiling again.

"Thanks for comin' by," he whispered. I took a deep breath, breathing him in. "Come over anytime."

"You mean that?" I asked, pulling away from him. "Because with the way he snores, you might have a roommate soon." I tilted my head toward Dean, and it took them a second before they erupted with laughter.

"I don't fucking snore," Dean scoffed, sounding insulted.

"You do," I said.

"You do, man," Micha agreed. "Heard you down the hall when I lived in the main house."

"You did not!" Dean huffed, but he was smiling. I gave Micha another quick hug, and he walked us to the door.

"Really," Micha said quietly as he caught my arm. "Thanks for comin' over. Maybe we can talk again soon. About him." I smiled and nodded before Dean and I walked home, hand in hand.

# Julia

I was curled up on the couch in Dean's office while he, Micha, Cory, and a few other men I didn't know sat around his desk looking at a map. It was hilarious, cute, and totally unexpected when Dean pulled out a pair of reading glasses, giving me a shy look before sliding them on his nose. They should've made him less intimidating, but they didn't. They only added to his intensity.

"If we can take money from here," Dean said, pointing at the desk, "we can set up a new warehouse over here." He pointed to another spot on his desk.

"That's on the Southside," Micha said, and Dean leveled a look at him.

"We own the Southside."

"But Costa—"

"Costa will continue moving in on our territory if we don't push back," Dean said darkly, and chills rippled down my arms.

"They'll—"

"What?" Dean barked. "What are they gonna do?"

"Kill more of our own," one of the other men said. "We've already lost too many. It's not worth the risk." Dean's jaw tensed as he stared at the other man.

"I won't back down from Costa," he said. "If he or any of his men step foot on the Southside again, they're dead. I'm done catering to him, and I'm done playing nice." Cory nodded a few times, a slight grin playing on his lips.

Slowly, I stood from the couch and made my way to Dean's side. He absently wrapped his arm around my waist and held me to his side, his thumb absently rubbing up and down. It was such a casual and intimate touch, like we'd been together for years instead of days.

"What was the warehouse for?" I asked as I scanned the papers and map on the desk. The layout of the dots scattered along the map looked familiar.

"It was a holding warehouse. Companies pay us to hold their stuff until it can be shipped," Dean said. "Thankfully, we didn't have any stock inside when it was burned down." I slid my hand over his shoulder and gently kneaded the hard muscle, and he let out a soft breath. His hold on me tightened, and my heart squeezed.

"Is it legal?" I asked, and all the men turned their eyes to me. Dean chuckled under his breath, then nodded.

"Yeah, darling, it's all legal," he said. He slid the glasses onto his head and turned to look up at me. "That's why we're able to have insurance on it." I nodded slowly, my eyes flitting around the desk again. "What're you thinking?" He turned his chair and gently tugged me onto his lap, balancing me on his thigh. His arms wrapped around my waist as he stared at me.

"Why not share the Southside?" I asked, turning to look at him.

"It's my territory." His eyes narrowed. "It's on the water, and if I'm controlling it, that means Costa and his men can't get in to recruit any of my guys. I've been trying to avoid conflict for years, but it seems inevitable."

"So, you want to recruit more men for yourself," I said, and he shook his head.

"I hate this line of work and don't want anyone to get mixed up in it if they don't have to. That story Matt told you about paying off debts is a common occurrence in Costa's Family. It didn't happen to him, but it's happened to countless others. I don't like it."

"So, why not go straight? Get out of this line of work?" I turned fully toward him. "Why not just let him take over the Southside so you can walk away?"

"If he takes over, he's going to force every man here to be in his Family, and the ones that refuse, he'll kill. No," Dean shook his head, "no, I can't let that happen. These are my people, and I won't walk away from them."

"We've been buying more legit warehouses," Micha said. "The more legal businesses we own, the easier it'll be for people to not be a part of this. We can stay in control of the area and keep people safe."

"If I can create legit jobs for people, they won't have to turn to Costa or me or other Families, to try to make money. It's been a cycle in the city for decades, and I want it to stop."

None of this was what I'd expected. I hadn't thought Dean wouldn't want to recruit more men. I thought he'd want to have more and become more powerful than Costa. But it seems like he really just wanted peace.

"Right," I breathed as I looked back at the map. The maps I saw in Costa's bunker flashed through my mind, and I glanced at Dean, biting my lip.

"What?" he asked, his brows drawing together.

"When I was at the cabin, I went downstairs," I started, glancing at the other men. "They had this bunker underground where all the men slept. But there was this room in the back with all these monitors on the walls."

"What was on the monitors?" he asked, his arm tightening around my waist.

"Security feeds," I said, closing my eyes as I relived watching Matthew kill a man. "And maps."

"Maps? Of what?"

"The city and state," I said. "There were dots in random places."

"Can you remember where they were?" His voice was urgent, and I opened my eyes, staring at him. I stood and leaned over the map and ran my finger around a cluster of dots.

"I remember seeing these marked," I said, and Cory swore under his breath. "What do they locate?"

"Here."

"What?" I turned to face him, my brows raised. "Here?"

"Yeah, that's my property," he said, pointing at the cluster again. "That's the guy's homes, the weapons building, garages one and two, the helipad, everything. It's my property."

"You're sure you saw this?" Cory asked, and I nodded. "Anything else?" I turned and scanned the map again, then pointed along the waterline. "Fuck."

"What?" I asked again, locking eyes with Micha.

"That's the warehouse that was attacked," he said.

"So, they know where all of your properties are," I said, and Dean sighed.

"Seems that way," he said. "Can you remember anything else?" I looked at the map again, my eyes scanning the paper quickly. Everything was jumbled, and I couldn't remember exactly what else I'd seen.

"No," I said. "I don't know." I shook my head, feeling frantic.

"That's alright, Jay," Micha said gently. When I looked at him, he gestured for me to calm down, sensing my growing anxiety.

"What if—"

"Look, no offense, why should we even trust you? You could be lying for all we know," one of the other men snapped. Dean's body tensed, his hand on my waist tightening.

"Excuse me?" he said, deathly low. "You'll watch how you speak to her."

"Dean, it's alright," I hissed under my breath. "He's right." I turned toward the man. "You're right. You have no reason to trust me. But I have no reason to lie." I started to move back toward the couch, but Dean yanked me back down on his thigh, keeping me pinned there.

The man flicked his eyes between us, then glanced at the other man, then Micha. They had the sense to not look at him.

"I just meant that—"

"Apologize," Dean said, and I whipped my head to him.

"It's fine," I said firmly, but he ignored me.

"Apologize," he said again. I turned toward the man, giving him an apologetic wince.

"It's okay," I said again. "I didn't take offense to it. You're right—"

"Not the point," Dean growled as he scooted forward in the chair. "Apologize."

"I'm sorry, Miss," he said, dipping his head.

"I promise, it's fine." I looked at Dean, but he was still glaring at the poor man.

"We're done here," he said as he reclined in the chair, pulling me with him. I braced my hand on his chest and pushed myself up, so I wasn't lying on top of him in front of his men. "We'll finish this later." The men nodded as they got to their feet.

"Gala's this weekend," Micha said, his lips curving in a small smirk. I glanced at Dean, finding him glaring harder at Micha.

"Gala?" I asked, interrupting their stare-off.

"I was going to talk to you about it tonight," Dean gritted out, still glaring at Micha. He grinned before bowing his head slightly and walking backward toward the door, a boyish grin on his face.

"See you tomorrow, Jay," he said, and I smiled.

"Goodnight." He smiled back before he slipped from the room. As soon as the door shut, my smile fell as I turned toward Dean, my brows furrowed. "What was that about?"

"What?"

"Forcing him to apologize," I said. He took the glasses from the top of his head as he flicked his eyes between mine, folding them and setting them on the desk.

"I didn't like how he spoke to you. You'll be spoken to with respect," he said. "I won't have one of my guys insulting you or accusing you of being a traitor." I inhaled sharply and bit my lip, trying to keep calm.

Wasn't that what I always did with Matthew, though? I stayed quiet, bit my tongue to keep the peace? And look what happened there—he lost all respect for me, not that he'd had much to begin with.

That wouldn't happen this time.

"No," I shook my head, "I don't like that." His brows hitched up, a small grin playing on his lips. "If I have a problem with the way someone talks to me, I can stand up for myself. I don't need you to do it. And he was right—"

"I will not have anyone speak to you like that," he said again, more firmly. "I know you can stand up for yourself, but it's my job to make sure these men remember their place. And their place is under me, which makes them under you. We're all under you, darling. You're the Queen here, and you'll be treated with respect. Nothing less."

"I didn't have a problem with it."

"I did."

"You're not getting it, Dean," I groaned.

"No," he smiled, "*you're* not getting it, darling." He pulled me closer to him, pressing his lips to my forehead. "I know it made you uncomfortable, but I'm going to protect you, even if that means telling one of my guys to apologize for their tone."

I pulled back slightly to look at him, and he smiled lazily at me. His eyes scanned my face, lingering on my lips as he licked his, then back up to my eyes. He wrapped his hand around the back of my neck and tugged me to him, kissing me gently.

"Alright," I said when he pulled away, and he laughed. I kept my eyes closed as I leaned forward again, capturing his lips with mine.

"Alright?" he repeated as he rubbed his other hand up and down my thigh. "That easy?"

"You're stubborn and won't change your mind," I said as I shifted to face him more. "It's not worth the argument." He paused and pulled away, his brows furrowing.

"If it bothers you, I want to know," he said firmly, his eyes flicking between mine. "I can't promise I'll do what you want me to, but I will always listen to you."

I swallowed heavily, then nodded. I kissed him again, harder, and he groaned. Lifting up, I straddled his lap, my legs squeezed between his thighs and the arms of the chair, and wrapped my fingers around the back of his thick neck.

He gripped my hips as he bit my lip, dragging it away from my mouth and through his teeth. "Get on the desk." Gently, he pushed me back on his thighs, his hands flexing. "On the desk."

Slowly, I pushed myself back on the desk, the papers sliding under me, some of them spilling to the floor. He grabbed my ankles and rested them on the arms of his chair as he moved closer. I let my legs fall apart as he dipped his face between them, inhaling.

"You smell so fucking good," he groaned. "I've been thinking about your pussy all day. I need to taste you again." I leaned back on my hands as he lifted my hips, dragging my jeans off and dropping them to the floor. Roughly, he pushed my legs far apart. "Such a pretty little pussy." He spread me apart, and I whimpered as I lifted my hips slightly. "Did you learn your lesson? Did you learn that this is my pussy?"

"Yes," I breathed, nodding. Slowly, he pressed a thick finger inside me, and I bit my lip, stifling a small cry.

"I want to hear you say it."

"It's your pussy, Dean. It's yours. I'm yours." A low growl rumbled through his chest, and he pushed a second finger inside me, stretching me. I writhed in front of him, and he grinned, fucking me harder. "Please!" He lowered his face between my legs, his other arm wrapping around my hips as he pulled me closer to the edge.

"I like when you beg me," he said before licking me slowly. Gently, I put my hand on his head and threaded my fingers through his thick hair. I pushed his face closer to my pussy as I lifted my hips. He laughed breathily, then dropped his mouth to my clit, sucking it roughly in his mouth. I rolled my hips, grinding against his face.

"God," I tipped my head back, "that feels so good."

He moved his tongue faster, and I moaned louder, the sound echoing around the room. My orgasm started to build, and my fingers tightened in his hair, making him groan. My hips moved in time with his fingers, his mouth moving with my movements.

I fell back on the desk, wrapping my legs around his head, holding him where I wanted him. He ate me like a starved man, not coming up for air. My other hand found his hand resting on my hip, and I wrapped my fingers around one of his, squeezing it as my orgasm began to rise.

"Fuck," he muttered, then gripped my hip tighter and dragged me closer to him. His mouth was relentless, and soon, I screamed his name as I came.

Finally, my legs fell away from his head, and his tongue slowed, his fingers gently pulled from me, then he kissed his way down one thigh and up the next. He hovered over me, pressing his lips to my neck, slowly kissing his way to my mouth. My back arched as he slid my shirt off and dropped it to the floor.

"I want to see you," I murmured, and his lips faltered before he stood, towering over me. "I don't care about the scars. I want to—"

"No." He shook his head, lowering his eyes. I folded my lips between my teeth, my eyes flicking between his lowered ones before I nodded. "Not yet. I can't—"

"It's okay," I said, grabbing his hand. "It's okay." His throat bobbed, then he looked at me. There was something there. Pain. The memories of what gave him the scars, probably. But I nudged him with my knee, smiling softly. "Come on." He shook his head slightly, and that look disappeared. Flexing his hands on my hips, he smirked, then lowered himself again, kissing me harder.

His hand slid between us, and he undid his belt and jeans, roughly yanking them down enough to pull his cock out. I hesitated before wrapping my hand around it, my thumb brushing over the piercing. I stroked him slowly, and his head fell back, a long groan leaving him as he jerked his hips forward. Suddenly, his hands landed on my waist, and he effortlessly flipped me, pinning me to the desk.

"I need to be inside you," he rasped as he rubbed the head of his cock against me. I arched my back, glancing over my shoulder at him. "Don't look at me like that."

"Like what?"

"Like you need a good fucking."

"Maybe I do."

The words barely left my mouth before he shoved himself inside me, making me scream. He thrust in and out, slowly pushing his way deeper until he was fully seated inside me. His hand landed on my ass, and I cried out.

"Fuck, I like the way you scream," he rasped as he slowly pulled almost all the way out. "Scream for me, darling." He slammed back into me, and I screamed for him. Again, he slammed into me, and again, I screamed and clawed at the desk.

He continued fucking me slow and hard, scooting the desk with each thrust. My toes brushed against the floor, barely touching it. More papers slid off the desk and crumpled under me, but he didn't care. He didn't stop until his cock thickened, and he suddenly pulled out.

"I'm not ready for this to end," he said breathlessly. Carefully, he helped me stand on shaky legs, and I tipped my head back, resting my chin on his chest. He smoothed my hair away from my face before he kissed me softly.

Lifting me, I wrapped my legs around his waist as he walked toward the couch. He set me against the arm, right in the corner, and braced one knee on the cushions, his other foot on the floor.

"Put your legs on my shoulders," he said as I scooted down. He slid my ankles onto his broad shoulders and pressed his body over mine, folding me nearly in half. "Hold onto me. I'm not going to be gentle."

His cock slid into me again, and he was right—he wasn't gentle.

He fucked me harder and faster, his pierced cock hitting me

deeper than before. I bunched his shirt in my fists as I screamed. His face was buried in my neck, his hot breath making me shudder.

"Fuck," I cried as my orgasm began to build. "More, Dean. I need more." He growled as he bit down on my neck, his hands dropping to my ass and spreading me apart, letting his cock hit deeper. I tightened around him as that familiar warmth began to spread through my body.

"That's it, baby. Come for me," he grunted. My toes curled, and my thighs trembled. "Come on my cock." He moved faster and I tipped over the edge, screaming and digging my nails into his back. "I'm coming inside you."

I was writhing under him, but his words penetrated my mind clearly. We were playing a dangerous game, but I didn't care. I squeezed his cock tighter, and he pressed his face deeper into my neck, his hips moving faster, harder, against me.

"You want that? My cum in your tight pussy?"

"Yes!" I cried. "Come inside me."

His movements were frantic as he fucked me relentlessly into the couch, his breathing hot and ragged against my skin. He bit my neck again, growling as his hips rocked roughly against mine, burying his cock deeper.

"You want it so bad, don't you, darling?" he grunted. "Your greedy little cunt wants my cum." I moaned, arching my back as his pace quickened.

"I want it." I held onto him as he slammed into me a few more times.

"You're perfect," he breathed, then his body went taut, his thighs trembling. There was more lingering on the end of his words, but he slammed into me again, and they were lost. "Fuck. Julia." He came, shouting my name.

Later, Dean was lying on his back on the couch with me draped over him, his fingers trailing lightly up and down my back. His heartbeat was steady under my ear, the fabric of his shirt soft against my cheek. When his fingers moved to my head, gently massaging my scalp, I sighed.

"Do you really want to stay here?" he suddenly asked, and I lifted my head to look at him. The office was dimly lit, the lights turned almost all the way down. I traced my finger along his jaw, over the tattoo under his eye, then the one peeking out from his hairline.

"I think so," I murmured, and he closed his eyes. "This is a lot for me." His throat bobbed, and slowly, he opened his eyes. They were shadowed as he stared at me, his large hand moving to cup my face. He stroked his thumb over my lips, gently dragging the bottom one down.

"I want you here," he said, and I felt the truth of the words to my core. "I never want to let you go."

I couldn't say anything back. I didn't know what would be enough. I couldn't promise him forever, not when I was still tied to that promise with someone else, and that was a disaster. I didn't know if forever would even be something I'd want to promise anyone else. Still, I could see myself spending forever with Dean.

I liked the way he touched me, how he looked at me, and how his eyes lit up when I spoke. I liked the way he was overbearing and over-protective. I liked how gentle he was but also how deadly he could be. I liked...*him.* Everything about him. From the way he combed his hair in the morning to the way his lips stayed slightly parted when he slept.

*Everything.*

I stared at him a moment longer, my eyes scanning his face, then flicking between his. Something shifted in my chest—and while I wasn't sure this was where I belonged forever, I knew this was where I belonged for now. And that was enough for me.

# Dean

Julia sat across from me at the table. She gave me a shy smile as she lifted her glass of red wine. Bringing it to her lips, she took a small sip, the dark liquid staining them slightly.

"So," she said as she put it back down, "the gala?" I sighed and grabbed my beer before leaning back in my chair. Her eyes roamed over the room. We weren't in the grand dining room, just the casual one off the kitchen, but the way she'd gasped would've made you think we'd just entered Buckingham Palace.

"There's a gala this weekend," I said, then took a sip, watching her carefully. "It's to raise money for a local farm sanctuary. I thought you'd enjoy going." Her fingers tightened around the stem of the wine glass, her lips parting. "If you're not interested, we don't have to go."

"I've never been to a gala," she said, and I barely hid my grin behind my bottle.

"Would you like to be my date Friday night, then, darling?" I purposefully dropped my voice slightly. When I did it earlier, I noticed goosebumps rippled across her skin. I liked knowing the effect I had on her.

She primly cleared her throat and sat a little taller. "Yes. I'd like that."

I smiled broadly at her and felt some of that anxiety I wished would go away, tighten a bit more. This was my big gesture to her, to let her know this was real. That I wasn't interested in a fling with her, I wanted her forever. And it didn't make any fucking sense to me at all.

All I knew was that when I thought about her not being in my life anymore, I wanted to fucking die.

I'd bought a farm sanctuary a few miles from here that was on the verge of closing and renamed it *Darling's Farm*. The people who worked there fought for animal rights and welfare, educated the public about the harm factory farming has on our environment and the animals, and housed animals saved from factory farms and abusive owners.

With Julia being a vegetarian, I figured this would be something important to her, and I thought she'd appreciate it. I wanted to give her something more than a ring, more than a promise to love her until my dying breath.

I wanted to give her something to make her know I was in this forever, not just for now.

The word love was a siren going off in my head, blaring louder and louder the more I tried to ignore it. I hadn't meant to even think the fucking word, but now that I had, I couldn't ignore how right it felt. But it was wrong. It was too soon. Too fast. She didn't feel the same, and I couldn't risk telling her only to scare her away.

"I don't have anything to wear," she said, and I blinked a few times, refocusing on her. I opened my mouth as Micha walked into the room.

"Oh, hey," he said, flicking his eyes between us. "Was just coming to grab some food."

"Chef hates when you do that," I said as he walked past my chair. He gave me a half-grin, then shrugged.

"He loves me."

"He'd kill you if I let him," I said, and he laughed. Julia sat quietly, a small smile on her face as she watched us. "Just have dinner with us." I told Micha, and he nodded but headed toward the kitchen anyway. "What is it?"

"He reminds me of Drake," she said. "His smile. I don't know how I didn't see it before."

"His laugh is the same," I said, and she smiled softly before nodding.

"It is," she agreed. "He looks like his mother, but there's something about him that's unmistakably Drake." I nodded again and took another sip of my beer, swallowing past the tightness in my throat.

Sometimes, looking at Micha made me miss my best friend more than anything. I'd give anything to have Drake back, but the man Micha had become was one I respected and valued. He was more of a man than I ever was at his age.

He came back in, Chef on his heels with a slight scowl. Micha slid onto the seat next to mine, across from Julia, and grinned as Chef set our plates down.

"Gruyere and mushroom ravioli in a white wine cream sauce," Chef said proudly to Julia. She smiled up at him, her tongue tracing along her bottom lip. The gesture went straight to my dick, and I looked away. Micha gave me a knowing look, then cleared his throat.

"It smells and looks amazing," she said sincerely. "Thank you, Chef." He preened at her praise and gave her a deep bow. He set Micha and my plates down without as much care, shooting us both a look that said not to hurt her or we'd get poisoned, and made his way back to the kitchen.

"Does he ever sit and eat with you?" she asked, and we both shrugged.

"Not really," I said. "He and his husband like to keep to themselves." I cut a ravioli in half and took a bite, anticipating hating it. Mushrooms were not my favorite thing. In fact, I didn't know if I'd ever had them. But the flavors that erupted on my tongue had my eyes closing.

Chef outdid himself yet again.

"You don't have to eat what I eat," Julia said shyly. I opened my eyes, finding her cheeks flushed. "I know my diet is restrictive. I'd make Matthew meat for dinner, even though I hated it. But he would've eaten out every night if I didn't. So, you really don't have to eat what I do just to accommodate me."

Micha and I stared at her. His hand tightened around his fork, but his face and body looked casual.

"Why are you a vegetarian?" he asked her, and she shrugged with one shoulder as she took a bite.

"I had a friend whose parents owned a farm. When I was over at her house one day, we watched her mother slaughter chickens. Some of the blood got on me, and I threw up. I'll never forget that smell." She shuddered slightly, then took a long drink of her wine. "I haven't eaten any meat since."

"Not even fish?" he asked, and she shook her head.

"If it has a heart, I don't eat it."

Micha and I glanced at each other, then I looked back at her. "I don't mind having what you're having." I ate the other half of the ravioli. "And Matt's a fucking asshole for making you cook meat when you don't eat it. He should've made it himself or not eaten it. Not that fucking hard."

The beer bottle shook as I brought it to my lips. I already hated the asshole, but the more stories she told me about him and their marriage, the more I wanted to kill him.

"I like this," Micha said around a mouthful, pointing at his plate with his fork. "Don't bother me any." Julia's eyes flicked between us, her throat bobbing again. I wanted to read her fucking mind. What was she thinking?

"Your dress," I said, changing the subject. "I've already asked Indigo, Chef's husband, to style you. He's a stylist."

"You have a stylist," she said slowly, then laughed slightly as she shook her head. "Why am I not surprised?"

"He's not *my* stylist," I said. "He's *a* stylist. As in, he gets hired by other people. He just happens to be married to one of my guys and lives on my property." She stayed smiling as she took another sip.

"Alright," she sighed. "I have two days to try to not look like I'm healing from a boxing match." She was being dramatic. She was mostly healed from her injuries from the cabin, and from what Justin had done to her. Just the thought of him made me want to bring him back from the dead to fucking slaughter him again.

"You'll look beautiful," I said. "You always do." A slight blush crept across her chest and up her neck, into her cheeks. She hid her smile behind another sip of her drink, her eyes lingering on mine.

She really had no idea what she did to me.

"Have you painted anything yet?" Micha asked before taking a long pull of his beer. She shook her head as she chewed.

"I haven't, um, I haven't been back to the studio since Dean showed me," she said shyly. "Inspiration hasn't struck, I guess."

It was a lie, and we all knew it. She was still holding back, even if she was telling me, and maybe herself that she was all in...she wasn't. And there was a part of me that feared she'd never be.

"I can always pose nude for you," I said, and she choked on her wine, her eyes flicking quickly to Micha and back to me. "If the subject is nude, the artist is, too, right? We wouldn't have to waste time taking clothes off after that."

"Dean," she hissed.

"What? It's not like he doesn't know," I said, jerking my chin to Micha. "Just because he's a virgin doesn't mean he's an idiot. What else did he think we were doing? You've been in my bed for...how many nights now?"

She was silent, her face redder than a tomato as she looked back at Micha. His chest was vibrating, trying to keep his laughter in. None of the guys were shy about who they were sleeping with. They gave probably too many details, honestly. I'd never talk about my sex life with Julia with anyone else around, but it was Micha. And I liked teasing her. Both in and out of the bedroom.

As the meal progressed, I couldn't help but stare at her in

wonder. She was free with giving her smiles and laughs away. She was effortless, unhurried. Utterly perfect. And even long after the meal ended and Chef grabbed our plates, we still sat at the table, laughing and talking and just getting to know each other.

I knew her intimately. I knew what made her legs shake and toes curl. I knew what words to say that would send her over the edge. I knew how to make her come with just my tongue.

But to know what her soul was made of...I was still learning that. And it seemed it was as fucking perfect as she was.

# Dean

"I have great news," Cory said gruffly as he walked into my office. He quickly glanced around, and when he didn't find Julia, his face turned hard.

Leaning back in my chair, I slid my glasses off and rested them on the desk. She was in her studio—inspiration finally struck, she said. So, off she went while I stayed in my office to deal with the fucking mess Costa and Blackwell made for me.

"Why do I think I'm going to hate this news?" I groaned as I rubbed my hand over my face.

"Because you are." He walked forward, then unceremoniously dropped his phone on the center of my desk. I snatched it up, and as soon as my eyes locked on two familiar names, I nearly threw the thing across the fucking room.

"How the fuck were they sold tickets? I thought I gave explicit instructions that they were not to be there," I said, tossing the phone back on the desk. "Fuck. Julia's going to freak the fuck out. Goddamnit!"

I pushed my chair back as I stood, my jaw tight as I tried to calm down. Cory looked as pissed as I felt. "How the fuck did they get tickets?!" I shouted, and his eyes met mine.

"No one thought twice about the names," he said. "These people aren't in our fuckin' world. They don't know—"

"I gave them a list of fucking names—no, it wasn't a list; it was two names," I held up two fingers, "two fucking names, Cory!" I banged my fist on the wooden bookcase behind me. "Get them off that fucking list. They're not allowed in. And if they show up, make it very fucking known they won't be leaving that building alive."

"I tried to tell the stupid fuck in charge of the event that they weren't welcome," he said, his voice tight. "Apparently, Costa made a substantial donation, so they won't revoke his tickets or not allow him inside."

"Are you fucking kidding me?" I turned toward him. I hit the bookshelf again, a little harder, not feeling any pain. I was vibrating with anger. "I'll talk to him. What's his number? It's my—"

"He won't budge," Cory said, and I let out a hard breath. "He won't fuckin' listen."

"You told him they were dangerous?" He was nodding as I spoke. Taking another deep breath, I slowly let it out. "What do we do?"

"Tell her," he said immediately, and I rolled my eyes.

"Obviously," I deadpanned. "I mean, how the fuck do we not let them in?"

"We could cancel," he said, but I shook my head.

"No, she's really looking forward to this," I sighed. "She was up all night looking at dresses."

"We can try to keep them away from her," he suggested, and I shrugged.

"We can't let them in," I said. "I want extra security, all the guys we can spare." He nodded as he started typing on his phone. "If Costa and Blackwell are going, they'll have their guys around, too. I need eyes on Julia at all fucking times. She goes nowhere alone. Even if she goes to the bathroom, I want someone in the room with her."

"How do you think she'll react?" he asked, his head still bowed over his phone, but his eyes lifted to mine.

"I don't fucking know," I sighed. I opened my mouth to say something else, but a soft knock at the door drew our attention.

"Hey," Cory said, his voice gentler than I'd ever heard before. She had one of my t-shirts on, and it was covered in paint. Her hair was tied up with a paintbrush, and a smear of light blue paint was on her forehead, right above her eyebrow.

"What's going on?" She tilted her head to the side, her teal eyes zeroing in on me. I cleared my throat and gave her a tight smile.

"Nothing," I said, and her eyes narrowed. "How was painting, darling? Did you create the next great masterpiece?" She snorted as she walked further into the room, wiping her hand on the front of the shirt.

"Scrapped it," she said.

"Hey, I wanted to hang it up in here," I said, and she rolled her eyes.

"Trust me, you did not want that hanging anywhere near you." Cory and I laughed, and her smile was bright. "I'm going to get fitted by Indigo tonight. Where do I meet him? All Chef said was to meet Indigo at six."

"I'll show you," Cory said, surprising me. "Need to talk to him about my outfit anyway."

"You're going, too?" she asked, shocked. Then she bounced on her toes as she smiled broadly. "It's going to be so fun! I've never dressed up this nice for anything before." I'd never seen her look so giddy, so carefree and happy.

I stopped breathing.

I'd never seen her happy.

And now that I had...I never wanted to see her unhappy. But I knew that these next few words would send her back to that place inside herself. The place that made her stay looking broken.

"Julia, sit down," I said, and her smile immediately fell. Cory shot me a look, but I didn't need to be a mind reader to know what he was thinking. "Cory, your phone." I held my hand out, and he hesitated before putting it in the center of my palm.

"What?" she asked, looking between us. I stared at their names on the screen.

*Dominico Costa.*

*Matthew Blackwell.*

Sighing, I handed it to her, but she didn't look at it for a moment. She just stayed staring at me. Finally, when she lowered her eyes, her hand began to tremble. I rounded the desk and sat in the chair beside hers, pulling hers closer to me. Cory sat on the edge of my desk, leaning forward slightly.

"Matthew," she said, then turned frantic eyes to me. "And Dominico. They're going?"

"Yes," I said. "I didn't know they were going until a few minutes ago. But it's going to be okay. I'm adding extra security to us, to you. They won't be able to even look in your direction without someone stopping it."

"I'm not worried about that," she said as she looked back at the phone. "Matthew wouldn't hurt me."

"You're not his wife anymore," I said, and she turned her head toward me again. "You're with me now, and he's not gonna like it."

"He won't hurt me over that, though," she said, and I glanced at Cory.

"He'd do a lot fucking worse than just hurt you," he said bluntly, and I tightened my grip on the arm of her chair. Just the fucking thought of Blackwell's hands on her made me sick with rage. Her brows pinched together as she stared up at him, then slowly looked at me again.

"You think he's going to hurt me?"

"I don't know what the fuck he's gonna do," I said. "I don't know why they're going or how the fuck they knew it was our event."

"Our event?"

*Shit.*

Cory and I glanced at each other again.

"Well, it's not ours," I said quickly. "But I did help out the cause a bit." Her eyes narrowed again.

"What aren't you telling me?"

"Nothing," I said too quickly.

"Dean." She tossed Cory's phone back on the desk, letting it clatter on the wood. "Our event?"

"It's really nothing," I said more calmly. "I gave a large donation, so we were added to the host list." Her brows bunched tighter like she didn't believe me. And I didn't blame her. It was a terrible fucking lie.

"Come on," Cory said as he stood and grabbed his phone. "I need to meet with Indie." He held his hand out to her, but she stayed staring at me for another moment. Then, she took a deep breath and followed him out the door.

# Julia

Dean just lied to me. I don't know why he would lie to me about something as simple as this, but it only made me wonder what else he'd lied about. Cory and I were quiet as we rode the elevator down, both too tied up in our own thoughts.

There was something disheartening knowing Dean had lied. But the fact that Matthew and Dominico were going was in the forefront of my mind more so than his lie was.

Were they working together? Was he trying to figure out a way to send me back to Matthew? Or, worse, had Matthew finally agreed to Dean's demands in exchange for his wife back? And Dean agreed to it.

I didn't know, and I wasn't sure I wanted to find out. I'd been so excited since he'd told me about the gala. I thought it would be a night of glamor, but now all I could think about was that I'd be coming face to face with Matthew. Forget Dominico. He wasn't who I was worried about.

I knew Matthew wouldn't hurt me, but would he hurt Dean? Or Micha? Or Cory? I didn't know if he knew that I was with Dean now, and if he found out tomorrow night, things could turn bad to deadly quickly. I didn't know what to do.

Cory led me from the elevator and down the hall in the opposite direction from the dining room we'd eaten in. The lower level was the same as upstairs. All marble walls, hardwood floors, darkly accented pieces, and an overall theme of Dean. Nowhere in his home could you escape him. Even though there weren't a lot of photos, there was no mistaking whose place this was.

We stopped abruptly at a set of double doors, and Cory pushed them open, letting me enter first. The room was all white, completely opposite from the rest of the house, but it felt warm and inviting instead of feeling sterile and cold.

A platform sat in the middle of the room, several mirrors in front of it with lights above and below them. The rug was lush and looked like a cloud. I wanted to roll around on it and forget about the last fifteen minutes.

Cory stood beside me as we looked around. No one was there.

"I thought we were supposed to be meeting Indigo?" I asked, and as Cory turned to answer, the side door flew open.

"Please, call me Indie, dear."

A man with sepia-colored skin in his mid-fifties waltzed into the room dressed in white slacks and a light blue button-down. His shoes were shined to perfection, his dark hair cropped close to his head.

"Hey, Indie," Cory said with a small chin-lift, and the man turned his dark eyes on him.

"At least you're on time," he said, exasperated. "Micha was two hours late for his fitting. How Dean trusts him to never be late is beyond me. He'll be late to his own funeral! And you must be Julia." He turned toward me, a bright smile on his face.

"Yes," I said. Something about him screamed regal, and I had the odd urge to curtsey, but I managed not to. His eyes scanned me slowly, and I shifted uncomfortably. "Sorry about the paint. It's dry. It won't get on anything."

"Please get paint on everything in this room," he said as he waved his hand out around. "I've been begging Dean to get new furniture for months now. I need to redecorate. This room is starting to feel a bit stale." I laughed breathily and glanced at Cory, finding him smiling, too. I stared at him a moment. I'd never seen him smile before.

"I still have my tux from the last event," Cory said. "I'll just wear that."

"Ah, no, you will not, young man." Indie rolled his eyes. "Julia will be a bombshell in a red dress, which means all of her men must be matching."

"I'm not wearing a red tux," Cory said dryly, and I bit my lip to not laugh.

"You're right." Indie nodded a few times. "But your accessories will be red, and they don't quite match your last tux." He gestured to the platform in the middle of the room. "You know the drill. Up you go."

I sat in a chair behind the platform and sipped wine while watching Indie take Cory's measurements. It didn't take as long as I'd anticipated, and soon it was my turn.

"I need to do something, but I'll come by in an hour for you," Cory said.

"It's alright." I waved dismissively at him as I stood. "I know my way around." He gave me a skeptical look, and I laughed. "Alright, I know my way around the top floor, but I need to learn the layout of this place. It's fine. If I get lost, I'll call Dean." Cory shrugged and said a quick goodbye to us both before he left.

"Wait here," Indie said. "Your dress is in the back." He left through the door he'd come in from, leaving me staring at myself in the mirror.

While I still had some bruises and scabs, I didn't look that bad. The dark circles I'd come to know and hate over the last five years appeared less dark, and I felt like I'd filled out a bit. Which was interesting, seeing as I spent nearly my first week here not eating.

That felt like forever ago, not just a few weeks ago. I'd been so scared of Dean, but now I couldn't imagine my life without him. I couldn't imagine not being in this house anymore. I couldn't imagine ever going back to the suburbs and living that life again.

It felt like that person hadn't existed. It felt like I'd read her in a book or dreamt her in a dream. She wasn't real. How could she become a hazed memory in such a short amount of time? But she had. And more than that, I didn't miss her.

I always thought I'd miss who I was before—before the truth, before the fire, before Dean. But I didn't. I didn't miss her, and I was glad she was dead and gone and never coming back.

Indie walked back into the room, a black dress bag in his arms. "Hopefully, this will be close enough to your size, so I won't have to make too many alterations. My lovely boss waited until last night to tell me about this event."

"Me too," I said, laughing. "Does he do that a lot?"

"What? Not tell anyone what's going on? Sometimes." He shrugged as he hung the dress up beside a mirror. My stomach sank a bit at that, but I swallowed thickly and tried to ignore it. "Alright, out of those clothes." I hesitated, and he threw his head back and laughed. "Trust me, dear, you have nothing I want."

He turned back to the dress bag and dragged the zipper down. My mouth fell open as more of the dress was revealed. It was...beautiful. A deep red, strapless gown that fell to the floor with a high slit on the side. I hadn't noticed Indie had gone to the back until he returned with a pair of heels.

"I hope that look on your face means you like the dress," he said, grinning when I turned to look at him.

"I—yes," I breathed, turning my attention back to it.

He gestured to Dean's oversized t-shirt, lifting his brow in admonishment. Quickly, I slid it off over my head and tossed it to the chair in the corner. "Bra and panties, too."

I stiffened, then turned curious eyes to him. "Why?"

"I have to measure you with the undergarments you'll be wearing. And there won't be any," he said, his back to me.

"Is that a joke?"

"No."

"A request from Dean?" I asked dryly, and his shoulders shook as he laughed.

"No, dear, this dress is silk and form-fitting, and it'll show panty lines." He held the dress in his hands as he turned toward me. "Now," he jerked his chin at me, "take them off."

I hesitated but slid my bra and panties off. Indie's eyes or hands didn't linger as he helped me into the dress and up onto the platform. Carefully, he turned me around so I couldn't see myself.

He kneeled beside me, a pincushion wrapped around his wrist and a tape measure around his neck. He snapped his fingers and turned to grab the heels before he came to my side again.

"If you would," he said as he held one shoe in front of me. I put a hand on his shoulder for balance and slid my foot into the stiletto. It'd been years since I'd worn anything this high, but I'd be lying if I said I didn't love it.

Indie quickly and efficiently pinned the dress, but it didn't need a lot of work. As much as I'd been upset about Dean's lie and finding out Matthew would be there, I was still looking forward to it.

Indie had me stand with my back to the mirror. A surprise, he'd said. When he was done pinning the fabric, he stood in front of me and let his eyes roam over my body.

"Take a look."

Slowly, I turned. And when I met my eyes in the mirror, my throat got tight. I'd never seen a more gorgeous dress, and I'd never dreamed of ever wearing one. But here I was, standing in front of floor-to-ceiling mirrors in a fantastic gown, perfectly fitted to my body.

"It's beautiful," I said, smoothing shaky hands down the front.

"The woman makes the dress, dear." I met Indie's eyes in the mirror, finding him smiling softly at me. I cleared my too-tight throat and nodded.

"Thanks, Indie," I said, and he waved dismissively as he rounded me to grab my clothes.

"Don't thank me," he said, then grinned wolfishly at me over his shoulder. "I want you here tomorrow morning, bright and early. We have a long day ahead of us." I took a deep breath and another look at myself in the mirror before nodding.

# Dean

A soft knock at the door drew my attention, and I looked up as I slid my glasses off. Julia leaned against the doorframe, her arms crossed over her chest.

"You have a ridiculously large house for a single man, you know that?" she asked, and I let out a breathy laugh.

"The better to impress you with, my darling." I leaned back in my chair, tossing my glasses on the desk and resting my hands on my thighs. She snorted a small laugh, the laugh I've come to crave, and pushed off the doorframe.

"I wandered for fifteen minutes," she said, and I cracked a small smile.

"You got lost?"

She gave me a mischievous grin, her eyes glittering. "I wanted to snoop."

"That's what I thought," I laughed, shaking my head. "And what did you find?" I patted my leg, and she walked to me and slid onto my lap. My arms went around her, and I pressed a quick kiss to her cheek as she rested one of her arms around my shoulders.

"I found out that you have a lot of empty space," she said, and I scrunched my brows. "There are things everywhere, but things don't make a home. Everything in this place is so totally you, but not at the same time. There's something missing."

"You," I said without thinking. "You're the thing missing."

Her eyes flicked between mine, her smile falling slightly. I wanted those three words to fall from my lips, then I wanted to press mine to hers. I wanted to tell her what I felt. I wanted to rip away the curtain and show her me—scars and all.

But the words never came.

"I lied earlier," she said. I stiffened, my blood turning icy. "I didn't really scrap that painting." I let out a hard breath, laughing slightly.

"Let me see it," I said. She shook her head before the words left my mouth. "Let me see!" I dropped my fingers to her waist, tickling her ribs. She squealed, then bucked her body as she tried to run from my touch. I held her tightly, not letting her fall but not allowing her to escape me, either.

She maneuvered out of my arms and ran across the room, her hair wild around her face, her chest heaving, and a glint in her eye I'd never seen before. She grinned at me as she took a few steps back toward the door.

"What are you doing?" I asked as I slowly rose from the chair, already preparing myself for a chase.

"Nothing," she said sweetly, and I narrowed my eyes at her.

"Darli—"

She sprinted from the room, her laughter echoing off the walls. I shook my head, mostly at myself, and took a deep breath before taking off in a full sprint after her.

I slid out of the room, catching myself on the doorframe. My heart was pounding as I watched her wink at me before flying down the stairs. I didn't know where the fuck she was going, but I was excited as hell to find out.

At the stairs, I decided to slide down the banister. My best idea? Probably not. Did I fall and make a fool of myself? Thankfully, no, I didn't. She nearly stumbled and fell as I slid past her, her eyes widening and mouth opening. But she caught herself and went down two more steps before turning and sprinting back up the steps.

Fuck.

My feet hit the ground, and I took a heaving breath as I chased her back up the stairs two at a time. This time, I didn't know where she'd gone. When I got to the landing, she was nowhere to be seen. All the doors were closed, including my office door, which I knew I'd left open.

"Darling," I called mockingly. No answer and I knew there wouldn't be. I smiled wickedly, thinking of all the depraved things I would do to her once I found her. "Ready or not, here I come!"

Stalking down the hallway, I went to my office first, not expecting to find her there. As suspected, I did a quick sweep of the room, found it empty, and then moved on to a few other rooms. There was Micha's office he never used and his connected bathroom, a spare bedroom, another bathroom, and her studio.

I peeked inside each room, leaving the studio last. I had a feeling that's where she was. As my hand wrapped around the doorknob, I paused.

I hadn't stopped smiling.

It was the first time in a long fucking time that I'd smiled this much. That I'd felt anything other than nothingness. And she'd brought this out in me. If she ever thought she was leaving me, she was fucking crazy. There was no fucking way I could let her go. Not when I know having her can feel this good.

Slowly, I turned the handle and pushed the door, letting it swing open and gently hit the wall. I leaned on the doorframe, feigning nonchalance as I stared into the dark room. I had no fucking idea if she was in there or not, but I'd rather her think I was all-knowing.

"Darling," I drawled into the darkness. "Are you really playing hide-and-seek with me?"

I was met with silence.

Sighing, I pushed off the frame and swaggered into the room, flicking the light on as I went. As soon as the light was on, I froze, and my mouth fell open. My cock immediately lengthened in my jeans, pressing painfully against my zipper.

"Fuck," I breathed, my eyes roaming over Julia's naked body. She was lying in the middle of the floor on a canvas, surrounded by paint tubes. I stared at her, at everything surrounding her, then her fucking body again, and breathed, "Fuck," again.

"Would you like to paint with me?" she asked, her voice low. It was a voice I hadn't heard yet, and I'd be fucking damned if it didn't make me want to come in my jeans. I nodded as I floated toward her, as if in a daze. She was a siren, singing me her song. "I think this painting will be much better than the other one."

Stopping at the edge of the canvas, I flicked my eyes over her body again, and she effortlessly got to her knees. She was at the perfect height to take my cock down her throat.

"Julia," I said, my voice strangled.

"I want to see you," she murmured, and I swallowed thickly.

I was covered in scars—fucking covered. Every inch of my torso, arms, and legs was scarred and a constant reminder of the shit I'd been through. There was no explaining away my past. So, I took a deep breath and leveled a look at her.

"Are you sure you want to open this door, Julia?" I asked quietly. "You're not going to like what I tell you. It's not a pretty story. And there's no going back after I tell you."

She gave me a confused look, her eyes narrowing as she tilted her head to the side. I sighed and glanced around the room, finding the t-shirt she'd been wearing hanging on the back of a chair. Grabbing it, I gave it to her and waited until she'd slid it on to hold my hand out.

I didn't know what the fuck to do or say. How to start this story. It was one I'd never told anyone. Micha generally knew what had happened but nothing else. Chef had been there, but he'd never seen my healed body—my scars.

I sat on a table and pulled her up with me, but not on my lap. I couldn't bear it if she moved away from me, if she was disgusted by me. I'd never recover from that.

She leaned her shoulder against mine, and I took a deep breath, not looking at her but at the floor.

"Do you remember how I told you my father died, and I was the one to take over?" I asked, and she nodded a few times. "Right, well. As much as I hated that fucking bastard, it was my fault." I quickly glanced at her, wondering if I'd find disgust on her face, but it was blank. Calm. And somehow, that was worse.

"How?" she asked, her hand moving to my thigh. She stroked her thumb back and forth, soothing me slightly. I rubbed at my chest, but I wanted to claw at it. I wanted to claw at my lungs to get the phantom smoke out.

"We were in Brazil at the time. He'd fucked over another Family, and we were hiding. I didn't know that, and I wouldn't have cared even if I had known. I was more interested in girls and partying; I didn't give a shit about this life. That night, he'd told me to stay home. He said that he needed all the help he could get. I ignored him and left anyway, taking a few guys with me.

"My father didn't know, of course. So, when the compound was attacked that night, he was left without many defenses. I'd taken five of the ten men with me. Like me, they were young and dumb and more interested in getting their dicks wet."

I was staring at the floor, at my shoes, but saw the burning house, the smoke that tainted the night, the disgusting smell of burnt flesh forever stuck in my nose.

The sight of my father's body.

"When we got home, it was late. The house was engulfed in flames. It wasn't a big place; he hadn't wanted to draw attention. I wasn't even thinking. I ignored the guys as I ran inside to find my dad. I didn't know if he was even in there or if he'd gotten out, but I had to save him if he was alive. He was a piece of shit, but he was still my fucking dad.

"I got to his room, but it was empty. Every room in that fucking place was empty until I got to the study at the back of the house. He was hanging on the wall, and even though his body had been burned, I could still see that his skin had been filleted off him."

Bile rose in my throat at the memories, at the smell, at the fucking sight. His legs limply hanging, his head down, what was left of his skin melting from him.

"I froze. I didn't know what to do. But that was my stupid fucking mistake." With a deep breath, I slid off the table and stood in front of her. Staring at her, I reached out and cupped her face, wiping a tear away I hadn't realized had fallen. Slowly, I dropped my hands to the hem of my shirt.

This was the first time I was showing anyone this.

My guys had seen glimpses of my scars, and Micha had seen the ones on my arms when we worked out. But no one, except my tattoo artist and doctors, had seen these fucking scars.

I held my breath as I ripped it off my head and tossed it on the table beside her. I kept my eyes squeezed tightly shut. I didn't want to see her face, the disgust that would twist it and stab me in the stomach.

"How?" she whispered. "How did you get them?" Her feet barely made a sound when they landed on the floor. Then her cold hands were on my stomach, gently caressing me.

"I got trapped in the study." I opened my eyes and looked down at her. Tears were falling freely from her eyes as she scanned my body, her shaky hands lightly trailing my skin. "The ceiling collapsed, and the fire spread through the room. I barely made it out. When my guys found me, they said they almost left me because I looked so fucking dead. But one of them—it was Chef, actually—said they had to get me to the hospital. And they did. He saved me."

Her hands didn't stop moving over the rough skin. I wished I could be smooth and perfect for her. I wanted to be someone she'd want to show off, not some fucking burned, tattooed freak. When she got to my chest, I closed my eyes again, sucking in a sharp breath.

They were the worst there.

"Does it hurt?" she whispered, her voice strangled. I shook my head, my eyes still squeezed tightly shut. The tip of her finger traced the flames tattooed there, a constant reminder of what happened that day.

"No," I said, shaking my head. She rested her palms against the center of my chest, and I finally opened my eyes. She was staring up at me, her watery eyes flicking between mine. I took a deep breath, then covered her hands on my chest with my own. "I'm not—I'm not whole. I'm not a whole man anymore, Julia. I have issues. PTSD, my shrink said. I have nightmares, and sometimes still have pain, and—"

She pressed her lips to the center of my chest, right over my heart and the worst of my scars, and my words got lodged in my throat.

"You're not broken, Dean," she murmured as she pulled away to look at me. "You think I don't have issues, too? We all do. But they make us who we are. And I really love who you are."

*Love.*

She loves who I am, but that doesn't mean she loves me. Right?

"I love who you are, too, darling," I said, my voice choked. Her eyes fell to my chest again, and I waited. I waited for the twist of disgust, or the pitying look, or...*something*. But nothing came. Instead, she kissed my scars again and stepped away, grabbing my hand.

Slowly, wordlessly, she led me to the canvas in the center of the room again.

"Make something beautiful with me," she said, stepping onto the flat canvas. She slid the shirt off over her head, tossing it to the floor, and again, she stood before me naked.

My feet felt like lead. I wanted her. My painfully hard cock was proof of that. But my mind told me it was a joke. She'd seen my scars, how hideous I was under my shirt, how marred and imperfect my skin was, and she wanted me? I couldn't understand it. How could someone who looked like her even give me the time of day?

She carefully watched me, waiting for my response. She was waiting for rejection. I didn't want to reject her, though. I wanted to give her the fucking universe. I wanted to give her every fucking universe in every solar system in all of existence.

With a deep breath, I forced myself to push my fears aside. This was Julia—*my* fucking Julia. She wouldn't hurt me.

I untied my boots and kicked them off but hesitated when I got to my jeans. When I looked at her again, there was a soft smile on her face. One I wasn't sure she was even aware of.

After taking the rest of my clothes off, my heart pounding wildly in my chest, I joined her on the canvas. She tipped her head back and gave me the brightest smile I'd ever seen, and it nearly fucking killed me. She kissed my chest again, then rested her hand over it, like she was trapping the kiss, forcing it to be absorbed through my thick, scarred skin.

"What's with the paint?" I finally asked, trying to break the tension, wanting this heaviness to leave my shoulders. She laughed breathily and looked down, then back up at me. There was a glint in her eye, the same one she'd had earlier, and I grinned.

Taking a few steps from me, she grabbed a few paint tubes. I thought she would start pouring them on the canvas or put them away. But she didn't. Instead, she uncapped one, aimed it at me, and squeezed.

Paint covered my chest and stomach, dripping from me onto the canvas. I blinked at her, then looked down at my paint-covered body. Another splash of the cold paint landed on me, and when I looked at her again, she threw her head back and howled with laughter.

"I can't believe you did that," I said, trying to sound angry, but she could see through it. Moving forward, I grabbed her around the waist and crushed her to me. I lifted her off the ground as I turned us in a circle, her arms going around my neck as she laughed.

"You're getting paint on me," she giggled.

"Oh, am I? I'm so sorry," I said, and she laughed harder. Tears danced in her eyes, laughter induced tears, and I felt all the anxiety, all my fear and insecurities melt away. The way she looked at me, like I was something special to her, made everything fall away. And all that was left was a warmth in my chest, in my heart. All that was left was her.

I pressed my lips against hers, silencing any lingering giggles, and her body melted against mine. My hand slid down her back to her ass, and I squeezed, making her whimper into my mouth.

The words were going to fall from my lips, and I wasn't going to be able to stop them. When she pulled away from me, when I was able to speak again, I was going to tell her I loved her. I didn't know if I could stop it.

Setting her on the ground, we got to our knees, our kiss never breaking. She licked at the seam of my lips, and I eagerly let her in, letting her take control for once. It wasn't something I did often, but I wanted to. I wanted to do anything for her.

Her tongue moved fluidly against mine, our lips slick. I laid her down on her back, cradling the back of her head to soften the landing on the hard floor. I rested my forehead against hers and breathed her in.

"Darling," I rasped before I opened my eyes. Her ocean eyes were depthless, and I felt myself falling further. The words danced on my lips, but they never came. Why wouldn't they come? Why couldn't I say it?

We stared at each other for a moment, silently waiting for the other to say something. But when the air became too tense and the moment passed, I kissed her again. Reaching between us, I pressed my hand between her legs, finding her clit. She let out a startled whimper when I pressed my fingers roughly against it. I circled it, coaxing her pleasure from her.

"Does that feel good, baby?" I murmured as I pulled away to watch her. She nodded, her eyes hooded as she stared up at me. "I should spank you for covering me in paint. Or maybe I won't let you come."

"Dean," she whined, her back arching.

"I could force my cock down your throat," I mused, and her eyes darkened. "But I think you'd enjoy that too much, wouldn't you?"

She dragged her bottom lip through her teeth, making me groan. "Yeah, you're such a filthy girl. So fucking dirty." My fingers moved faster over her clit, making her moan loudly. Her pussy was dripping now, covering my fingers with her arousal. "You love my cock down your throat, don't you, darling?"

"Fuck," she groaned, her eyes rolling back as her back arched off the ground again. "Yes, I love it down my throat."

"And in your pussy?" I asked, and she nodded. Her thighs trembled, and her hands dropped to the canvas, clawing at it. She nodded fervently as she spread her legs more. I lowered my face to hers, running my nose along her jaw. Moving my lips to her ear, I growled, "In your ass?"

She cried out as her orgasm shot through her, her back lifting off the ground completely. Her body convulsed, and her legs clamped around my hand. I forced my fingers to keep moving, driving her pleasure up more and more until she finally collapsed and whimpered with every rough pass of my fingers.

I'd never loved making anyone come as much as I loved making her come. She looked fucking gorgeous, like she was glowing, and I was addicted.

Kissing her roughly, I settled myself between her legs. My hands slid down the outside of her thighs, then hooked under her knees and pushed them to her chest. I sat back on my knees and stared down at her spread open and dripping for me. We were both covered in blue and green paint, and the canvas was smeared with it.

"Hold your legs," I said, and she hooked her forearms under her knees, pulling them back more. "You didn't answer me." I ran my hand down the back of her thighs, then brought my hand down on her ass, making her swallow a scream. Moving my fingers to her pussy, I gathered her wetness before dropping my finger to her ass.

Her body stiffened, and I lifted my eyes to look at her, but she didn't say anything. I circled her hole, wanting her to relax. Our eyes stayed locked as I gently forced the tip of my finger inside, stretching her. Her breathing was heavier, and the more I twisted my finger, the more she relaxed.

"Do you want my cock in your ass?" I asked as I pushed my finger further inside. It was only the tip, but she was moaning and writhing like it was my cock stretching her. "You're so fucking tight. You've never been fucked here?" Slowly, I dragged my finger in and out, twisting it with each push and pull.

"No," she whimpered. "Never." I grinned at her as I moved my finger faster. "Dean—"

"It feels good, doesn't it?" I asked, narrowing my eyes. "You like me playing with your tight little ass." It wasn't a question. I knew she loved it, loved the way it felt, loved the dirtiness of it, the foreign and tabooness of it.

"Yes," she whispered. I grinned, my finger moving at the same slow speed.

"I didn't hear you," I said. "What was that?" She glared up at me, but I just lifted my brow, then added, "And be specific. Tell me what you like, darling."

"Yes, I like you in my ass," she said shyly.

"Another time," I said and slipped my finger from her. "Maybe if you're my good girl, I'll fuck your ass while you wear your pretty dress tomorrow night." She groaned as she closed her eyes and nodded. I laughed and kissed the tip of her nose.

"Please," she said as she wiggled around, silently begging me to fuck her.

"Please, what?" I gripped my cock and dragged my pierced head against her clit, making her moan. Her fingers tightened around her thighs until the tips were white.

"Please fuck me," she said. I played with her clit a little more, slapping my cock against her, then moved to her entrance. I pressed inside, and her pussy swallowed my head.

"God, I forget how good you feel," I groaned, pressing deeper inside her. "So fucking tight." She moved her ankles to my shoulders, and I slammed the rest of the way inside her, making her scream.

Each thrust was more brutal than the last. I was fucking her into the floor, and she took it the way I knew she would.

"You're so fucking big," she cried, arching her back. I slammed my hips against hers, then stilled, letting her feel all of me. She gently shoved at my shoulders, "Get on your back." Her legs slid off my shoulders, and I dipped to press my lips to hers before slipping out and falling beside her.

Far too gracefully, she got to her knees and crawled over my body. I rested my hands on her hips and watched with hooded lids as she gripped my cock and positioned it at her entrance. Slowly, she lowered herself, hissing as I stretched her.

"I love stretching your cunt," I said, and she whimpered, pressing herself further down. Moving my hand to her lower stomach, I pressed slightly and felt my cock slowly filling her, then dropped my thumb to her clit.

"Dean," she groaned and grabbed my wrist with both hands. "It's too much." I ignored her as I strummed my thumb back and forth, making her pussy spasm around me. I jerked my hips up, forcing her to take all my cock at once. She screamed and dropped her hands to my chest, her eyes widening.

"Ride my cock," I growled, smacking her ass with my other hand. Her body was shaking, but she forced herself up, then dropped down, crying out each time. She moved her hands behind her, resting them on my thighs as she rode me. It gave me the perfect view of her tits bouncing. Her head tipped back, her hair tickling my legs.

Her pussy tightened around me until it was hard to move, but I forced my hips up, fucking her through her orgasm. She screamed and shook her head, incoherently begging me to stop, but I wouldn't. I couldn't. Not until I'd filled her with my cum.

I moved my thumb faster, my breathing harder. My legs shook as my own release built. "Fuck, baby, I'm about to come." She dropped down, landing on my chest. I wrapped my arms around her, hugging her tightly to me, and bent my legs, fucking her relentlessly as I chased my orgasm.

"Oh, God. Too much," she cried into my neck. Her body was malleable, completely boneless.

"So close, baby," I grunted, squeezing her tighter. I fucked her faster, my fingers tightening on her sides. "I'm so fucking close."

Her teeth sunk into my neck, and that was what toppled me over the edge. I groaned as I slammed into her a final time, then filled her with my cum, pushing it deeper inside her with each shallow thrust.

"You okay?" I breathed, smoothing my hand up and down her back. She nodded against me, her sweaty forehead slick against my skin. "Did I hurt you?" She shook her head. "I need your words, darling."

"I'm okay," she said tiredly. "I'm not hurt." I nodded, then settled slightly, holding her to me.

It wasn't comfortable lying on the floor, covered in sweat and paint, but I'd stay here forever if this was where she wanted to be. And from the way her body was limp against mine, the way her breathing was evening out, I was starting to think this was where we were going to be sleeping.

"It wasn't your fault," she finally murmured, her words slightly slurred. "You didn't start the fire, you tried to save him, and you hurt yourself. It wasn't your fault." She nuzzled her face into my neck with a small sigh.

Then she fell asleep.

# Julia

I paced at the bottom of the stairs, my hands twisting in front of me as I waited for Dean. My heels clicked against the floor, echoing around me mockingly. The dress's silk slid against my bare skin with each step, and when I met Micha's eye, I sighed.

My stomach had been in knots all day. Tight, painful knots that made me want to die. I hadn't been this nervous since...well, I'd never been this nervous.

"Where is he?" I asked Micha for the fifth time in the last five minutes.

"He'll be down in a minute," he said again. "Calm down, Jay." I paused in front of him. He barely hid his smirk, then folded his arms over his chest.

He looked incredibly handsome. He wore a fitted tux with a little red pocket square, the same shade and fabric as my dress. His face was clean-shaven, with no trace of his usual stubble, and his messy blond hair had been trimmed and neatly styled.

"I've never seen you so nervous," he said. "You look great. You're gonna do great tonight. Calm down, you got this."

"Do I?" I murmured, mostly to myself, but I knew he heard.

Turning back toward the stairs, I took another deep breath. My dress felt too tight. Maybe Indie had made it too tight, and that's why I was having trouble breathing. "I'm just going to check on him. Maybe something's wrong."

"Jay—"

Micha reached for me, but I jerked my arm out of the way before he could. But if he'd wanted to stop me, he would've. Carefully, I opened the dress a little wider so I wouldn't trip, thankful for the high slit, and made my way up the steps.

My hands were trembling, and my teeth chattered. I didn't know what to expect. And I didn't know how Dean would react to my outfit. I loved the dress, it was fitted on top, molding perfectly to my torso and hips, and the slit showed off my legs and dangerously high heels. I felt beautiful, sexy, and powerful. I felt like someone else. I felt like someone strong and worthy enough to be by Dean's side.

Indie instructed the hairdresser to keep my hair in loose waves but pin it away from my face. He told the makeup artist to keep it simple but bold. Which didn't make sense to me, but it must've made sense to her because I looked...simple yet bold.

I got to our bedroom door and paused. Why was I so nervous? And had I really thought of his room as ours? Was it ours? Was this place *our* place?

I shook myself. I'd worry about that later. Right now, I needed to get Dean so we could leave. He was taking too long, and I didn't want to be late. Micha assured me it'd be hard to be late to an event like this, but I was punctual.

The door was pulled open as I pushed it, and Dean and I abruptly stopped, our eyes wide. Then his eyes dropped to my body, and he bit his bottom lip. Taking a step back, he lazily checked me out, which was fine because I was doing the same to him. Because...*damn.*

His tux was nicer than Micha's and fitted him like a second skin. It was tight around his massive biceps and shoulders, but he made it work. Even his tattoos added to his beauty. To his perfectness. His pocket square was like Micha's, but my name was stitched to it in bold black letters. There would be no mistaking who I belonged to, but more than that, who belonged to me.

"Goddamn, darling," he breathed as he held his hand out to me. "You look fucking incredible." I slid my hand into his, and he turned me in a slow circle. I could feel his eyes searing me everywhere, and my heart pounded faster in my chest.

"So do you," I said breathlessly when facing him again. He gave me an arrogant grin, then kissed the back of my hand, his eyes locked with mine.

"Come here." He walked further into the room, and I glanced over my shoulder at the empty hallway. I firmly shook my head, and his grin broadened. "What?"

"We're going to be late."

"We have plenty of time," he said, taking a small step toward me. He lowered his mouth to my ear, and his cologne surrounded me, making me float. His hands were warm through the silky fabric as he ran them over me, then to my ass, squeezing slightly. "Are you wearing panties? I told Indie not to let you." My breath stuttered, and I shifted on my feet, pressing my thighs together.

"No," I whispered, and I felt him smile against my hair.

"Good girl," he purred, and I melted. "I want easy access to your pussy all night."

"Dean." I tipped my head back, and he crowded me, walking us backward and pinning me against the wall.

"Darling," he said in a low voice. His fingers brushed against my bare thigh, slowly trailing up. "Let me taste you." My breath was sawing in and out of my chest, but I couldn't let us get carried away. Things with Dean were never quick. He'd have me here for hours, and we'd miss the gala altogether.

"We're going to be late," I said again, and he laughed breathily. "Please." He shook his head, his too-handsome-for-his-own-good smile still on his face.

"You know I can never deny you anything," he said. "Even if I'll have blue balls for the rest of the night."

"Oh, you'll be fine," I laughed, swatting at his chest. He quickly pressed his lips to mine. Then he ran his thumb under my lip, fixing any smudges from my lipstick, and took a step back, wrapping his hand around mine.

"I have something for you," he said, and I lifted my brows. He slipped his hand inside his jacket and pulled out a long black box. He handed it to me, and I shook his hand off mine to open it.

It was a thin gold chain with a small demon pendant on it. The eyes were rubies, and the horns were tipped with diamonds. I glanced up at Dean, finding him looking nervous.

"It's pretty," I said, and he groaned.

"You hate it." He reached for the box, but I yanked it away.

"I don't hate it," I laughed, swatting his hand when he tried to take it from me again. "I just never wear jewelry, but I'll wear this. Thank you." He eyed me skeptically. It was a beautiful necklace, but I was serious; I never wore jewelry. I never even wore my wedding ring. "Will you put it on me?"

He cleared his throat and took the dainty chain between his thick fingers. I wanted to laugh when the tip of his tongue slid between his lips as he pinched the bracket open.

"Turn around." I turned and gathered my hair, lifting it for him. He draped the chain around my neck and clasped it together, then fluffed my hair when I let it go. "There's a tracker in it."

I turned toward him again, my brows furrowed. "A tracker? Like I'm a dog?" I laughed, but he didn't. "Do you think something will happen tonight?" He sighed and scrubbed his hand down his face.

"I don't know," he said quietly. "I doubt it, but I want to be prepared. If anything happens to you, I need to know where you are at all times. Don't take it off."

"Alright," I said, resting my hand over the small pendant. It felt heavy now, and I took another breath. "I won't." His eyes flicked between mine, then he nodded before kissing me gently.

"Ready?"

# Julia

We walked down the stairs, my eyes locking with Micha's halfway down. He grinned and shook his head as Dean wrapped my hand around the crook of his elbow, mindlessly patting it.

"Are the cars ready?" he asked. Micha covered his laugh with a cough, and Dean's eyes narrowed. "What?"

"Nothing," Micha said quickly. "Just never seen you look so..." He glanced at me, then shrugged.

"So?" Dean's brows pushed together as he looked down at me, then to Micha.

"Just don't lower your guard tonight," Micha said, and Dean nodded slowly.

"When have I ever?"

"You've never had a girl on your arm," he retorted. "Stay aware." He turned on his heel, and we followed him down a long corridor to a part of the house I hadn't been to yet.

We entered a massive garage, finding it full of cars and men bustling about. All of them were dressed similarly to Micha and Dean, all of them with the same color pocket squares, but they were strapping weapons to their bodies before putting their coats on. Dean ignored them as he walked me to a black SUV and opened the door.

"Is there something I should be worried about tonight?" I asked, looking up at him.

"Nothing at all," he said. "You're to enjoy yourself, that's it."

"The men—"

"Are there for added protection," he said. "I don't think we'll need them, but I want you safe." I swallowed heavily, then nodded before he helped me into the car and shut the door. I turned and watched him from the back window tell a few of the guys something, using his arm to point at one of the cars. They nodded before going to a weapons rack, grabbing a few more, and getting into the car behind ours.

Dean's door opened as the front two opened. He slid in beside me, Micha was in the driver's seat and Cory into the passenger seat. Cory turned around, his face hard as he gave me a quick once over.

"I'll be your shadow tonight." With that, he faced forward again and left me blinking after him. Dean chuckled softly, then rested his arm across the back of the seat.

"Come here," he said. I swallowed heavily but rose and carefully shuffled to the middle seat beside him. He helped me put the seatbelt over me, then wrapped his arm around my shoulders, pulling me tightly against him.

Micha glanced at us in the mirror before he pushed a button and the garage doors opened. Slowly, he rolled forward. We sat in silence for a few minutes, then, surprisingly, Cory turned the radio on. Not loud, but enough to drown out the silence.

"You look beautiful," Dean said low in my ear, his breath warm and minty against my skin. Goosebumps rippled over my body, and I shuddered. He grabbed my hand and rested it in his lap, right over his diamond-hard cock under his pants. "See what you do to me?"

I gave him a gentle squeeze, and his hand tightened over mine. He made a choking sound in the back of his throat and rested his head against the headrest.

"Don't start something we can't finish," he warned. I smiled sweetly up at him, and he shook his head. His piercing was hard, and I ran my thumb over it, feeling it shift. He groaned again, and Cory shifted uncomfortably. Laughing, I drew my hand away.

"Maybe if you're good, I'll take care of your problem later," I whispered, and Dean's brow flicked up.

"If *I'm* good?" He shook his head, grinning. "I'm always good." His hand went to my bare thigh under the slit in my dress, and I grabbed his wrist. He easily slid his hand between my thighs, and his finger ran along my pussy, making me gasp.

"You two need to fuckin' cool it," Micha snapped. Dean ignored him as he slid his finger inside me.

"Why are you so wet, darling?" he murmured. "You're going to ruin your pretty dress." He pumped his finger in and out a few times. I tried to keep my breathing steady and not draw any more attention to us, but it was impossible when he slid it out and ran it in a circle around my clit.

Cory glanced back at us and our eyes locked. He quickly looked down at where Dean's hand was hidden beneath my dress and cleared his throat before turning forward again.

"Dean," I breathed, not meaning for it to come out as a moan as he pressed two fingers inside me, hooking them up. I wanted to tell him to stop, but I also wanted to come. He was making me feel so good, especially when he was licking and kissing my neck in time with his thrusts. I was about to combust.

Suddenly, he slid his fingers from me and pulled away. His eyes clashed with mine as he sucked his fingers clean, then straightened his jacket. My body was vibrating, and my mind was whirling. What the fuck was that?

"What—"

"We're almost there," he said, his lips twitching. "And you were teasing me. It was just payback." I narrowed my eyes at him.

"I'll remember that when you're begging me—"

"I don't beg," he interrupted, and the look he sent me had me clenching my thighs together. I cleared my throat and looked ahead, shifting slightly. He kissed my temple before he and Cory started talking about the venue's layout and where everyone was to be stationed.

I sat quietly and barely listened. I didn't need to know the details of Dean's security; I was going to be by his side all night. Wherever he went, I went. Micha's eyes found mine periodically, but we both stayed quiet.

"Do you know how to shoot a gun?" Dean asked, and it took me a moment to realize he was speaking to me.

"Um, no," I said. "Well, I've shot one once before, but otherwise, no." He nodded a few times like that's what he'd been expecting.

"Then it'll do no good to arm her with one," he said, lifting his eyes to Cory. "Let me see one of your shoes." I gave him a curious look but bent over and slid my foot from my shoe, handing it to him. Then, to my horror, he popped the heel from it.

"Dean!" I reached for it, but he pulled it away. I paused, my mouth falling open as he twisted the broken heel piece in half, exposing a small blade.

"It won't do much damage, but it'll do enough to get away," he said, handing it to me. "Your other shoe has one, too." I twisted the blade back and forth, the street lights reflecting off the knife. "Aim for the neck." He tilted his head back and pointed at the base of his tattooed jaw. "You want to try to kill them." I swallowed thickly and nodded.

He stared at me a moment longer, his eyes flicking between mine before he grabbed my free hand. "Be safe tonight. Don't do anything stupid. Don't go anywhere alone. Don't trust anyone except for the three of us."

I looked at Dean, then turned to look at Micha and Cory. Micha and Dean, I trusted, more so than I'd realized, but Cory...I didn't know him well enough to trust him. But if Dean said I should, then I would.

"We're here," Micha announced. I looked out the windshield, finding the street full of cars and beautifully dressed people.

"Stay with me tonight, darling," Dean said quietly, almost a plea. His words sent a chill down my spine, and something cold began to bloom in my chest. Something I was scared to acknowledge. I gave him a gentle smile and slid my shoe back on as the car came to a slow stop.

# Julia

Conversation greeted us as we entered the venue, the full-bodied scent of rich food and spiced drinks floating in the air. I'd never seen so many beautifully dressed and wealthy-looking people before, and I felt painfully out of place. I felt like I screamed commoner, or worse, Dean's escort for the evening.

My hand tightened around Dean's inner elbow as we walked down the steps, Cory and Micha behind us, scanning the crowd. Dean rested his hand over mine, his thumb stroking back and forth reassuringly.

Banners hung from the ceiling, the name of the charity on them. Bar height tables were scattered around the room, and people stood around them talking and laughing. The floor was white marble, and the walls were a creamy off-white color, with massive marble columns at different points in the room. A set of double doors stood closed at the back of the room, probably where the actual event would occur.

Dean took my hand in his and led us down the marble steps. I hesitated for a moment, my fight or flight response kicking into overdrive. And flight was winning.

"It's okay," he whispered, leaning down to my ear. My eyes met his, and I immediately calmed.

"Hello, Mr. Austen. We hope everything is to your liking this evening," a man said as he approached us. It took me a moment to realize he was speaking to Dean. Then it hit me like a semi—I'd never asked Dean what his last name was. I always stupidly assumed it was Demon. Dean Demon? Ridiculous.

*Dean Austen, though?*

I glanced up at him with new eyes, hiding my smiling behind a polite face to the stranger. Dean nodded a few times, a polite smile of his own as he quickly scanned the room and then looked down at the older man.

Dean looked just as out of place as I felt. Even if he wasn't covered in tattoos, he towered over everyone. He looked like his biceps were going to burst from his tux jacket at any moment. But more than that, there was a static around him that made him dangerous, and people knew that. Their eyes wandered to us periodically, but quickly, they'd divert their attention again.

"Yes," is all Dean replied. "Come, darling, let's explore."

As we stepped onto the floor, I looked around. I wished I could tower over everyone the way Dean could, then I'd be able to see what was happening.

"Is that Dean?" A woman said loud enough to draw our attention to her. I turned my head in that direction, my stomach sinking. "It is!" she squealed, yanking on her date's arm.

They were both middle-aged, probably married, and actually quite kind-looking. She had bouncy auburn curls piled on top of her head with a floor-length sleek, black dress. Pearls lined her neck and wrists, and she wore matching pearl earrings. Her date was bald, his eyebrows dark brown. A pair of thin, silver-rimmed glasses sat perched on his nose, hiding his hazel eyes. He was wearing a traditional tux, his hand on the woman's lower back, the other holding a champagne flute.

They came to us, the woman leaning up on her toes to air kiss both of Dean's cheeks. The man only clapped his hand against Dean's before shaking it enthusiastically. Both of them smiled broadly at him before turning their attention to me.

"My God," the woman said, putting her hand against her chest, making my stomach immediately drop. "Has *the* Dean Austen finally settled down and found a woman?" She threw her head back and let out a bright cackle.

I let out a breath of relief. I really thought that was about to go in a totally different direction. Dean chuckled beside me, his hand tightening around mine momentarily.

"I have," he nodded proudly, then turned his soft gaze on me. "Tom, Anna, this is Julia Chamberlain. My...*fiancée*." He hesitated on the word, then glanced down at me like he wasn't sure of my reaction.

"Wow!" Anna squealed. She reached both of her hands out and grasped my free hand, her eyes darting between us with a broad smile on her face. "You didn't tell us you were even dating!" She playfully swatted at Dean's arm. How well did these people know him?

"It was sudden," he admitted, smiling. "Love at first sight, you could say." Tom chuckled and shook his head at Dean as he took a sip from his champagne.

"You've never been one for patience," he said. I looked up at him and tried to hide the shock on my face. He gave me a weak smile.

"Don't make me look bad in front of my girl, Tom," Dean teased, his tone light.

"I'm sure you do that enough yourself." Tom barked a laugh when his wife swatted his shoulder.

"I've worked with Tom for several years," Dean said to me. I nodded a few times and kept a polite smile on my face. I'd played this game before, the doting wife. I could be this for Dean. But his brows twitched, then he cleared his throat. "The warehouses I told you about?" I nodded again.

"Oh," Tom said, sounding startled. "She's in the business, too, then?" He looked me over again, more critically.

"Bringing her in," Dean said. "She's still new but is a fast learner." I loved that he had faith in me, but I didn't want him hyping me up to his business partner.

"I'm sure you have nothing but the best," he said, lifting his champagne to me. I dipped my chin slightly, feeling uncomfortable.

"So," Anna said, dragging the word out, her voice high and excited. "How did you two meet? I love hearing how couples meet!" Her eyes were on me like she expected me to tell the story. Dean followed her gaze, a mischievous grin playing at his lips in a challenge. He wanted to know what I'd say.

At first, I thought of telling them the truth: he kidnapped me and stole my heart from my husband. But with the way Dean was grinning at me, *challenging* me, I wanted to show him I could play, too.

"Oh, Julia loves to tell the story. Go on, darling, don't be shy." Dean nudged me gently with his elbow. I looked up at him and cocked an eyebrow, accepting his challenge. If he wanted to put me on the spot...

"Dean was a regular at the club I worked at," I started and watched as Anna's eyes widened. Dean stiffened beside me, but that smile was still on his face.

"Club?" Tom asked.

"Strip club," I clarified, making him choke on his champagne. Dean's hand tightened around mine again. Not in warning, I didn't think, though. I smiled sweetly at the couple before continuing. "One night, he came in and bought a private dance. Of course, I had to go with him. He was a paying customer, after all." I nudged Dean's arm playfully with mine.

Anna's eyes were saucers, her lips straining to stay in a smile, but she was struggling. Poor woman, I really shouldn't be tormenting her. The torment was more aimed at Dean, and she just happened to get caught in the crossfires. Something told me he was loving this, though.

"After the first dance, he came in Every. Single. Night," I said, enunciating the words. "He bought dance after dance after dance. I had no other customers for three months. At one point, the bouncers thought they'd have to ban him from the club because they thought he was a total creep." I looked lovingly up to Dean. "They were right, of course." Dean wasn't hiding his smile, his eyes dancing with pure happiness. He was an odd man, but he was mine.

"Eventually," he took the story over, and the couple turned their attention to him, "they did kick me out. I couldn't get in to see her. So–"

"So he found all of my social media accounts and messaged me on each one," I interrupted. Anna's eyes darted between us, her smile fallen and forgotten. Instead, she looked absolutely enthralled at the story unfolding.

"She never responded." Dean rolled his eyes, exasperated. "One night–"

"One night," I said, interrupting him again. "He was waiting by my car behind the club."

"I knew what time her shift ended, so I waited for her." He wrapped his arm around my waist and pulled me to him. His attention was solely on me, and the world fell away.

"When I got to my car, I'll admit, I wasn't shocked to see him." I smiled.

"But then I got down on one knee, and you were shocked," he said and I let out a breathy laugh, nodding.

"And he asked me to marry him. Right there in the parking lot of the club." I shook my head like I couldn't believe it.

"The ring?" Anna asked, her eyes still wide as she looked frantically at my hand. I gave her a tight-lipped frown.

"It's getting resized," I sighed. "But, it's beautiful."

"A beautiful ring for a beautiful girl," he said and I rolled my eyes. Then, to my horror, added, "Spent well over a million on it." Tom choked on his drink again, and the color drained from Anna's face. Even my eyes went wide at him. He only stayed smiling at me, looking completely unphased.

"Million?" Anna croaked, and he shrugged.

"Nothing's too much for Julia," he said, and she sighed, then looked at her husband.

"Maybe you should take some notes," she said, elbowing him. Tom shot Dean a look that had us both laughing. We spent several more minutes in polite conversation before breaking off toward the bar. He ordered us a glass of red wine, then leaned on the bar, looking effortlessly cool.

"You know," I said as I toyed with the stem of my wine glass. His eyebrows rose as he waited for me to continue. "I'm holding you to it." I grinned as I took a sip of my wine. He cocked his head to the side, studying me.

"Holding me to what?" he asked.

"The million-dollar ring," I teased. A broad, eye-crinkling, blinding smile spread over his face, melting my heart and soul completely.

"I promise, it'll be much more than that," he said, bringing his glass to his lips. "I can't wait to see you panic when I give it to you." I rolled my eyes and took another sip.

"I won't panic," I scoffed. "And don't think I'll forget about this conversation if you get me drunk." He laughed as he shook his head, then leaned forward and gently pressed his lips on mine. I leaned into his kiss, enjoying the comfort he brought me. "Also," I said when I pulled away, "I didn't know your last name was Austen."

"You never asked," he said.

"You never told me, either," I replied and he nodded a few times, then gently clinked his glass to mine before taking a sip. I laughed as I set the glass down and toyed with the stem.

"What?" he asked again, his voice dropping. He took a small step toward me and rested his hand on my hip, his thumb rubbing up and down like it always did.

"You have two first names." I laughed again, turning my eyes down to my glass.

"One day, you will too."

My eyes snapped to him, finding his cheeks tinged slightly pink.

My heart was in my throat, but when I opened my mouth to say something, *anything*, nothing came out. Instead, I took another drink, a much longer one, and turned my attention to the crowd.

I looked around the room, stared at the banners hanging from the ceiling with *Darling's Farm Sanctuary* written on them. There were tables set up around the room with people crowded around them. Others were in small groups talking and laughing amongst themselves. I knew who our guys were by their red pocket squares, and they were all on high alert.

"*Darling's Farm?*" I asked, glancing at Dean. "I've never heard of it before." He took a long drink of his wine, nearly finishing it before he wiped his mouth slowly with the palm of his hand.

"It's yours," he said, and I blinked at him.

"Mine?" I choked on a laugh and looked at the banners again.

*Darling's Farm Sanctuary.* I tried to find a board or a banner with more information, but there was nothing. Instead, Dean rested his hand on my hip again, drawing my attention.

"There was a small farm sanctuary close to the house," he said quietly. "They were close to having to shut down, so I bought them out." I couldn't swallow, or breathe, or really even think.

"You bought me a farm?" I asked with a small laugh, then looked around again.

"A farm sanctuary, but yeah." He nodded, his eyes narrowing slightly. "Do you hate it? Was it the totally wrong move?" My mouth fell open, and even when I tried to close it, I couldn't. "I know you don't eat animals, and I assumed it was because you loved them, so I wanted to give this to you. And then you told us that story about the chickens at your friend's farm and–why are you laughing?"

"Dean." I rested my hand on his forearm that rested on the bar. "You're rambling." His face flushed red, and I shook my head, smiling. "This is incredible." I looked around the room again, taking it in with new eyes. This was for me. All of it was for me.

*He did this for me.*

"No one has ever been this thoughtful before," I said quietly, lowering my eyes to my wine. "I've never had anyone care about this part of my life. It's always been an inconvenience or a joke. It's never been something that's been taken seriously. So," I looked up at him, finding him staring intently at me, "thank you."

"Baby," he rasped, his voice tight. "I know you've had to spend the last five years with a complete fucking asshole, but you need to get used to this. Everything I do, every breath I take, is for you. And this is something important to you, so it's something important to me."

I nodded a few times and tried not to let the tears in my eyes drip down my face. It would ruin my makeup, and Indie would be royally pissed. But I had noticed Dean's lack of meat at the meals we spent together. I assumed he was doing it out of politeness, but now I don't think he was. He was doing it because he wanted to, because, like he said, it was important to me.

Resting my hand on his chest, I gently tugged him down and pressed my lips to his. He didn't hesitate to sweep me into his arms, crushing me against his body and taking control.

A throat cleared behind us, and I pulled away from Dean and glanced over my shoulder, finding Cory with his hands clasped behind his back. He was scanning the crowd, but his neck and face were a deep red shade. I laughed when Dean chased my lips with his, kissing me again. I leaned against him, and his arm circled me, tucking me tightly to his side as I sipped my wine.

# Julia

"What's going on over there?" I asked, using my glass to point at the largest group of people standing around a booth. Dean cleared his throat before picking his glass up.

"Let's go see, shall we?" I tipped my head to look up at him, finding him already staring down at me with soft, silver eyes. I wanted to read his mind and know exactly what he was thinking and feeling. But I didn't want to ask.

Instead, I nodded and let him lead me toward the crowd. We weaved through people, Cory and Micha carefully keeping them well over an arm's length away from us. I tried to keep my eyes up, but I couldn't. I felt uncomfortable. Even though the dress made me feel beautiful, this wasn't me.

This wasn't me with lavish parties, wealthy people, expensive wine, and galas. Would a life with Dean mean becoming this person? Would I be trading the politics of suburban life for the politics of this world? I wouldn't survive it.

We stopped behind the crowd, but I couldn't see over the people, even in my heels. Dean easily looked over everyone, and his face lit up before he smiled down at me.

"Puppy and kitten adoption," he said, and my heart warmed.

"Really?" I turned toward the crowd again. "I want to see." He wrapped his arm tighter around me, anchoring me to his side as he began pushing his way through the crowd.

We got to the table and found a nice-looking girl behind it, holding a sleeping gray pitbull puppy. I grabbed Dean's hand, mostly to keep from reaching across the table and stealing the dog.

"He's adorable," I cooed, leaning forward.

"This little guy is Diego. He has a sister and brother, too," the girl said. She held the dog out, but I didn't reach for him. There was no use in getting attached when I couldn't take him home.

I'd begged Matthew for years for a dog, but he never wanted one. Too much mess, he'd said. It was always about the mess with him. Not that he was the one who would've been cleaning up anyway.

"Can we see them too?" Dean asked. She hurried away, putting Diego back in his cage, and grabbed the two other baby pits.

"Daisy and Devil," she said. Then quickly added, "Don't let the name fool you. He's a total sweetheart." Dean laughed breathily.

"I think it's a sign," he said, nudging me gently. "What do you think, darling?"

"A sign?" I looked up at him.

"A Devil for The Demons?" He lifted his brows, and I laughed before looking back at the dogs. Daisy was tan, and Devil was all black.

"He would make a good mascot," I said, nodding.

"They all would."

The girl and I snapped our heads toward Dean, my eyes widening.

"All?" I repeated, and he gave me a weird look like I was dense.

"We can't break them up. They're a family," he said, and I nearly died from how sweet he was. He was stealing my heart, my love, my soul, and I was happily letting him.

"That's the sweetest thing I've ever heard," the girl said, her voice dreamy. A surge of jealousy shot through me, and I took a step closer to him, grabbing his hand. He let out a startled laugh but didn't pull away. A small part of me had been expecting him to pull away from me or apologize to the girl for my behavior—the way Matthew would've—but when was I going to learn that Dean wasn't Matthew?

"Sir," Cory said from behind us, but Dean ignored him.

"We'll take all three of them," he said to the girl. I squeezed his hand and tore my eyes from her. He looked down at me, a small grin on his face as he said, "If that's what you'd like, of course, darling?"

Butterflies swarmed my stomach, they always did when he called me that, and I nodded. I couldn't help the broad smile that spread across my face.

"Really?" I asked, and he pulled me tighter against him, wrapping his thick arm around my waist.

"Anything you want," he said quietly. "You want them all?" I looked at all of the puppies and kittens being fawned over by the people around us. "They're yours."

"Sir," Cory said again, and I glanced over my shoulder at him.

"We'll need you to fill out some paperwork—"

"I'll send someone over to do that," Dean said dismissively to the girl before he turned toward Cory, his brows lifted expectantly. "What?"

"They're here."

"Who?" I asked, then froze. It could only be two people, and they were here. I looked up again, finding Dean's face like stone.

"They stay the fuck away from her," he growled. "Keep him away from her. He comes near her, fucking kill him, I swear to God, Cory. I'll fucking bathe this room in his blood."

"Yes, sir," Cory said, nodding.

"Matthew?" I squeaked, and they both looked at me. "Kill Matthew? Dean, no." His jaw tensed under his thick beard, but he looked back at Cory and Micha.

"He doesn't come near her," he said again. Micha nodded and

weaved through the crowd, his finger pressed to his ear as he barked orders at the men on the other side.

"I've got you," Dean said, and I nodded mindlessly.

We were surrounded by people. I couldn't see Matthew or Dominico, but if they said they were here, then they must be. Just knowing I was in the same room as them made me feel sick. My teeth began chattering, and Dean swore under his breath.

"Send someone to finish this," Dean said to Cory, and he nodded before he pressed his finger to his ear and began talking. "Come on, darling. Come with me."

He quickly pushed his way through the crowd back toward the bar. He ordered me water and pulled me to his chest when we got to it, holding me tight.

"I've got you," he said again. "Drink something." He held the glass to my lips, and I took a small sip before pressing my cheek to his chest. A shadow fell over me, but I didn't pull away. I waited for Cory or Micha to update Dean. Instead, the voice I heard sent a bolt of panic through me.

"Well, aren't you two cozy?"

# Julia

I froze, every cell in my body going on high alert at the voice I once loved. I kept my face buried in Dean's chest, telling myself if I ignored him, he'd go away.

"Get the fuck out of here, Blackwell," Dean growled, shifting to put his body between us.

"Nice to see you, Jewels," Matthew drawled, ignoring Dean. Finally, I forced myself to look at him. I barely looked around Dean's arm, right into Matthew's eyes, and felt my stomach drop to the floor.

"Matthew." My voice was hoarse, nothing more than a faint croaking sound, but it was loud around us.

"Get the fuck out of here," Dean said again.

"I paid for my ticket just like you." Matthew's lips curved into a grin, a cold, mocking one that sent a shiver down my spine. "But you didn't have to pay for your ticket, right? Not if you own the place. Not if it's your event." I glanced up at Dean, finding him glaring harder at Matthew, his jaw flexing.

"Ah, *amor*, how are you?" Dominico stepped up beside Matthew, a crystal tumbler full of amber liquid in his hand.

"Fine," I managed to say. Dean's back pressed against my chest as he straightened.

"Both of you are going to get thrown out," he said.

"I'm here to speak to my wife," Matthew said. "Or did you forget that you're still married?" His nasty words stabbed through me the way he knew they would.

"You're separated. You made that clear," Dean snapped. "She wants nothing to do with you—"

"Julia," Matthew held his hand out, ignoring Dean, "come." I felt myself take a step forward at his command, but Dean's body stopped me, returning to the present.

"Anything you have to say to me, you can say to us both," I said. Some of the tension in Dean's shoulders loosened, and I rested my hand in the center of his back, trying to soothe him.

"No." Matthew shook his head. "I'm not playing this game with you. Come with me. Now."

"You're fucking delusional if you think I'm letting her go anywhere alone with you," Dean scoffed.

"So, you're fine with him speaking for you? Apparently, all you need is some dick, and you'll comply—"

"Some good dick, yeah," I snapped, sidestepping Dean. "Some big dick, yeah. Not some barely-there dick."

"Julia," Dean said, barely hiding his laugh, putting his hand on my lower back.

"Classy, as always," Matthew said, and my blood heated. "Apparently, spending time with these low-lives has let the real you shine." He adjusted his sleeves with a small sigh. "Good luck trying to control this one." He looked at Dean, his expression bored. "She's fun in the beginning, a decent lay, too. But this shit," he waved his hand around at me, "gets old fast."

"I'm going to fucking kill you." Dean took a step forward. "Maybe not tonight, but when you die, it'll be by my fucking hand." I'd never heard his voice like that, so low and deadly. But Matthew just grinned up at him, not scared in the slightest.

"I need to speak to you," Matthew said, then his face softened. "Please." My gut twisted. Even with everything that's happened in the last month, when he gave me that look I felt myself lowering my guard for him. Why was I like this? Why did he have this power over me?

"Alright," I said. Dean inhaled sharply, then opened his mouth to say something, but I rested my hand on his chest. "I'll come back to you. I promise." I tugged on his jacket and he lowered his mouth to mine. Matthew snorted in disgust behind me, but I chose to ignore it. Even if he had power over me, he wasn't mine and I wasn't his. I never had been. But Dean? I whole-heartedly belonged to him.

"You touch her," Dean said, wrapping his arm protectively around me as he glared at Matthew, "You're dead. If you even reach for her, it's a bullet between your fucking eyes."

It wasn't the ferocity in Dean's tone that shocked me. No, it was the laugh Matthew barked that had my spine stiffening. Did he have a death wish?

Dean bent lower, putting his lips to my ear, and murmured, "Remember your heels. Stab any fucker who tries to harm you." I swallowed thickly, my eyes locking with Matthew's before he turned toward Dominico.

"I know," I rasped. "I will."

"That's my girl." He pressed his lips to my temple before pulling away and straightening to his full height. "Cory," he jerked his chin at me, "follow them."

"I said alone," Matthew barked and Dean's hand tightened on my waist.

"I don't give a shit what you said," he growled. Matthew swallowed, his Adam's apple bobbing as he narrowed his eyes. Then, with a huff, he turned toward Dominico, dismissing Dean.

"I'll be back in a moment."

"Take your time," Dominico said as he scanned my body, his eyes heated. Cory took a step forward, placing his large body in front of me.

"I suggest you look elsewhere."

I glanced over my shoulder at Dean, still feeling his chest against my back. He was glaring between Matthew and Dominico, his face hard. He grabbed my hand before I could move, and kissed me again, harder than before.

Matthew made another sound, then when I pulled away from Dean, Matthew opened his mouth to say something. But whatever he saw on Dean's face, or maybe mine, had him shutting his mouth again.

Cory walked with me toward Matthew. I glanced quickly up at Cory, finding him with a face like granite as he glared down at Matthew. Cory's anger and disgust were palpable, and they washed over me like armor. I stood a straighter and pushed my shoulders back, thankful my heels made me a few inches taller as I stepped up to Matthew.

"Let's get on with it," I said.

# Julia

Cory and I followed Matthew deeper into the crowd and further away from Dean. And with every step away from him, my stomach twisted with more and more unease. Finally, we stopped by an arch that led into a long hallway.

"I'd like to speak to my wife alone," Matthew said. Cory snorted.

"Don't give a fuck."

"Julia, please," Matthew said tiredly. Reluctantly, I turned toward Cory and patted his arm.

"I'll stay in your line of sight," I said, pointing through the archway. "We'll be right there." His jaw tensed as he stared down at me, then at the area I'd suggested.

"I don't know," he said and glanced over his shoulder. "Don't think Dean will like that."

"The quicker we get this over with, the better," I said quietly. "Let me just speak to him alone. He's not going to hurt me." Cory took a deep breath, and his full lips tightened into a thin line. He glared down at Matthew, who only looked impassively back at him. Finally, Cory nodded.

"Fine. Stay where I can see you." I patted his arm again, then gestured for Matthew to lead the way.

"Care to explain what the fuck is going on?" Matthew snapped when we were in the hall. He whirled to face me, his arms folded tightly over his chest.

"Explain what?" I asked, trying to muster up as much braveness as I could. He let out a humorless laugh before letting his arms fall to his sides.

"Don't fuck with me, Jewels. Not tonight. Not after seeing another guy with his tongue down your throat." I blinked at him. I was at a complete loss for words, then his face softened, and he took a step closer to me. "Why are you doing this to us?"

That snapped me right the fuck out of whatever I'd been feeling.

"I wasn't the one to lie for five fucking years," I snapped, taking a step back. "I wasn't the one who said I wanted you dead. I'm done." I took another step away, ready to flee, when he grabbed my hand.

"You're choosing some asshole you've only known for a few weeks over me? Your husband?" he scoffed. "Let me guess, he told you some sob story, right? Told you we were the bad guys? Said he was innocent in it all?"

I gnawed on my bottom lip as he spoke, but I kept quiet. I wasn't going to indulge him with this conversation. This was about Matthew and me, not Dean. One side of Matthew's mouth lifted in a sarcastic grin.

"Did he tell you about all the men he's killed? Did he tell you about killing my dad? About killing Dominico's nephew after torturing him for information?"

I shook my head, not wanting to listen to him. I knew who Dean was, and I knew what he was capable of. He never tried to hide it from me, and he never tried to pretend to be something he wasn't.

"Micha killed your dad," I said coldly. "And rightfully so, too." His brows shot up, then he laughed.

"You think so?" he spat, then roughly let go of my hand, pushing it away from him like it was dirty. Rage filled my chest, and I stepped toward him, getting in his face.

"Fuck your dad," I snarled. "He killed my fucking cousin!" I shouted, throwing my arms out as I stepped away again. I couldn't stand being so close to him anymore. "Fuck you, too! You fucking knew, Matthew! How many times had I mentioned trying to find Drake? How many fucking times had I said I wanted to rekindle a relationship with the only family I thought I had left? And you let me hold on to the belief that he was alive. You fucking knew he was dead!"

"And?" Matthew drawled. "You really wanted to know him? That fucking scumbag?"

"Don't," I growled. "Do not talk about him." He laughed and shook his head.

"You're away from me for a few weeks, and you suddenly forget where your loyalties are supposed to lie. Dean's what you want? Really? You want to be a fucking Demon?" He shook his head like he couldn't believe it, like I was an idiot.

Dean's exactly who I wanted, who I needed. I hadn't realized it before, but I couldn't imagine my future without Dean. I couldn't imagine ever loving someone else.

The man in front of me wasn't the same man I'd married all those years ago. He didn't even look the same. He looked mean, with an ugly sneer on his once handsome face.

How had I ever let myself fall for him? And worse, how had I ever let myself get dulled and muted by him?

I took a deep breath, readying myself to tell him to go fuck himself. Opening my mouth, the words were about to fall out, then the room went black, and hands grabbed me from behind. I kicked my legs out and let out a scream that was cut short when something hard hit my stomach.

"Shut the fuck up," a man growled in my ear.

Screams and chaos erupted from the banquet hall as I was dragged further away from Dean.

"Julia!" Cory's voice rang out. I couldn't reply, not with the hand that was clamped over my mouth. "Where are you? Answer me!"

A metal door was pushed open, and the balmy night air greeted me, prickling my skin. I blinked, letting my eyes adjust to my surroundings. Matthew stormed past me and slid into the backseat of a black town car while I was hauled to the back. The trunk popped open, and the man holding me lifted it.

"Ready for a ride?" he asked, his hot breath skittering along my neck. I sank my teeth into his meaty hand, and he let out a startled shout before bringing his other hand down on the back of my head. Tears welled in my eyes at the impact, and I let go. "Fuckin' bitch."

Even though I was flailing and purposefully making it hard to lift me, he still did so easily. He dropped me unceremoniously into the trunk of the car. The last thing I saw was his ugly, sneering face peering down at me before he slammed the lid shut.

# Dean

The room went black, and screams pierced the air. I looked frantically around, then a hand landed on my arm, and I shot my fist out on instinct. The person made a grunting sound, but their hand tightened.

"It's me," Micha croaked. "Fuckin' hell." I let out a breath, then grabbed my phone and turned the flashlight on as I began pushing my way through the crowd of people. I needed to get to Julia. Micha followed behind me, shouting things in the earpiece at the guys.

As people rushed past me, I shoved them out of my way, frantically searching the sea of faces for the one I needed. But when my eyes met Cory's dark ones, my stomach sank.

"Where is she?" I shouted. He shook his head, his face filled with regret and rage. I looked around in the pitch dark, my flashlight still pointed toward Cory, frantic to find her. "Julia!" I reached out again, and people ran into my arms as they scurried by. She had to be fucking close. She couldn't have gotten that far away from me. She was right fucking there.

"Boss," Cory said when he reached me, and I took a deep breath. "She's gone."

"What the fuck do you mean she's gone?" I yelled. A few more women screamed, but I ignored them. The doors at the top of the stairs were open, and the lights from outside poured in. "Cory!" I grabbed his shirt and dragged him toward me. "Where the fuck is she?"

"I followed them out the back and saw her get put into the back of a car," he said in a low voice.

"And you're still here. Why?" I shoved someone out of my way when they ran into my chest. "Why the fuck are you talking to me, Cory? Go fucking find her!"

"I don't know which car she was in," he said, and I paused.

"What the fuck do you mean you don't know which car she was in?" I repeated as calmly as I could. "You either saw what car she was loaded into, or you didn't."

"There were four cars, and she was put into one of the two in the middle. I didn't see which, and they all went in different directions." He at least had the sense to sound worried.

"Fuck, Cory!"

I stormed through the building, not caring who I was shoving out of my way or where they were ending up. I needed to find my guys and get the fuck out of here.

I needed to find Julia.

The warm night air hit me when I got outside, and my lungs seized. It was too thick, and I couldn't breathe. I ripped the top buttons of my shirt open, letting them fall to the ground. I began pacing as my guys surrounded me. Running my fingers through my hair, I paused in front of the two men I wanted to talk to.

"Is the tracker still on?" I asked, looking at Micha. He nodded, then shoved his phone in my hand. Sure enough, she was still online and headed toward a property we knew Costa owned. We could get there before they were able to do any real damage to her.

*Hopefully.*

"Round up the Demons," I said. "We need them all."

"We're not prepared to go to war tonight," Cory said slowly, and I shifted my eyes to him.

"Then give me the keys, and I'll go get her myself." I stepped forward, but he held his ground like I knew he would. As much shit as I gave him, Cory was a hard motherfucker. Four tours overseas, a Marine through and fucking through, as logical as they came. But right now, I didn't need fucking logic. I needed my fucking girl.

He'd never once thought with anything other than his brain. He never let his emotions lead him, and right now, my emotions were leading me. I was going to kill everyone in Costa's Family. I was going to fucking ruin them. I was going to save my girl and bring her home tonight, and if Cory wanted to be the one to stand in my way, if he wanted to try to talk me out of going tonight, he'd find himself dead, too.

"No, sir," he said, straightening slightly. "She's a Demon. We'll get her back." I stared at him a moment longer, studying him, then looked around at the guys. They waited for my orders, orders I didn't know how to give. Orders that might send these men to their fucking deaths.

I wouldn't mind giving my life up for her. I didn't have to think about it—but I had to think about their lives. They had families and people counting on them. If I died, Micha would take over, and the world would keep spinning. I'd have no one to mourn me. No one would care. But these men had people who would care.

I'm a selfish bastard, though, and I needed her back.

"Everyone armed?" I asked, looking around. Everyone's expression was bloodthirsty. They might've not known Julia, might've not given her a second glance, but they knew what she meant to me, and that was enough. Micha nodded for them, then Cory. I gave my men a final look over, and they nodded their final agreement.

There was no turning back now.

# Julia

"Get your hands off me, you fucking asshole!" I shouted as I flailed my body around. My dress was ripped, my hair was a matted, tangled mess, and I was sure my makeup was streaked all over my face. But a fight isn't what they'd expected, and it was exactly what I was giving them.

A man grabbed my shoulder, and I turned my head, then sunk my teeth into his hand, not letting go even when he roughly jerked his hand away, making my jaw pop painfully. I stayed latched onto him, biting down harder until his warm, metallic blood pooled in my mouth.

If I was going down, I was injuring as many of these fuckers as possible.

They say you never know how you'll react in a life-or-death situation. Will you freeze, fight, or run? Apparently, I scream obscenities at the men with guns aimed at me. Not the smartest tactic, I'll admit. But I'm not making it, whatever *it* is, easy for them.

I spat a mouthful of blood onto the concrete floor before laughing. The emotions coursing through me were ones I didn't recognize. Laughing was the only thing keeping me from crying, and these men wouldn't get my tears. I'd never been so close to death that my body knew my time was limited. And even though it was an idiotic move, I spat on the man I'd just bitten next.

"You fucking bitch," he snarled, roughly wiping my bloody spit from his face. "Tie her up. I'm fucking tired of her."

"What? Too much of a pussy to deal with me untied?" I mocked, grinning at him. Two men grabbed my arms, and I let them drag me backward, but my eyes stayed locked with the man who'd dragged me from the gala and shoved me into the trunk.

When we got to this fucking place, a warehouse, by the looks of it, I was untied and told to walk. Which I did not do. So, I was dragged inside, kicking and fucking screaming.

If Dean found me too late, I wanted him to know I put up a fight. I wanted him to be proud of me. I wanted him to see that I was a Demon—and Demons fucking fight.

I was shoved onto a table, my hands tied above my head and my ankles tied together at the bottom. It was better than apart, I guess. But I needed to get to my heel, to that blade, then I could start stabbing.

"Fucking pussy!" I shouted again. "Can't get any, so you have to tie me up? I doubt you can even get your shriveled dick up." I turned my head to glare at the man I'd bitten. His hand was wrapped in a towel, stained with his blood. He gave me a cold smile, and I gave him one back.

"*Amor*, please stop provoking my men," Dominico's voice was mocking, as it always was, as he walked out onto the floor, his shoes clicking against the concrete. "I can't be responsible for what they'll do to you."

"Untie me," I demanded, and he laughed.

"Oh, you're not the one calling the shots here," he said.

"Where's my husband? Matthew!"

"I'm your husband now?" Matthew drawled as he moved closer. He was still in his tux. They both were, and they looked fucking stupid.

"Unfortunately," I muttered. "Untie me." I jerked on the bindings, the ropes rubbing against my skin.

"Not a chance."

I glared up at him, but he only stared smugly back. Any trace of the man I once knew and loved was gone. And I didn't fucking miss him. He didn't come for me when I was taken, but I knew Dean was on his way. I trusted him to come for me. I loved him.

*I loved him.*

"I hope you're not waiting on your Demon," Matthew said. "He's not coming." I stared passively up at him, and he cracked a small smile. "He was seen heading back to his house. That's in the opposite direction of where we are."

"You're lying," I said, and he shrugged.

"Believe me or don't," he said. "Don't you think if he would've wanted to grab you at the gala, he would've? Don't you think one of the many guards he had there would've saved you? Cory could've easily gotten to you." I looked away from him. Dominico was standing behind Matthew, his hands clasped behind his back and that cold, shark-like grin on his face. "Isn't it possible this was his way of giving you back to us?"

"He wouldn't do that," I said, tears stinging my eyes. I squeezed them shut. Dean was coming. I knew he was.

"Are you sure? You're not the first woman he's left behind, you know. You're not the first he's given to us—"

"Shut up."

"You thought you were special to him?" Matthew laughed coldly. "Oh, Jewels. I thought you were smarter than that. What? Did he buy you something pretty? Or tell you about his scars? And you thought that meant anything?

"Let me tell you something, sweetheart. He does that with all of them. He tells them all the same sob story and buys them luxurious things. Hell, he probably fucks them however they want, too. But you're just another whore on a long list. You're nothing to him."

I stayed silent, not trusting myself to speak. Matthew was lying.

He had to be. But Dean told me that he'd slept with over a hundred women. Someone didn't get a list like that without becoming a master manipulator. Was I just a pawn? Had I been right from the very beginning? Had he been using me as a way to get back at Matthew?

I shook myself. No. Dean cared for me. Even if he didn't love me, he still cared about me, right? That was obvious with the way he touched me and by the way he kissed me and looked at me. He couldn't fake that. Could he?

And Micha wouldn't let him do that to me, would he? Maybe he blamed me for Drake's death. Maybe he thought I was lying. Maybe he thought I knew more about it than I'd told him. But I didn't. If I would've known about it, I wouldn't have stayed with Matthew. I couldn't have stayed with someone responsible for my cousin's death, by his hand or not.

Was Micha even Drake's son? Was Drake still alive?

"Have you met his mother?" Matthew asked, and my eyes flew open.

"She's dead." I glared up at his grinning, triumphant face.

"That's what he told you?" he laughed and shook his head. "You never were one to look further into things. You took everything anyone said at face value. You're naive, Jewels. His mother is not dead. She's very much alive."

I was shaking my head as he spoke. That was a lie. Dean wouldn't have lied to me about that. Why would he? There was no reason for it. It wasn't like I would've forced him into letting me meet her. I would've let him do that in his own time.

But if he had been lying about everything...

"No," I said again. "He—he loves me."

"Does he?" Matthew said, folding his hands in front of him. "Has he told you he loves you?" I squeezed my eyes shut, and he laughed again. "I'll take that as a no, then. God, you must feel like a real fucking idiot right now. You could've come back to me, and I would've taken care of you, you know that. But no, you wanted him. The Demon King."

My throat was too tight to swallow or speak, let alone breathe. I wanted to scream at him that he was lying, that I knew Dean, and Dean wasn't like that. Dean wouldn't betray me. He was coming for me. Even if he'd gone to his house first, it was to regroup. I told myself that he was coming and I had to believe it. Otherwise, what was the point of fighting?

If I fought and won and got out of here? What then? Where would I go? Who would I go to? Who would I have left? What life would I have left?

I'd have nothing, and I'd have no one.

So even if it was a false hope, I had to believe that Dean was coming. And even if everything he'd done and said to me had been a lie, I had to believe it wasn't because if I let myself spiral, I was as good as dead.

# Julia

I was left alone some time ago. I don't know why, but surprisingly, I found my eyelids growing heavy. Maybe it was the evening's intense up and down emotions and everything that had happened in the last few weeks, and I just wanted to sleep and forget everything.

Maybe I wanted to pretend this was all a dream and wake up beside Dean.

Familiar footsteps echoed around me, and I braced myself for Matthew. He put doubts in my head, then left me to brew, like he always had. He was good at making me feel stupid and second guess myself. But the more I thought about it, the more I refused to believe it.

And even if Dean hadn't gotten there yet, he would. He'd be here. I couldn't imagine that everything I felt for him was one-sided. He couldn't fake that. Matthew wanted to get in my head, to make me doubt Dean, but I wasn't going to let him do that. I wasn't going to let him win.

Without a word, Matthew went to the head of the table and easily sawed through the ropes binding me. When my hands were free, I brought them down too fast, crying out at the pain. I rolled my shoulders a few times, then rubbed at my wrists as he sawed through the ropes on my ankles.

"What's going on?" I asked when he pulled me up. He didn't answer me. He just helped me stand, then he let go and began walking. I looked around the dark room.

We were on an open warehouse floor. It was empty, except for a few crates in the corner and some pallets along another wall. Otherwise, it was empty. There was a giant garage door on one end of the room, but Matthew led me in the opposite direction.

Sighing, he grabbed me and pushed me in front of him when we got to the stairs. "All the way to the top," he said, putting his hands on my hips.

"Matthew, please—"

"Go." He shoved me, and I stumbled up a step, bracing my fall with my hands. Pain shot through my wrist, but I ignored it as I straightened. Glaring at him over my shoulder, I slowly made my way up the stairs.

I needed to figure out how to take the heel off my shoe. But if I did that, I'd need to use it. And could I use it on Matthew? I didn't think he'd have a problem using a weapon on me, but I couldn't use it on him. I'd have a hard time using it on anyone. But my husband? I couldn't.

"This way," he said as he pushed past me. We were on a metal grate walkway with thin railings on the sides. It was narrow and swung slightly with each of Matthew's stomps. My stomach dropped when I looked down. If I fell, it was a long drop to the cement floor.

I followed Matthew, and something about the familiar set of his shoulders, his familiar gait, his scent—it sent me back to that complacent, submissive place I'd been in for the last five years.

If I wanted to survive, I needed to behave like the quiet housewife he'd molded me to be. And even if I found out that everything had been a lie and that Dean truly was a monster, at least I'd be free.

Free to do what I wanted, to go where I pleased, to live the life I'd always dreamed of.

So, I let that blank mask slide over my face as I walked into the room behind Matthew. He stepped aside and gestured to a chair across from Dominico. Carefully, I slid into it and straightened my dress as much as I could. I crossed my legs, bringing my heel up close enough to grab in an instant.

"I'm sorry about your dress, *amor*," Dominico said, sounding unapologetic. The glint in his eye was a wicked one, but I didn't shift under his gaze. I forced myself to stay still.

The things I'd seen and done in the last few weeks had ripped the blindfold off my comfortable life. I wasn't as naïve as I once was. Dominico didn't scare me like he had. I'd felt true terror when Justin was on top of me, and I'd seen true rage when Dean killed him. I'd lived in a house with armed men, and they didn't try to hide it.

Dominico was a shark, but a shark without teeth. He might be scary, but there was always someone bigger and more dangerous out there. And I knew exactly who was–Dean.

I smiled coldly as I smoothed my hand over the torn silk fabric. "It's fine." Lifting my eyes, I scanned the room, taking in the few men I recognized from the cabin and Matthew standing around us, then looked back to Dominico. "What can I do for you?"

"That's the question, isn't it?" He leaned back in the metal chair, looking unbothered. "What *can* you do for me?" I mimicked his posture, leaning back, letting the cold metal dig into my skin.

I once read that if you're trying to assert your dominance in a conversation, to force the other person to speak first. You just watch them silently and wait. Eventually, they'll break.

Dominico laughed under his breath, then shifted his eyes to Matthew. They had a silent conversation with their eyes, one I couldn't understand. When the attention was back on me, the first pang of unease settled inside me.

"I'm sure you learned a lot during your time with The Demons," Dominico said conversationally. I didn't agree or disagree. "Tell me."

It wasn't a request but an order. A harsh demand from a man not used to being told no.

"I learned that I prefer acrylics to oil paints," I said, and he blinked at me. My heart was in my throat, but I wasn't giving anything away. Even if I had information, I wouldn't give it to them. Dominico's eyes narrowed as he leaned forward and rested his forearms on the small metal table.

"Has your wife always had a mouth on her?" he asked Matthew, but his eyes stayed on me. "I find it very unattractive."

"Good." I couldn't stop the word before it tumbled from my lips. But it was true. I didn't want him to find anything about me attractive.

"I thought she grew out of it," Matthew sighed. "Apparently not."

"How you put up with it for so long is beyond me," Dominico said, shaking his head. "I'm not going to play this game with you, Julia."

"And what game is that, Dominico?" I asked sweetly. He bared his teeth for a moment, then he relaxed into his unphased role again.

"I have no problem letting my men take turns beating you until you decide to cooperate," he said casually. "It's your choice how far we take this." I clenched my jaw as I glared at him. He could send in all his men. I wouldn't say a word.

One of the men took a step forward, flexing his hand. I lifted my eyes to him, then to Matthew, before finally looking back at Dominico. The threat was clear.

"What do I know?" I looked at Matthew and smiled. "I was nothing but his whore."

# Dean

There was a static charge in the air as Micha, Cory, and I moved toward the doors in a crouch. The guys with us at the gala had the building surrounded and were to enter at my count. The rest of my guys would kill off anyone who tried to leave.

My instructions were clear: save Julia and kill everyone.

On the drive over, I covered every fucking inch of myself with weapons. The building was quiet, but I knew that didn't mean shit. This was a trap, they were expecting me to come for her, and I knew it. They probably had cameras on my guys and me. They might've had the advantage of knowing my location, but they weren't tight with rage like I was.

They stole from me.

They took what was *mine*.

They stole her, and I would blow the fucking place up, killing everyone inside. I was going to wipe The Costa Family off the map. This was my city now, and I was going to rule it with my Queen.

They'd be nothing more than a faint memory, a scary story

mobsters told each other about The Demons and what would happen if we were crossed.

My finger rested against the side of my AR-15 pistol and slipped onto the trigger as Micha and Cory stood beside the double doors, then each grabbed a handle. Our eyes met, then I gave a brief nod, and they yanked the doors open.

A bullet landed between the guard's eyes before he realized we were there. Tonight, I wasn't hesitating. Tonight, I wasn't worried about sparing lives or taking prisoners. Tonight, I was killing everyone.

The rest of the doors flew open, and our guys rushed inside, gunfire echoing off the walls. Micha and Cory stood behind me, back-to-back, with their guns raised. I calmly looked around, ready to spill more blood. Most of the men were running away from us, toward the rest of our guys.

"We need to find her," I said. One of them grunted their agreement, and we began to move forward. We'd done this a million times, moved as one deadly machine. Micha dropped a guy as he rounded the corner, and I shot the one who followed.

Cory took the lead as we entered a narrow hallway. Three directions. One led out onto the main floor where we could hear most of the fighting, one led to a set of metal stairs, and the last was where we'd just entered.

"I'll head that way," Cory said, tilting his head toward the main floor. Micha and I glanced at each other before I gave him a stiff nod.

"I'll head upstairs," I said, then looked at Micha with raised brows. He jerked his chin at us.

"I'll be here. Stay alive. Both of you."

We didn't waste any more time as we separated. Typically, we'd never do this. It wasn't good to leave each other unprotected, but we needed to find Julia. The longer she was alone, the more likely it was that she would be hurt. And if something happened to her, I'd never forgive myself. If she died tonight, I'd fucking kill myself. It would be

my fault, and I couldn't live with that. I couldn't live knowing I was
the reason why my girl had been fucking killed.

"Get the fuck off me!" Her voice sliced through me like razor
blades. I moved faster, not caring about how much noise I was
making on the metal walkway. My palms were sweaty against the
gun, and I regripped, then blinked rapidly as I approached the room
at the end. I paused in the doorway, taking in the scene before me.

One man was lying on the floor with her blade sticking out of his
neck. Dominico stood in the corner while Matthew had his arm
pinned around her throat, her back to his chest. She was struggling in
his hold, and I saw fucking red.

"She said to get off her," I said as I stepped into the room. They
froze, and even Dominico looked stunned. "Hey, darling. You miss
me?" Her eyes were wide as she stared at me, her chin wobbling.

"You came," she breathed, sounding shocked. I wanted to look at
her again, but I couldn't risk taking my eyes off Blackwell. If I did,
he'd do something irreversible.

"Course I did," I said. "Let her go." I took another step forward,
and the sound of a gun cocking stopped me. Dominico's pistol was
pointed at me from where he stood in the corner. "One shot is all it'll
take, Costa. Drop your fucking gun."

The fucker laughed.

My eyes stayed locked with Blackwell's, but I could still see Costa
moving closer. I needed to deescalate this before it was a fucking
blood bath. Once Julia was safely behind me, then I'd kill them. I'd
fucking obliterate them.

Matthew squeezed Julia's throat a little tighter, and she made a
choking sound. She clawed at his hand, her face turning a deep red. I
took another step closer and paused when my foot hit the body on the
floor.

"What do you want?" I asked. "You want my territory? It's yours.
You want me to disband The Demons? Done. Give her to me."
Matthew's lips twitched. He knew he had the upper hand. We all
knew it. There was no sense in hiding it. I'd give up everything for

her, and he knew that. "You want to kill someone tonight? Kill me. Let her go."

She tried to say something, but no sound came out. Her throat was being crushed, and it was fucking killing me. It felt like my throat was being crushed with hers. I didn't know how much longer she had. Her foot reared back and hit Matthew's shin, but he barely flinched.

"I'll kill you," Matthew said, grinning, "right after I kill her." Dominico stood beside him, silent for once. His gun was aimed at me, and it was putting me on edge. From what I could tell, Matthew didn't have a weapon on her. It was a massive risk I was about to take, but I couldn't take the chance of Dominico shooting her or me.

So, I pointed my gun at Dominico's head and pulled the trigger.

# Julia

I was going to die.

My husband was going to kill me.

He was going to squeeze my throat until he crushed it, and then I was going to die in front of Dean. He came for me like I knew he would. All the doubts Matthew had been trying to put in my head left me when my eyes met Dean's icy ones.

I knew he'd come for me.

Dominico kept his promise and sent the first guy after me when I wouldn't give them the information they wanted. I broke my heel off, twisting it and revealing my blade. It shocked everyone in the room, including me, that I'd been so quick. Matthew was the one who'd broken the silence, telling them I didn't know how to use it.

The man stepped forward and grabbed me. When he hauled me against him, I reached up and jammed the blade through his neck where Dean had told me to.

As soon as it sunk into his flesh, he let go and stumbled back a step before putting his hand to the wound, then falling to the floor.

Matthew and Dominico were in shock, and I took the opportunity to grab the blade from my other heel. They weren't going to make the same mistake twice, though. Matthew pounced on me before I'd been able to break it off, and he pressed his forearm across my throat, crushing it.

"What do you want?" Dean asked. "You want my territory? It's yours. You want me to disband The Demons? Done. Give her to me." Matthew's hold on me tightened, and I clawed at his wrist until I felt his skin open under my nails. "You want to kill someone tonight? Kill me. Let her go."

My blood turned to ice.

*No.*

He couldn't die. I wouldn't let him die for me. He needed to live. I needed him to live.

"I love you," I tried to tell him, but my words were nothing but a breath. I needed Dean to know before I died. I needed to tell him. Dean's face was furious as he slid his eyes from Matthew to Dominico, then back.

Frustrated, I pulled my bare foot forward, then reared it back, hitting Matthew in the shin. I was hoping it was hard enough for him to loosen his grip, but the opposite happened. He squeezed me tighter, shaking me in warning.

"I'll kill you," Matthew said, "right after I kill her."

My vision started to darken around the edges, and the ringing in my ears almost drowned out the gunshot. It jolted me, making me alert again. It wasn't Matthew or Dean who'd been shot, though.

Dominico's blood poured out of his head and pooled around our feet. I wanted to scream—images of Justin's bloody body flashed through my mind, the way he'd touched me, the way he'd held me down.

Terror rose in my chest, the same terror I'd felt that day, and the only thing I knew was that I needed Dean. He was my protector, the one who would save me. He saved me from Justin, and he'd save me now.

I jerked my head back, hitting Matthew's face, and felt something crunch. He roughly let me go, throwing me forward as he cursed. I stumbled and tripped over the guy I'd stabbed in the neck and fell to my hands and knees. I took a deep, ragged breath, then felt hands on my shoulders, yanking me to my feet.

"Stay behind me," Dean ordered. I wasn't in a place to argue, so I stood behind him as I tried to catch my breath. My hands shook as I bunched Dean's untucked dress shirt in my fists, needing him to ground me. I tugged on him, silently telling him to leave. We needed to go before anyone else got hurt.

"I told you if you touched her, you were dead," Dean said in a low, deadly voice.

"Yeah?" Matthew taunted. I glanced at him, finding his face bloody and nose broken, and a surge of satisfaction flooded me. "You're gonna kill me over some bitch?" Matthew took a small step forward, shaking his head as he prodded at his nose. "You know, you could've been better than your father. You could've had this city-- probably the whole fucking East coast under your thumb."

"Wasn't interested in that," Dean said gruffly.

"Yeah, that's what makes you a fucking idiot," Matthew laughed, then grunted as his nose stretched. "We can work together now that he's out of the way." He jerked his chin toward his boss' still-warm dead body. Dean let out a frustrated sound.

"I'm not interested in working with you," he said.

"No, you're more interested in fucking my wife," Matthew said, his eyes sliding to me. There was nothing behind them, no warmth or hint of love. How had I been so blind?

"I'm not your wife," I snapped, and he grinned.

"No? And what are you going to do when he's gone?" he asked, jerking his chin at Dean. "Will you still pretend to not be my wife then?"

"He's not going anywhere," I said, tightening my fists in Dean's shirt.

I heard the gun before I saw it.

Matthew lifted it, cocking it as he did so, and didn't hesitate to pull the trigger. Everything happened in slow motion. It hit the center of Dean's chest and sent him stumbling back a step.

The scream that ripped from my throat was one I'd never made before. It was one I'd never heard before. And it was one I never wanted to make again.

"Julia—" Dean breathed my name, and tears pooled in my eyes. I stumbled around him and wrapped my arms around his waist, holding onto him. I tried to push him back, but he was too big. I needed to get him away. I pressed my chest against him, my ear resting over his heart. The steady thumping of it was the only thing bringing me comfort—*he was alive.*

Dean dropped the big gun he'd been carrying, then grabbed a pistol from his pants. His other arm wrapped around my waist as he lifted his weapon, but Matthew was quicker.

A searing hot pain shot through my shoulder, then Dean grunted out a breath. The pain coursed down my arm and through my body, and for a moment, I didn't realize what it was. But then I saw my blood stain the front of Dean's white shirt.

"Motherfucker!" Dean roared.

He easily lifted me and shifted, keeping his body between us. I pressed a shaky hand to my opposite shoulder, feeling my stomach lurch when my hand came back crimson.

"Dean," I croaked, but my voice sounded far away. "Blood."

Another gunshot, the final one of the night, echoed around us as I fell to the floor.

# Micha

atthew's gun was raised but wasn't pointed at anyone. He was so consumed watching Dean make sure Julia wasn't fucking dead that he hadn't noticed I'd stepped in the doorway. His face looked pained. Truly pained. And if I was a better man, I might've felt sorry for him.

But I wasn't a good man. I'd done bad things, seen bad things, and would continue to do bad things. And I'd do them unapologetically. I'd ask for forgiveness from God, but only from Him. If anyone had a problem, they could take it up with the other end of my fuckin' gun.

I don't know what Jay ever saw in him. Before I knew her, I'd always wondered what kind of person would marry a psychopath like Blackwell. But when I saw her for the first time, so fuckin' scared but wanting to be brave in front of us...I knew *that* was the type of person who'd marry him.

Someone far braver than the rest of us.

I'll admit I was pissed when I learned she was Blackwell's wife, after all his father was responsible for. I wanted to see every Blackwell burn, and she was one. But she was also a Chamberlain. She was my family. My only fucking family left.

And it made me even angrier at her for marrying into the family responsible for taking my father from me. I was mad at her for marrying my boogeyman. For marrying my fuckin' monster. But it wasn't her fault. She didn't know.

And when I saw Dean start to fall for her, I knew it was only a matter of time before she did, too. I told him as much, too. The night before he killed Justin I'd told him as much. He hadn't wanted to believe it, but it was plain to see. Even Cory, the fuckin' emotionally stunted asshole, could see Dean's infatuation with her.

"YOU LOOK AT HER LIKE SHE HUNG THE MOON," I LAUGHED. DEAN *shot me a look over the rim of his glass before throwing his whiskey back.*

*"Don't," he growled. "She's married. To Blackwell, no less." I shrugged, knowing their marriage was obviously fucked if he was willing to let us keep her.*

*"She looks at you the same way." I smiled, remembering how her eyes had lit when he walked into the room. Only for a moment, but I saw that spark. She'd tried to hide it, but I saw the rosy flush that bloomed on her cheeks, how her chest heaved just a little too much when his knee brushed against hers.*

*Dean didn't want to believe it. He never thought women were attracted to him for him, only for his power and money. And a girl like Julia, he'd never let himself believe he could land a girl like her.*

*"You like her."*

*"Yeah," he admitted with a small sigh. "I like her."*

"YOU'RE NOT FUCKING BLEEDING OUT," DEAN BARKED, HIS VOICE frantic. "I love you, Julia, and you're not dying on me. You're not doing this, darling."

Matthew shuffled a step forward, peering over Dean's shoulder. Julia was lying on the ground, surrounded by her own blood. Dean was kneeling beside her, his hands pressing firmly against the bullet wound.

Dean brushed her hair from her face with a bloody hand, streaking her cheek with her own blood. I still hadn't been noticed, not when both the men in this room were focused on the woman connecting them.

I hoped Julia would forgive me for it, for killing her husband. But I needed to save her and Dean, and, more importantly, I needed to avenge my parents. I wasn't good at many things, but killing was something I'd been born for.

And taking Blackwell's life was something that I'd been dreaming of.

Dean shushed her when she tried to say something, her hand limply falling back to her side. "It's alright, darling. Hush. I'm here." Her head lolled to the side, her eyes rolling back.

He shook her slightly, trying to wake her up. When she didn't make a sound, he banged his fist against his chest, a pained sound ripping from his throat.

"I'm going to fucking kill you, Blackwell!" Dean roared, his bloody hands slipping against her skin. "If she dies, I'm killing you, then myself. You fucking hear me?!"

*BANG!*

I didn't hesitate as I pulled the trigger. I watched Matthew's face go from worry to anger, to confusion, to pain in seconds. His eyes shifted to mine, then widened. He knew me, and he knew the promise I'd made him.

It was his father's order to kill my parents, but Matthew's bullet had killed them. The first time I saw him after that, I vowed to kill them both.

"Fuck!" Dean shouted as he looked over his shoulder, reaching for his gun. When he saw it was me, he relaxed and turned his attention back toward Julia again.

"Sorry for takin' your kill," I said as I stepped over a guy with Julia's knife in his neck. Matthew fell to his knees, his hands clutching the center of his chest. His blood was spilling between his fingers, staining his shirt. His breathing was labored as I walked to him, the death rattle in his chest music to my fuckin' ears.

"It's fine," Dean said. I glanced at him, finding him standing with Julia in his arms. "Knew we should've put a fucking vest on her, too. Fucker shot me right in the center of my chest. Stopped the bullet, but it still hurt like shit. Come on, finish him and let's go."

"I should let you suffer," I said, lifting my gun. "But I don't have time to stand here and watch you die, much as I'd like to." The bullet landed between Matthew's eyes, and he fell backward, landing on top of Dominico. I didn't know who'd killed him. I'd get the full story later. I was just fucking glad these two fuckers were dead.

I smiled to myself.

The vengeance I'd carried with me for years, the need to kill my parents' killer, was lifted. But more than that, I felt the freedom that came with that.

And not just my own freedom. Julia's, too.

She was free.

# Dean

"You need to go faster!" I shouted.

Julia's blood covered my hands, sticky and warm. It made me feel sick. Her skin was a deadly shade of white, and her eyes were rolled back in her head. But she still had a pulse, and I held onto that with all my fucking hope.

"Cory! Drive faster!"

Cory had heard the gunshots and came running to find us, unsure if we'd been the ones who were shot. But when he saw me carrying Julia, he didn't ask questions. He just turned and sprinted for the doors and brought the car to us.

I'd barely shut the door when he'd peeled from the lot, leaving the rest of my guys behind to clean up the bodies. I told them to just burn it to the ground. I was done. I didn't give a shit what happened anymore. All I cared about was making sure the woman in my arms survived.

"Julia, come on." I smoothed my hand over her hair. It was beautifully curled hours ago, her makeup perfectly done...and now, she was knocking on Death's door. "You need to live, darling."

Her eyes found mine for the first time since she'd lost consciousness, but they were glazed and unfocused. The streetlights illuminated her ghostly face, making a choked sob bubble up my throat. Her lips parted, but no sound came out.

Tears dripped down my cheeks, landing on her ruined, pretty dress. The gold demon pendant lay in the hollow of her throat, glinting mockingly in the passing lights.

Why was I stupid enough to think someone I loved would live? Everyone I'd ever loved was dead. My mother, my brother, my father, my best friend. It was a fucking miracle Micha and Cory were still alive.

She opened her mouth again, this time a small breath leaving her. Another sob escaped me, and I hunched over her, pressing my forehead to her chest.

"Please," I cried. "Don't do this." I didn't know who I was begging to, but I'd continue to plead until I couldn't anymore. Her hand lifted, barely raising, her red painted fingernails blending seamlessly with the blood coating her hands.

"I lov—" her voice was a croaked whisper.

"No." I shook my head as I lifted it, looking down at her. "You're not telling me you love me like this. You're going to tell me tomorrow when you wake up and are still alive." She stared at me, her eyes seeing through me.

"I love you, Dean."

More tears flowed freely from my eyes as hers closed. Gathering her in my arms, I clutched her to my chest. "Cory!" I screamed. "Hurry the fuck up!"

"Here," he said gruffly.

I hadn't realized I'd been rocking us, not until the car lurched to a stop and I was still moving.

Cory and Micha flew from their seats and yanked the doors open.

"Give her to me," Micha said, holding his arms out. I looked down at Julia, then to him, and held her tighter.

"No," I said, shaking my head. "I can't. She's mine. No."

"You need to pull yourself together," Cory snapped. "She's going to die if you don't pull your head out of your fucking ass. Get her inside."

I didn't know what the fuck was wrong with me, why I was feeling so out of control. Lost. I stared at Cory, blinking rapidly. I squeezed her tighter. I couldn't let her go.

"Boss, I'm about to knock you the fuck out so we can take her—"

"Don't fucking touch her," I growled, twisting our bodies away from him.

"Then get her the fuck inside!"

His tone had me moving. With her still clutched to my chest, I slid from the car and sprinted after Micha. He ran into the ER lobby first, and the few people in chairs looked up as we rushed in.

"We need help! She's been shot!" he shouted.

"Bring her back here!" A nurse shouted. I didn't hesitate as I pushed past Micha and ran after her. She led me to a curtained-off area and motioned for me to lay Julia down. "Who are you?"

"Dean—"

"Boyfriend? Brother?"

"Husband."

Nurses hurried around Julia as we stared at each other. I silently dared her to call me on the lie we both knew it was. But she didn't. Instead, she gave me a slight nod and turned toward the bed.

"You need to leave. We'll get you when she's stable."

"I'm not leaving her."

"You'll leave, or I'll have security throw you out," she snapped, glaring at me. I stumbled back a step, my chest heaving with each angry breath. Then I dropped my eyes to Julia, and my anger disappeared. In its place was fear. A fear I'd never felt.

She was going to die. I could feel it. Death was lingering around us, around her, and I knew she wouldn't make it 'til morning. I couldn't leave her, but the more people that swarmed around her, the more I was crowded out.

"I'm not leaving you, darling," I called as I stepped back, the movement crushing me. I needed her to be alright. I needed her to live. And that's why I took another step back, trusting the nurses and doctors to save her. If they didn't...I had a bullet with my name on it. "I'll be right here when you wake up. I'm with you."

# Julia

An annoying beeping was the thing that woke me. I thought it was Dean's alarm, and I tried to lift my arm to shake him awake, but a searing pain shot through me.

"Don't move."

I cracked my eyes open and stared up at Dean, blinking a few times. Sunlight surrounded him like an angel. He smiled softly at me as he stroked my cheek with his knuckle.

"Hey, darling," he said, and I couldn't help but smile back. "I've been dying to see that smile." A chair was right next to my bed, and that's when I realized I was in a hospital room.

"Where am I?" I rasped, then cleared my dry throat.

"You're in a private suite at the hospital," he said. "You were shot." I looked around, blinking a few times to clear my vision. He was right —it was a hospital room. A very nice-looking hospital room, and one I'd never be able to afford.

Then the memories came rushing back, and I sat up, reaching for him with my good hand. I rested it on his chest, then looked up at him.

"You were shot, too," I said, my voice raspy. "I saw it."

"Bulletproof vest." He gave me a sad smile. "If I knew you were gonna try to shield me, I would've put it on you instead." He brushed my hair away from my face, his thick fingers warm against my skin. "How are you feeling, darling?"

"I'm okay," I said. Slowly, I laid back down but kept my hand wrapped around his. "How long was I asleep?"

"Only a few hours," he said, frowning. "It was a clean exit and didn't hit anything vital. You didn't lose as much blood as I thought. You were mostly in shock." I nodded a few times and looked around the room again.

"Micha?"

"In the waiting room with Cory," he said. "They haven't left."

I dropped my eyes to his clothes, finding them covered in blood. He looked exhausted. His hair was sticking up in random directions, and his under eyes were dark purple. The fine lines around his eyes were deeper, and his lips were pressed into a thin line.

"What do you remember?" he asked, sounding cautious. I lifted my eyes to his again, giving his hand a slight squeeze. I knew what he was asking. Did I remember telling him I loved him?

Even if I lost all other memories, that's one I'd never forget.

"I love you, Dean," I said quietly, repeating my words, and his throat bobbed before he dropped his head. He wiped at his face, pinching between his eyes.

"I thought I was gonna lose you," he croaked. "And when you said it, I thought you were saying goodbye." I nudged him with my knee, and when he looked at me, I gave him a small smile.

"You know it'll take more than getting shot to get rid of me," I said, and he shook his head, choking on a laugh. We smiled at each other, my heart full and warm. Then, I bit my lower lip. "Don't you have something to say to me?"

He laughed, then turned fully to face me. With my hand still in his, he brought it to his lips and gently kissed the back of it. His eyes were open and vulnerable in a way I hadn't seen before, and it made my breath catch.

"I love you, darling. More than I realized was ever possible."

The sincerity in his voice made the world stop. My throat got tight as tears welled in my eyes. I swatted at him with my good arm, laughing as I wiped the tears away.

"You weren't supposed to make me cry," I teased. But he wasn't laughing. He was staring at me with soft eyes—eyes that I was addicted to. Eyes that I was going to wake up next to forever. Eyes that were holding me captive and making my smile slowly fall.

"I don't know a lot, Julia. I'm not the smartest man. I'm not a good man, and I won't pretend to be. But I'm your man." His thumb stroked back and forth over the back of my hand, his eyes searching mine. I didn't know what he was looking for, but whatever it was, I'd give it to him. "And I know that I'll love you until my last breath, and even then, it'll take more than death to rip my soul from yours. You're stuck with me, darling. Forever." I grinned at him as the door opened and a nurse strolled in.

"Oh, you're awake," she said, stopping abruptly. "Great. I'll grab the doctor."

"When can I go home?" I asked before she could leave.

"Um," she glanced at Dean, then back to me, "I'm not sure, Mrs. Austen. You'll have to discuss that with the doctor." She left the room, and I slowly turned toward Dean, finding his face bright red.

"Want to explain that?"

"They wouldn't let me stay unless I was family," he said, shrugging.

"And you told them I was your wife?" I deadpanned.

"Well, I wasn't gonna tell them you were my sister." He laughed when I swatted at him again, harder.

"I'm not getting married again right after—" I paused, my stomach sinking. "Where's Matthew? What happened?" Dean's face shifted, and I knew. I knew before he said the next four words.

"He's dead. I'm sorry."

I closed my eyes, the weight of what he'd said heavy. I'd spent so long under Matthew's thumb, wanting desperately to get out and be my own person. And then, when I finally was free and fell for Dean, I thought that's all that would happen. That Matthew and I would move on with our lives and be with people we loved and loved us. I wanted him to be happy, and I wanted to be happy.

I never hated Matthew, even in the end. He was terrible, but he'd held my heart at one point. And that part he held he still owned, and I didn't think I'd ever get it back. Dean had to know that. But it was such a small part compared to what Dean held.

To know that Matthew was dead was...heartbreaking. It was hard to accept, and it was hard to know that I'd never see his smile or hear his laugh again. But there was a sick and fucked up part of me that felt relief. It was overpowered by the disgust and guilt that washed over me when I realized that I wasn't as sad as I should've been at the news of my husband's death.

I was now technically a widow. And I felt nothing. Did that make me a monster? To still love him and know that he'd always have a small piece of me but still not care that he was gone forever? I was relieved that I never had to deal with his bullshit again. I'd never have to hear him yell at me, put me down, or make me feel like an idiot again. He couldn't do that from the grave.

"You?" I asked as I opened my eyes. He shook his head, his eyes narrowed as he watched me. He was waiting for the blow-up, but it wouldn't come.

"Micha."

"Good," I said, nodding. Dean blinked a few times, then cleared his throat. "If anyone deserved to kill him, it was Micha." He nodded slowly, still watching me cautiously.

I wanted to feel more than I did, but I couldn't make myself. And now that the initial shock was wearing off, all that was left was relief. Even that guilt was starting to go away.

I didn't have any more room in my heart, or my head, or my soul for another man. Not when I had Dean. Not when he owned me entirely.

"You're okay?" he asked quietly, his eyes scanning my face. "It's okay if you're not. You don't have to be strong in front of me. You were married to him—"

"I'll be okay," I said. He clamped his mouth shut but looked like he wanted to say more. I smiled sadly at him, then shrugged. "I'll be fine."

# Julia

I'd been home for three weeks. It was still hard for me to think of this place as my home, but it was. I was still exploring the endless hallways and massive rooms. There were indoor and outdoor pools, a wet and dry sauna, and several private workout rooms. I'd found a library, and I nearly collapsed when Micha showed me the formal dining room. There was even a movie theater, a full basketball court, and even more buildings on the property than I'd first thought. It seemed everyone had a place to themselves. Everyone had a home.

We'd given Micha and Cory two of the dogs--Micha got Daisy, and Cory got Diego. We kept Devil, of course. I'd spent most of my time resting and cuddling Devil, then I started drawing again. Really drawing. And I couldn't wait to show Dean everything I'd been working on.

Dean spent most of his time either in his office, gym, or asleep. We hadn't spent a lot of time together, which upset me. He felt guilty for Matthew's death. Even though he hadn't been the one to kill him, he felt like he could've prevented it. It didn't matter how many times

I'd told him that I was okay, and I didn't blame him for his death. He still felt guilty.

He wasn't listening to me. He was assuming I felt one way and ignoring my words. He was shutting me out, and I wouldn't live this life again. So, when I woke up to an empty, cold bed, I'd decided that today was the day I would force him to listen to me.

I didn't bother knocking when I reached the office door. I just pushed it open and let it slam into the wall. Cory, Micha, and two other men were standing around Dean's desk, staring at the map like they had been a month ago.

They turned in unison when the door opened. I paused in the doorway, my eyes locking with Dean's. He slid his glasses off and clutched them in his hand.

"Everyone out." I kept my voice even as I stepped further into the room, out of their way. The men hesitated, looking between us. "Now." They scrambled to leave, not wanting to witness whatever was about to happen.

"Darling," Dean said cautiously, squaring his shoulders. I slammed the door behind Micha but didn't miss how he'd silently laughed. "What's wrong?"

"What's wrong is you're shutting me out, and that's something you're not going to do," I snapped as I turned toward him. "Sit." I jerked my chin at his chair, and he fell into it.

I hadn't expected him to obey me so easily, and I tried not to let it show on my face. Slowly, I approached him and rested my hands on the arms of the chair, gently pushing him back. The chair rolled until it rested against the bookcase behind him. His eyes were glittering as he stared up at me, waiting for my next move.

"Why have you been ignoring me?" I asked, bringing my face to his. His throat bobbed, and some of that light left his eyes.

"Julia—" He dropped his head forward, looking defeated.

"Dean," I said firmly. "Don't."

"He's dead."

"And?" I said, and his head shot up, his eyes wide.

"And? He was your husband."

"*Was*," I agreed, nodding.

"You're going to wake up one day and realize you hate me for killing him." I slid onto his lap, straddling him. I laced my fingers through his hair and yanked his head roughly back.

"I chose you," I said, lowering my face to his. "You didn't kill him. Micha did. But even if you had, I'd never hate you for it." He was growing hard under me, and I smirked knowingly at him. "Do I need to remind you who I belong to? Who belongs to me?"

His eyes darkened, and his hands slid onto my hips. He tried to push and pull me the way he wanted, but I kept still. I was in charge. He lifted his brow and relaxed his hands.

"And who do I belong to, darling?" he asked, his voice velvety. I ground my hips against him and pulled his hair harder. I ran my tongue down the taut skin of his neck, then bit down where his neck and shoulder met.

"Me," I said. "And your guilt over his death has no room in our relationship." His eyes searched mine, but when I rocked my hips against him again, he groaned and dropped his head the rest of the way back.

"You won't hate me?" he asked, his voice strangled.

"No, Dean, I won't hate you." I kissed along his neck as I slid my hand down his body to his jeans. I popped the button open and slowly lowered the zipper. "Are you done running from me?" He nodded as I slipped my hand under the waistband of his boxers.

"I'll agree to anything when your hand is wrapped around my dick," he said breathlessly. I laughed against his skin, shaking my head as I stroked him.

"I need to trust that you're not going to shut me out every time we come to an obstacle," I said as I released his dick. I leaned back and met his eye. "I need to know you're here."

"I'm here," he said immediately. "I'm always here." He cupped the side of my face, and I leaned into his touch, sighing. Tucking my hair behind my ear, he searched my eyes, then dropped his hand. "I know

I've pulled back, and I'm sorry. But I don't feel bad that he's dead. In fact, I'm fucking thrilled he's gone. And that's made me feel guilty. Guilty that I'm happy when you're hurting." I flicked my eyes between his, then lowered them to his chest.

"The truth is, I'm not hurting," I murmured. "And I'm not all that sad." He pulled me to his chest, and I melted against him.

"It's just us from now on," he said quietly. "No more ghosts. I won't let him ruin this from his fucking grave." I nodded, my cheek sliding against his shirt.

"Just us," I repeated, then pulled away, but he didn't let me get far. He wrapped his hand around the back of my neck and crushed his mouth to mine. I came in here with the intent to take charge, but I couldn't with Dean. He demanded control, and I willingly gave it.

"I need to be inside you," he breathed against my lips.

He stood, and when my feet hit the floor, he barely gave me time to steady myself before roughly yanking my jeans and panties off and tossing them across the room. I yelped as he lifted me and pressed me against the window next to the bookcase. Without warning, he slammed into me.

"Fuck!" I clawed at his shoulders and locked my ankles behind his back. He fucked me into the glass, each thrust harder than the last.

"I know I'm yours, baby," he said against my neck. "I know that. But I can't fucking lose you, not over him. I can't let him win."

He pulled away, his cock stilling inside me. "He's dead, Dean. Let him die." I pressed my lips gently to his, and he melted against me before he slowly started sliding his cock out. "I'm yours, only yours." My lips brushed against his with each word.

He pulled me away from the window and sat on the couch, staying inside me. Slowly, I sank onto him again, letting him fill me. I was never going to get used to his size, or his piercing, or how good he felt. Pushing my shirt up over my breasts, his mouth latched onto one nipple as I wrapped my arms around his head, holding him to me.

Slowly, I rose and fell at a steady pace. He trailed kisses to my other breast and gently bit down, making me cry out. I tangled my fingers in his hair again, tugging on the ends so he'd look up at me.

"I love you," I breathed. He gave me his best cocky grin as he reclined back on the couch, his hands falling to my waist.

"And I love you, darling," he said.

# Epilogue

## Julia
*Six Weeks Later*

"We've been wondering when you were going to be back." Alison's high-pitched voice pierced my eardrums, and I winced. Taking a deep breath, I turned, a fake smile barely plastered on my face. She was wearing her usual too-tight clothes with her hair pulled into a high ponytail.

"Hey," I said as Margret stepped beside her. They were both on my lawn, their hands on their hips. They were inspecting me closely, their eyes narrowed as they scanned me. "We're just clearing out the house." I threw my thumb over my shoulder. Dean and Micha were inside boxing up my past life.

It had been hard to walk into the house again, seeing it as it was the day we'd left. Our things were still scattered around, the book I'd thrown at Matthew still on the floor. I took one look around and bolted.

"I didn't see Matthew with you," Margret said accusingly. I smiled tightly at her and opened my mouth to reply when I felt a large, warm, reassuring hand on my lower back. The women lifted their eyes to Dean, Alison's brow lifting slightly as hunger took over her features.

"Alison Hawkins," she said as she extended her hand, batting her lashes. I took a deep breath. He didn't take her hand, he only looked passively down at it, clearly not interested in touching her.

"The kitchen is all packed, darling," he said, then leaned down and pressed his lips to my temple. The women exchanged an obvious look before turning back to me.

"And you are?" Alison asked, trying to make her voice pleasant, but I could see through it. I hoped he could, too.

"Dean," I answered for him. They stood waiting for me to elaborate. I didn't.

"Her long-lost brother," he said with a small smirk. I folded my lips between my teeth to keep from laughing. Their faces shifted from confusion to alarm to disgust. "I'll wait for you in the bedroom."

His silver eyes twinkled with mischief before he scooped me into his arms and kissed me long and deep. Setting me back on my feet, he slapped my ass as he walked back inside the house, throwing a casual wave over his shoulder at the women.

"It was nice to catch up," I said, taking a step back. "But as you can see," I looked back to the house, "I'm a little busy."

I hurried inside, not wanting to prolong my conversation with them further. I found Dean and Micha in the kitchen. They quieted when I entered the room. Folding my arms over my chest, I leaned in the archway.

"Brother? That was a nice touch," I said, smiling at him. Dean was sitting on the counter with a water bottle in his hand. Micha leaned against the wall, chuckling softly to himself and shaking his head. "We're going to be the talk of the neighborhood for the next year." Dean shrugged.

He was starting to get more comfortable with his body and the scars. Today he was wearing a short-sleeved t-shirt. It was the first time I'd seen him wear anything other than a long-sleeve out of the bedroom since I'd known him, so it was a big deal. I loved seeing his thickly muscled arms and all of his tattoos.

Micha was in his usual blue jeans and white t-shirt, a baseball hat folded and tucked into his back pocket.

"So?" Dean said, swinging his legs, his booted feet banging against the cabinets. "Let them talk. We won't be here anyway." I sighed and rolled my eyes before cracking a bigger smile at him.

"You need help in the bedroom?" I asked, looking between them and Micha shook his head.

"Nah, I told him to go save you," he said. "I gotta get going, though. My boss is a real hard ass and is making me go over paper-work." A knock on the door had us pausing, and I gave the guys a weird look before I pushed off the wall. "Stay there. I got it."

Micha waved at me as he untucked the back of his shirt and grabbed his gun from his waistband. He cracked the door open slowly, and I smiled when I heard the voice.

"Oh, I'm sorry. You must be the new homeowner." I stood behind Micha, gently trying to shove him out of the way, but he looked starstruck. "I'm Sophie Russo. I live right across the street."

"Hey, Soph," I said, sidestepping him. I nudged him in the ribs with my elbow, and he shook himself before he tucked his gun back in his jeans.

"I'm Micha," he said quickly. He shot his hand out toward her, and she let out a startled laugh. I'd never seen him so clumsy and awkward. I smiled at them because they were blushing and stumbling over their words. "I'm Jay's—Julia's cousin."

"Really?" Sophie looked at me, her smile bright. "It's so nice to meet you!" She took his hand, and he gave it a gentle shake. She took a step closer to him, then stopped. She glanced over her shoulder, and I flicked my eyes to her house, finding Gio standing on the porch.

"Everything okay?" I asked as I looked back at her.

"Oh, fine," she laughed, but it sounded forced. "I just hadn't heard from you in weeks, and I wanted to make sure you were alright." Guilt twisted my stomach.

"Right," I sighed. "I'm sorry. A lot has happened, but I promise to tell you all about it. Maybe we can grab lunch this week." She nodded a few times, her eyes constantly returning to Micha.

"That would be lovely," she said, nodding. She glanced over her shoulder when Gio called her name, and she sighed.

"I'll call you later, Soph," I said. She was smiling when she looked back at us, but it was forced. There were fresh bruises around her wrist that I chose to ignore. I'd figure out a way to get her away from him, but I'd need Dean's help.

Micha left shortly after Sophie did. I knew he had a million questions, but he kept quiet. From the tense set of his shoulders, he'd seen the bruise when she stuck her hand out, too.

I followed Dean to the bedroom. Everything was white, or beige, or gray. It was lifeless. I used to think it was cozy, but now it felt cold and depressing. Everything was still on the floor, just as we'd left it. Seeing what was left of the destruction brought me back to that day.

"I can't be in here," I croaked, my throat tight. The air in my lungs emptied, and a flash of heat washed over me, leaving my head a spinning mess of anxiety. "I need to get out. Dean—"

Without a second thought, he lifted me into his arms and hurried through the house. When we got outside, he set me on the hood of his Porsche and knelt between my legs.

"Stay out here," he said, his hands rubbing up and down my legs. "I'll box everything up. I won't throw anything away. You can go through it when you're ready." I shook my head and started to stand, but he put his hands on my hips, lowering me back down.

"It's my house," I whispered. Tears stung my eyes as I looked past him at the navy blue door. I laughed softly. "The door," I gestured to it with my chin, "Matthew and I fought about the color for weeks. I wanted something different, you know? I was so tired of living in a carbon copy of my neighbor's house. One day, I had enough and went to the store and grabbed the first can of paint I saw. When he got home, the paint was everywhere on the porch, on me, on the grass... just everywhere."

I shook my head, letting my smile fall as I remembered Matthew's catastrophic blow up. Dean's hands tightened around my knees, anchoring me to him.

"That day, I realized the type of person I'd married. It was only a year into our marriage. He'd gotten so angry with me then he didn't speak to me for a month. After that, I took every opportunity to change something about the house, or my appearance, anything, just to provoke him. I don't know why. I just wanted something different. Maybe it was just to rebel. Eventually, I stopped. Maybe because I knew none of it mattered in the end. It wasn't the house I wanted to change; it was my life.

"I gave up. When I looked at the other couples and their families, I felt trapped." I shook my head, then dropped my eyes to my lap. "It's not that I didn't love him at one time. I did, and that's why I stayed. That's why I put up with everything. I wanted him happy even if it was killing me." My voice broke, the tears finally falling. I looked at him, and his face was soft.

We hadn't talked about Matthew since that day in his office. He might still hold guilt, but he was getting past it. And I hadn't realized I was shoving it down until I walked into the bedroom we'd shared.

"I hate him. I hate that he made me hate him. I hate that I'm not more upset. How can I not feel anything about his death, Dean? Does it make me a monster?"

"No, darling," he said gently. "If you're asking yourself that, then you're the opposite of a monster. I'm glad he's gone. I'm glad he can never take you away from me again. I hate that you spent so many years hurting, but I'm glad that you married him. If you didn't, we wouldn't have ever found each other."

I blinked at him, then cupped the side of his face. He leaned into my touch, kissing the palm of my hand.

"We don't have to sell this place," he murmured, tucking my hair behind my ear. I sighed and dropped my hand back to my lap. "We can keep it for a while. Maybe rent it out."

"It's time to leave this life behind. For good."

He pressed his lips to mine before he smoothed my hair away from my face. His eyes searched mine for a moment, and before I could say anything, he kissed me again. A tear dripped from my eye, but it wasn't that I was sad. Not entirely. And it wasn't that I was even mourning my husband.

I was closing this chapter of my life. And for the first time in a long time, I was excited for what was to come. Looking at the house— my first home, the home that had seen the beginning and end of my marriage—I let out a long, cleansing breath. The tears fell, and my lips curled into a smile.

I was finally getting out, just like I'd always wanted.

I was free.

**THE END**

# About Haley Tyler

Haley Tyler is a dark romance author who loves to write swoon-worthy book boyfriends and badass, strong heroines. She lives in Texas with her boyfriend and dog, Maverick.

When she's not writing, you can find her reading or listening to books, playing with her dog, watching Bob's Burgers, eating chocolate, or scrolling TikTok for an endless amount of time.

www.haleytyler.com

instagram.com/haleytylerthewriter

tiktok.com/@haleytylerthewriter?

goodreads.com/haleytyler

amazon.com/author/haleytyler

bookbub.com/profile/haley-tyler

pinterest.com/haleytylerthewriter

# Also by Haley Tyler

## The Salvatore Brotherhood MC Series

*Killing Calm*

*Little Bear*

*Lost and Found*

## A Salvatore Brotherhood MC Short Story

*At First Sight*

*Say I Do*

*Just One Night*

## Standalone

*Queen of Demons*

## Coming soon

*Safe House (Salvatore Brotherhood MC Series Book Four)*

*Calling on the Reaper (Reapers Book One)*

# Acknowledgments

Thank you for reading and (hopefully) enjoying *Queen of Demons!* I've had Dean and Julia in my heart for years, but have put off telling their story until now, and I couldn't have done it without a few amazing women helping me along the way.

*Queen of Demons* was always meant to be a standalone, but as I wrote and fell in love with these characters and this world, I found myself falling HARD for Micha and Cory. So, I'm planning their own book! It'll be another standalone, so be sure to look for it in the future.

I hope you loved these characters and their story as much as I did. Thank you so much for your support and for taking the time to read my book.

Haley Tyler

**Macie (@mhmhoneyreads on TikTok and Instagram)—**
You've quickly become one of my greatest friends and I will never stop thanking you for all that you've done. You're my sounding board, and rock, and the person I know will appreciate all of the tatted men on TikTok with me.

**Melissa (@rubyjeandesigns14 on TikTok and Instagram)—**
I have told you a million times, and I'll probably tell you a million

more, but thank you!! You've been such a big supporter and great friend since the very beginning. And without your help, my books would not be what they are today. So, thank you *so* much for everything!

**Courtnee (_dirtylittlesmut on TikTok and Instagram)—**
As with the others, you've helped me with so many things and I can't ever thank you enough for it. I don't know how we've gotten so close so fast, but I'm glad we did! I always look forward to our conversations, and what new cringey videos we can find.

I feel insanely lucky to call the three of you my friends. Thank you all
for everything you've done.
Seriously.
You're the best.

# Playlist

## *Official Queen of Demons Playlist*

*Be Alone - Acres*
*Friend of the Devil - Adam Jensen*
*I Can Hold a Grudge Like Nobody's Business - Adam Jensen*
*Let Me Down Slowly - Alec Benjamin*
*Demons - Alec Benjamin*
*Monsters (feat. Blackbear) - All Time Low*
*Fallen For - Another Day's Armor*
*Black Lungs - Architects*
*Animals - Architects*
*Holy Hell - Architects*
*Royal Beggars - Architects*
*The Time Is Now - Atreyu*
*Party With The Devil - Attila*
*HEAT - AVOID*
*Sail - AWOLNATION*
*Dethrone - Bad Omens*
*Killing Me Slowly - Bad Wolves*

*Devil - Barren Gates*
*The Past Is Dead - Beartooth*
*Knees - Bebe Rexha*
*Cinema (Skrillex Remix) - Benny Benassi, Gary Go, Skrillex*
*i love you - Billie Eilish*
*Into The Ocean - Blue October*
*Dance With The Devil - Breaking Benjamin*
*Parasite Eve - Bring Me The Horizon*
*Go to Hell, for Heaven's Sake - Bring Me The Horizon*
*True Friends - Bring Me The Horizon*
*Blasphemy - Bring Me The Horizon*
*Four Walls - BROODS*
*They're Coming to Take Me Away - Butcher Babies*
*The Red - Chevelle*
*BLURRY (out of place) - Crown The Empire*
*lil blood - Dana Dentata*
*Welcome To The Family - A Day To Remember*
*I Feel Like A God - DeathbyRomy*
*Devil's Den - DEELYLE*
*Change (In The House of Flies) - Deftones*
*Iris - DIAMANTE, Breaking Benjamin*
*The Devil Within - Digital Daggers*
*I Feel It Too - Dream State*
*Devil's Callin' - dying in designer*
*Demon Eyes - ENMY*
*ONE OF US - FEVER 333*
*Demons - Fight Like Sin*
*Devil - Fight The Fade*
*Darkness in Me - Fight The Fade*
*Us Versus Them - For The Win*
*Victim - Halflives*
*Villain - Halflives*
*Curse Me with Your Kiss - Holding Absence*
*Bullet (Single Version) - Hyro The Hero*

*Face Your Demons - I Prevail*
*Scars - I Prevail*
*Gasoline - I Prevail*
*Never Lose Your Flames - Issues*
*Demons - Jacob Lee*
*Drown - Jeris Johnson*
*roses red - Jeris Johnson*
*Your Life and Mine - Just Surrender*
*ANGELS & DEMONS - jxdn*
*Devil On My Shoulder - Kelsy Karter*
*F\*CK YOU, GOODBYE (feat. Machine Gun Kelly) - The Kid
LAROI*
*Alpha & Omega - King 810*
*King - Lilith Czar*
*The Devil is a Gentleman - Merci Raines*
*Devil Devil - MILCK*
*Voices - Motionless In White*
*Demons - Our Last Night*
*Let Light Overcome The Darkness - Our Last Night*
*Lost - Our Last Night*
*Come Around - Papa Roach*
*Dark Days (feat. Jeris Johnson) - Point North*
*Man or a Monster (feat. Zayde Wølf) - Sam Tinnesz*
*Play with Fire (feat. Yacht Money) - Sam Tinnesz*
*Demon - Savage Hands*
*I'll Be There For You - Silent Child*
*Burn - Too Close To Touch*
*Deeper - Valerie Broussard, Lindsey Stirling*
*Me Against Myself - Wage War*
*To Tell You The Truth - Written by Wolves*
*The End - Zero 9:36*

Made in the USA
Coppell, TX
30 April 2022

77219866R00184